Praise for the Kitt Hartley Mysteries

'Cosy and amusing'
Irish Independent

'Brilliantly funny and charming'
Northern Life

'A great read with smart characters and a clever plot'
Candis

'Kitt is definitely not a woman to be messed with'
Belfast Telegraph

'Unique, atmospheric'
Woman Magazine

'A 2020 Miss Marple'
Woman's Way

Helen Cox is a Yorkshire-born novelist and poet. After completing her MA in creative writing at the York St John University, Helen wrote for a range of publications, edited her own independent film magazine and penned three non-fiction books. Helen currently lives by the sea in Sunderland, where she writes poetry, romance novellas, the Kitt Hartley Yorkshire Mystery Series and hosts The Poetrygram podcast. Helen's *Mastermind* specialism would be *Grease 2* and to this day she adheres to the Pink Lady pledge.

More information about Helen can be found on her website helencoxbooks.com, or on Twitter @Helenography.

Also by Helen Cox

Murder by the Minster
A Body in the Bookshop
Murder on the Moorland
Death Awaits in Durham
A Witch Hunt in Whitby

HELEN COX

A Body by the Lighthouse

QUERCUS

First published in Great Britain in 2021 by Quercus
This paperback edition published in 2022 by

QUERCUS

Quercus Editions Ltd
Carmelite House
50 Victoria Embankment
London EC4Y 0DZ

An Hachette UK company

A CIP catalogue record for this book is available
from the British Library

PB ISBN 978 1 52941 041 9
EB ISBN 978 1 52941 042 6

10 9 8 7 6 5 4 3

Typeset by CC Book Production
Printed and bound in Great Britain by Clays Ltd, Elcograf S.p.A.

Papers used by Quercus are from well-managed forests and other responsible sources.

A Body by the Lighthouse

CHAPTER ONE

'Kitt ...' Rebecca Hartley called up the stairs of thirteen Ouse View Avenue, York, a bewildered frown marking her brow. 'There's a ... a pirate at the door for you.'

The moment the word 'pirate' left her lips, Rebecca shot an almost apologetic glance at the man who stood on her twin sister's doorstep in York. She should have taken the man's name. That would have been the polite thing to do. It's just that his appearance was so utterly bizarre she had temporarily forgotten her manners. Still, perhaps she couldn't be blamed for being a bit flummoxed. The man was dressed in a black silk shirt and breeches. A scarlet headscarf covered his shoulder-length sandy hair which had strands of grey running through it. He also had a live parrot sitting on his shoulder. Calling the man a pirate may not have been polite but in Rebecca's defence, at least on the surface, it seemed accurate.

That said, her level of accuracy didn't stop a familiar

feeling of mild embarrassment from washing over her at how rude she'd just been. That same awkward feeling that she was fairly sure her somewhat bolshier sister had never experienced, and always left her unsure about what to do with her hands. She tried running one of them through her short, pastel-pink hair for something natural to do. The pink pixie cut was one of several superficial differences between her and Kitt that made them look quite different, even though they were genetically identical.

Mercifully, her somewhat flippant description didn't seem to have ruffled their visitor. His sea-green eyes remained steady and maintained the friendly light that had glimmered in them when he'd asked if Kitt was home.

Inside the house, however, Rebecca's choice of words caused quite a stir. In the time it had taken her to reach peak awkward, Kitt's boyfriend, DI Malcolm Halloran, her best friend Evie and her assistant Grace had come rushing through to the living room from the kitchen. They had been making some lunch when the knock came at the door. The moment Evie and Grace clapped eyes on the visiting mariner, their mouths fell open.

A moment later, Kitt herself came charging down the stairs.

'Bryce?' Kitt said. 'Is that you? I can't believe it after all these years. I was just getting worried. I . . . oh.' Kitt stopped in her tracks as she stared at the man on her doorstep. 'I'm sorry,' she said. 'I was expecting someone else.'

The man on the doorstep opened his mouth but before he could say anything Halloran cut in.

'You know more than one pirate?' he said, a slight edge to his voice. Now that Rebecca thought of it, police officers and pirates were sort of natural enemies. Thus, it probably wasn't a surprise that Halloran was less than thrilled at the thought of his girlfriend making friends with people who, in his eyes, were just criminals with access to a boat.

'No,' Kitt said, the edge to her voice even more noticeable than Halloran's had been. 'I've never met this man before.'

'Who's Bryce?' said Grace, who worked with Kitt at Hartley and Edwards Investigations and was, according to her sister, prone to bouts of spontaneous and disruptive giddiness. 'You know I have to be kept abreast of any new information about your life. Otherwise, how can I effectively ridicule you on a day-to-day basis? Do you know 'ow much planning it takes to fit banter around my duties at the agency?'

'I, for one, would be glad if you just focused on what you get paid for,' said Kitt.

'Woman cannot live on spreadsheet data entry alone, I tell you!' Grace said, shaking a fist at the ceiling.

Rebecca couldn't resist smirking at Grace's cheek, even though, from what her sister told her, it was deeply unfair to suggest that Kitt never let her do anything more stimulating than data input. The pair had a fairly lengthy working relationship. Originally they had managed the Women's Studies section at the Vale of York University Library.

Kitt still worked there two days a week while Grace worked full-time at the private investigation agency Kitt had founded. Even back when Grace assisted Kitt at the library, however, Rebecca remembered her sister talking about how important she felt it was to give Grace the more interesting jobs wherever possible. Say what you wanted about Kitt, she was a big believer in nurturing youthful enthusiasm. Although, if her reports about Grace's antics were to believed, perhaps in this particular case that well-meaning intention had backfired.

Duly, Kitt shook her head at her assistant's remark, unwilling to offer a verbal response to such a silly claim. Despite the number of times Rebecca had listened to Kitt rant about the recalcitrant nature of her assistant, in truth, from what she had seen, there was more than a grudging admiration between the two.

Glancing over at Evie, who was fiddling self-consciously with one of her short blonde curls, Rebecca realized she had been unusually quiet for the last few minutes. She had been good friends with Kitt for what must be going on for ten years by now. Perhaps she knew who this Bryce figure was and was keeping schtum. But why would Kitt not want anyone to know about him?

'Sorry to disturb you on a sunny Saturday afternoon like this one, Ms Hartley,' said the man at the door in a southern accent that Rebecca couldn't quite place. Maybe somewhere near Essex? But not quite that strong. 'I'm Errol Jackson.

I worked with Bryce and I'm afraid I'm here with some sad news.'

All prior amusement left Rebecca's face at those words and a chill came over her, despite the May sunshine streaming in through the doorway. It wasn't just the announcement that there was some sad news to come. There was something else: the man's use of the past tense when he talked about his association with Bryce. Rebecca had no idea who this Bryce person was. Kitt had never once mentioned him, but she clearly did know the man in some capacity. And from the sound of things, something unpleasant had befallen him.

Rebecca did her best not to openly sigh. She, Kitt, Evie and Grace were due to go on a jolly to the Scottish Highlands the next day. That's why they had all congregated at Kitt's that afternoon. They had arranged to have a leisurely lunch together and plan their various outings and walks, while making a list of restaurants they wanted to visit. This visitation from Errol, however, had all the markings of something that would at best postpone their trip. Hardly welcome news. Rebecca wasn't so much concerned about taking a break for her own enjoyment as she was for her sister's wellbeing. There had been several worrying signs lately that Kitt was long overdue a holiday.

'Call me Kitt, and please do come in,' Kitt said.

A disgruntled hiss sounded from the hearth as Errol stepped over the threshold. Kitt's black cat Iago had caught sight of the parrot perched on Errol's shoulder.

'Come on, you,' Kitt said, approaching the cat and scooping him up in her arms. 'You're going out if that's the way you're going to behave.'

Iago, never one to go down without a fight, screeched and scratched at Kitt all the way to the kitchen and then growled as she closed the door on him.

'Sorry about that. I've fed him and cared for him since he was a kitten but he's still somehow under the impression that he's the one doing me a favour,' said Kitt once she had straightened herself up after Iago's attack. 'Do take a seat.' She waved her hand over to the dark grey sofa Halloran had brought with him when he'd moved into the cottage. It didn't really go with anything else in the room, which was largely upholstered in shades of green and navy.

'Mechanic,' said a low, uneven voice.

For a moment, Rebecca was unsure where the voice was coming from but then she realized it was the parrot who had spoken.

'That's clever,' she remarked, watching the bird's head cock from side to side.

'Just spiffing,' said Evie, who rarely expressed herself without injecting some kind of old-fashioned slang, such was her love for all things vintage. According to Kitt, Evie had been vintage-obsessed for as long as she'd known her but as Rebecca had only met her a handful of times at Kitt's birthday and such, the old-fashioned lingo was still quite alien to her ears.

Errol nodded at Evie and flashed Rebecca a smile as he took his seat. 'He's a good lad.'

'It is a beautiful bird – a fine specimen,' Kitt said, sitting herself down in one of the armchairs near the fireplace while the others found seats either on the sofa or on the carpet.

Errol nodded, stroking the bird's head. 'Yes, but he's been through quite a lot of late, haven't you, little fella?'

'How do you mean?' asked Kitt. 'What's all this about? Has something happened to Bryce?'

Errol offered Kitt an almost imperceptible nod, his green eyes at once becoming watery. 'You might have heard there was a body washed up on the rocks by Flintbrim Lighthouse, up near Tynemouth, a few weeks back.'

Rebecca swallowed hard and took in a deep breath. There were only two reasons she could think of that would prompt Errol to bring that up when asked about Bryce. Either Bryce was somehow responsible for the body that had washed up by the lighthouse, or he was the body himself.

'I . . . I read about it, yes. I remember thinking that a shooting on a ship was very *Death on the Nile*,' Kitt said, slowly. 'It was a man's body. He'd suffered a gunshot wound. They didn't give a name, or any other details that I can remember.'

Working as a doctor in Ambleridge Hospital up in Northumberland, Rebecca had heard about this case too. Gunshot wounds in the region were exceptionally rare. The man had been taken to South Tyneside Hospital which was much closer to Tynemouth than Ambleridge. But other than the same details Kitt had read on the news, that was the extent of Rebecca's knowledge on the subject.

'Bryce never spoke to me about you directly, Kitt,' said Errol, 'but from the way you talked when you thought I was him, I'm guessing you were mates.'

'I haven't seen him in person for many years but yes, I was very fond of him,' Kitt said, casting a quick glance at Halloran. He was watching this conversation intently and his blue eyes were filled with obvious confusion. Whoever this Bryce was, it seemed Kitt had never mentioned him to Halloran either. This was something of a surprise as, seeing the two of them together over the past few years, Rebecca wouldn't have believed there was anything they hadn't told each other.

'He's quite a strange fellow, so I was never entirely sure why I warmed to him so much but we are friends,' Kitt continued. 'I mean ... we were friends. From all you've said, I'm assuming that the body washed up by the lighthouse was Bryce's.'

'I'm afraid so,' Errol replied. Rebecca tried to take in a deep breath but somehow couldn't quite fill her lungs properly. The weight of Errol's revelation seemed to hang in the air, making it thick and difficult to breathe. Naturally, as a doctor, Rebecca was no stranger to death. But her sister hadn't had the easiest of lives. Even just taking into account her time as a private investigator, she had lost people she knew and cared for. And now Kitt had lost another person she was close to and she hadn't had any of the mentorship Rebecca had received during her medical training to cope with this matter. Her sister had always been the curious type – that was an understatement! But curiosity could lead a person to problematic places and Rebecca was beginning to wonder just how many blows like this Kitt could take.

'Mechanic,' the parrot said again, twitching its head from side to side.

Rebecca noticed Evie open her mouth, likely to ask what they were no doubt all wondering: why the bird was so obsessed with that one word? But on seeing Kitt's pained expression, Rebecca gave a little shake of her head to let Evie know she should find another time.

'Bryce was shot,' Kitt said, her voice hollow as though she couldn't quite convince herself it was true. 'Why? By whom?'

'Nobody knows,' Errol said. 'Except that it was almost certainly someone working on the ship with us. Going on the little evidence the police found, the shooting took place in an area that only staff can access through a coded keypad. That's why they're convinced it was a crew member, though nobody on board can really believe it. The North East police service has been investigating all personnel who were on board when the shooting happened.'

'So crime at sea does fall under the police's jurisdiction, then? I weren't right sure about that,' said Grace.

'Ships are governed by the laws of whichever flag they're flying but if the body washed up in Tynemouth, the killing would likely have taken place close enough to UK shores for the responsibility to fall on the British police force, yes,' said Halloran.

'The *Northern Spirit* flies a British flag,' Errol said with a look of mild confusion on his face that Rebecca couldn't quite fathom.

'Then it would definitely fall to the North East police to investigate,' Halloran continued. 'Though such investigations aren't easy to solve. And they're not always made a priority because the police have enough on their plate solving crimes committed on dry land. The crime scene often isn't protected as it should have been and we just don't have the resources to send officers on to the ship to investigate for days at a time.'

'You're a police officer?' Errol said.

'Aye, but here in York. I haven't been involved in investigating this case,' said Halloran.

'I suppose if it is a crew member, that at least limits the number of suspects,' Kitt mused.

'It does, but not by as much as the police would like,' said Errol. 'Cruise ships the size of the *Northern Spirit*, you're looking at about a thousand crew members in round numbers.'

Kitt sighed. 'I suppose that's still better than trying to pick a killer out of the general population of millions. And how did someone get a gun on board the ship? Isn't there security?'

A frown that hinted at deepening confusion crossed Errol's face at Kitt's question but he answered it nonetheless. 'The . . . police can't be sure of much. As for how a gun might get on board, you're right to think it shouldn't happen. All crew and passengers pass through a slightly more relaxed version of airport security before they board. But there are measures in place to make sure weapons don't get smuggled through, obviously. I'm not saying it's impossible – once we were out at sea, someone who knew what they were doing, especially a crew member, might be able to smuggle something on board in one of the tender boats we use to shuttle passengers about on excursions. But it would take a lot of planning.'

Kitt nodded slowly, digesting Errol's explanation. 'Do they know exactly when Bryce was killed? How far from shore, I mean?'

Errol shook his head. 'Their current belief is that he was killed on the approach to Tynemouth, probably a mile or so out of the harbour, and pushed overboard. From there, they think his body drifted down the coast to Flintbrim Bay.'

'And, being a member of the crew and all that, you don't have any idea who might be responsible?' Kitt said, casting, what seemed to Rebecca, a stern eye over their visitor.

'I wouldn't know where to start pointing the finger, to be honest,' said Errol. 'Bryce was . . . well, I never had any trouble with him personally but he was just one of those people who was much better at making enemies than he ever was making friends.'

'Oh yes, I know all about that,' said Kitt, in a manner that left Rebecca wondering just how she knew that. 'And there was no CCTV? No eye witnesses or ear witnesses? Someone who heard the gunshot perhaps?'

'If any of those things were available, I think the police would have closed the case by now,' said Errol. 'There's no CCTV footage of the murder because there is only one camera in the staff area and the killer must have deliberately kept out of sight of it. I don't exactly know how but that's what I've heard. It's only really there in case of theft, which Crown Cruises are less interested in if it doesn't involve a passenger. There are a fair number of cameras in the public spaces where the passengers roam, because otherwise you get complaints that thefts can't be followed up. Theft is the biggest problem these cruise firms have.'

'And not one person heard the gunshot?' said Kitt. 'On a ship with that many people on it? What about lookouts? They didn't see the body fall?'

'Common theory amongst the crew is that the killer shot Bryce when the horn sounded out on the approach to Tynemouth. You wouldn't hear anything over that. We do have lookouts on the ship but at that point in the journey they are stationed at the ship's bridge at the other end of the boat from where he was shot. As for any other eye-witnesses ... well, nobody's stepped forward. Unless you count Skittles here,' Errol said, indicating the parrot.

'Skittles ...' said Kitt, looking the creature up and down. 'This bird was with Bryce when he died?'

'We think so,' said Errol. 'When we disembarked from Tynemouth the day Bryce was shot, Skittles came flying to me at the harbour as if from nowhere. It had been Bryce's turn to look after Skittles and he'd never flown to me randomly like that before so I knew something was up, but never in my wildest dreams did I imagine that Bryce had been ... that he was dead.'

'Not the most natural turn of events to fall into anyone's mind,' said Kitt.

'Too right ... I hope it doesn't upset you too much to hear it, given you were friends and all, but we found small specks of blood on Skittles' chest after the attack. The police tested it and confirmed it was Bryce's. Given that parrots are not known for their gun-wielding abilities, we're assuming he is a witness rather than the culprit.'

'Poor little thing,' said Evie. 'He's probably traumatized.'

'I think you might be right,' said Errol. 'Before Bryce's death, we'd trained Skittles to say a range of short phrases for our act. Now, for some reason, there's only one word he'll say, over and over again, and nothing else.'

'Mechanic,' Skittles repeated, as if on cue.

CHAPTER TWO

'Without wanting to state the obvious,' said Grace, at last breaking the silence that had fallen on the group, 'have the police interviewed the ship's mechanic? Because if Skittles is anything to go by, that's your culprit right there. I'm sure he's not in the 'abit of concocting wild stories, like, but if you ask me, it's worth checking into.'

Errol let out a little chuckle. 'As you might guess by the number of crew members on board a ship the size we're talking about, there isn't just one mechanic. A ship like that ... well, it's like its own little village with restaurants, a cinema, a theatre, several bars ... it's even got its own library.'

'A library?' Kitt said. Rebecca watched as her sister got that look in her eye she always got when the subject of books was raised. Though she had been running the investigation agency for just shy of eighteen months now she'd not been able to let go of her two days a week at the Vale of York

University Library. It seemed old librarian habits died hard. Kitt's somewhat glazed expression made it more than clear that she was drifting off into her imaginary on-board library when Errol spoke again and snapped her back to reality.

'Yes, it's really got everything. And as such, it's no small task to keep her in working order, so there's not just one engineer. There's a whole team with different specialisms for the engines, the generators, and the computerized elements of the machinery. But, to put your mind at rest, if the ship rumour mill is anything to go by, the police interviewed every member of the engine room crew when it became apparent that Skittles had witnessed Bryce's death and was left with only one word in his vocabulary.'

'The very least you'd expect from a thorough police investigation,' Halloran chipped in. 'Were any of the engine crew arrested?'

'No . . .' Errol said, the frown of mild confusion returning to his face. He paused before continuing. 'From what I understand, they were all able to provide an alibi for each other. Because the shooting is believed to have taken place within the thirty minutes before we reached the harbour, all of the engine crew were in the engine room at that point. Preparing to dock.'

'How strange, though, that the bird is manifesting its trauma with that word,' said Kitt. 'You mentioned that you trained the parrot for an "act" that you and Bryce were part of? What kind of role did Bryce play in that, exactly?'

'He worked with me as part of a pirate sideshow, you know the kind I mean. The passengers sit in rows in a small seating area shaped like a skiff and we tell them about the history of whichever ocean they're travelling, focusing on piracy. It's a performance art of sorts, and it pays well because by mid-afternoon the passengers are usually so merry on all-inclusive bottles of Pinot Grigio, the tips are pretty good.'

So that's why Errol was dressed as a pirate, Rebecca realized. Although you'd have thought he might have changed his clothing once the boat docked. Walking around York with a live parrot on your shoulder was guaranteed to cause a bit of a stir.

'Wait a minute,' said Halloran, seemingly unable to curb his curiosity about Bryce's relationship with Kitt any longer. 'You're friends with this bloke and you don't even know what kind of work he's doing? And if that is the case, why did you assume it was Bryce at the door when Rebecca called up to say there was a pirate here? Surely he didn't walk round dressed as a pirate as a matter of course?'

'Actually, his dress sense even on the average day was a bit eighteenth-century maritime,' said Kitt.

'What the bloody hell's that supposed to mean?' said Halloran.

'He was an eccentric, Mal. You know, a sort of romantic at heart. He revelled in adventure. While everyone in his generation was building a white picket fence, he was sailing the high seas, and getting himself into a fair bit of trouble I might add. And as for finding out what he did for work these days, it wasn't for the want of asking,' said Kitt.

'Did you even catch his last name?' said Halloran.

'Griffin,' Kitt said, a sharp note in her voice that Rebecca recognized well as a warning sign that her sister was losing her patience. She preferred to be the one asking the questions.

'Bryce Griffin?' said Halloran. 'I'll bet you a tenner that's not his real name.'

Kitt tutted. 'Why couldn't that be his name? You're one to talk, Malcolm Galfrid Halloran. Anyway, it's the only name he ever gave me.'

Evie and Grace started giggling at the mention of Halloran's middle name.

'Don't you two start,' Halloran said, though Rebecca could see he was fighting a smile behind his beard before turning back to Kitt. 'All I'm saying is, he wouldn't tell you what he was doing and his name sounds like it might be made up. He didn't strike you as a suspicious character?'

From what Kitt had said, as a police inspector Halloran was more than a little bit well-practised when it came to deconstructing personalities on little evidence. One had to wonder, however, if jealousy was playing a part in his assessment of this particular mystery man.

'He wasn't a saint, I wouldn't pretend that. But he was a friend to me,' said Kitt. 'If you're worried that I might have been mixed up in any of his less savoury activities, as I say, I haven't seen Bryce in almost fifteen years. We've kept in touch purely by post. A letter every six months at most.'

'So, that's who you've been writing to when you write your letters?' said Halloran.

'He's one of several correspondents, yes,' said Kitt.

'Dare I ask who else you write to alongside your pirate pal? A local arms dealer perhaps? A novice bomb-maker?'

'Must you be so dramatic? Anyway, when I knew him he wasn't exactly a pirate,' said Kitt. 'He was more of a smuggler.'

'Oh, that's much better,' said Halloran. 'How did you even meet somebody in that line of work? Or is it better you don't tell me?'

'Well, therein lies a tale,' said Kitt. 'But it was perfectly innocent on my part, thank you very much.'

'I'll be the judge of that,' said Halloran.

Kitt, seemingly realizing she was not about to get out of telling the story, let out a short sigh. 'About fifteen years ago, I had a summer job bartending at a pub in Seaton Carew.'

'Oh yeah, I remember that,' said Rebecca. 'The uniform was very . . . fetching.'

'Ugh, don't remind me. Who chooses radioactive green as the signature colour for their business? Anyway, Bryce and his crew came in one night. They were on this mad mission, looking for some silver dollars that had washed up on Seaton Carew beach back in 1867.'

'Silver dollars?' said Grace. 'What, like, American money?'

'Oh no, much older than that,' said Kitt. 'This was Spanish money, the coins the later American dollar was modelled on. There are several useful volumes I could—'

'Just get to the bit about you teaming up with a pirate,' Halloran said, holding up his hand.

'Smuggler,' Kitt corrected him, giving his cheek a squeeze before continuing. Halloran still had enough good humour in him left to laugh, playfully batting her hand away.

'Bryce believed he had stumbled across a map drawn by a smuggler at the time the coins had washed up. Apparently said smuggler had stashed a significant number of the coins in underwater caves and had died before he could come back to retrieve them. The only hitch was, Bryce and his . . . associates couldn't decode the map.'

Halloran narrowed his eyes at Kitt. 'But you could.'

'Well, of course she could,' said Grace, butting in. 'While we mere imbeciles spent every night of our youth out on the lash, nursing hangovers and wishing we hadn't gone home with whoever we went home with, Kitt was sensibly curled up at home with *The Big Book of Deductive Reasoning* and, in my imagination, she alternated this activity with knitting cashmere cardigans and sending important missives via carrier pigeon.'

'When you've quite finished,' said Kitt, shaking her head at Grace.

'It's true, though, you can be a bit of a peg-puff,' said Evie.

'A what?' said Rebecca, unable to keep from laughing.

'I think she's trying to imply, in her uniquely old-fash-ioned way, that I act older than my years,' said Kitt, before turning to Evie. 'I've got enough to contend with without you adding fuel to Grace's wild fancies, if you don't mind.'

'So, if I've got this right, you helped a gang of smugglers make off with riches that should have been declared to the local coroner?' said Halloran.

'Not . . . exactly,' said Kitt. 'I only agreed to help them if half the treasure was donated to the local museum, where all of it rightfully belonged. I was hoping that if we did find the treasure, I'd be able to convince them that the fame associated with the discovery was worth more to them than the coins themselves and they'd wind up giving all of the treasure to the local museum. Of course, it didn't quite turn out as I'd hoped it would.'

There was a pause as Halloran made some unspoken cal-culation. 'Bryce double-crossed you and made off with all the treasure.'

Kitt looked briefly at the carpet before answering. 'I sup-pose I shouldn't have been so surprised.'

'If he double-crossed you like that, why the bloody hell would you stay in touch with him?' Halloran asked.

'I . . . well, I don't know exactly,' said Kitt. 'Bryce never really pretended to be anything other than he was, which was sort of refreshing in its own strange way.

And although he did deceive me, at the time that whole

episode was the most adventurous thing that had ever happened to me. When I found a note from Bryce in my bag apologizing for what he'd had to do and giving an address to write to . . . I . . . suppose I just wanted to keep remembering that all that really happened.'

At this juncture, Rebecca noticed Grace and Evie, from their position on the carpet, looking back and forth between Kitt and Halloran as their bickering played out. Grace was pressing her lips together in a clear attempt not to giggle while Evie was chewing on a stick of celery she'd been munching on when she ran through from the kitchen. Odds were she would have preferred popcorn but still, it seemed, the show was no less engrossing to her for the lack of confectionery.

'Some years back he wrote to tell me he'd secured a steady job,' said Kitt. 'Something legitimate. But no matter how many times I asked what kind of work he was doing, those details were always missing in his replies.'

'Yeah, I got the impression he didn't exactly want to broadcast what he did outside the ship,' said Errol. 'I think his previous life afforded him a bit more of a rugged reputation than a family-friendly sideshow for the wealthy.'

'That sounds like the Bryce I know,' said Kitt. 'But what an awful way for him to die. I assume you've come because you want me to investigate the matter?'

'Which perhaps wouldn't be the best idea,' said Rebecca, jumping in even though she knew her comments would irk her sister – who didn't much like being told what to do by anyone.

'Really, and why's that?' said Kitt, her nose crinkling in just the way it always did when her unpredictable temper was aroused.

Rebecca did her best to keep her tone gentle. 'Besides the fact that this case has a personal element that might mean uncovering something about your friend you'd rather not know, you promised you were going to take a break,' said Rebecca, reminding her sister of the trip to Scotland.

A few months back, while staying in York for a long weekend, Rebecca had found sleeping pills in Kitt's bathroom cupboard. At first she'd thought maybe they belonged to Halloran. His work as a detective inspector meant odd hours and likely disrupted sleep patterns. On asking Kitt about her discovery, however, her sister had admitted that the sleeping pills were hers and that shutting her brain down after a long day working on a case was getting increasingly difficult. That's when the plan for an all-girl trip to Scotland had been hatched.

'Oh yes, I did promise that,' said Kitt, her voice softening. 'But what if the police don't find Bryce's killer? If they get away with it once, they might do it again at some point in the future.'

'I know sometimes you forget because of the work you do at the agency,' said Halloran, 'but the police are best placed to handle a situation like this. I'm sure they will find the culprit. They'll have conducted all the preliminary interviews and will now be in the process of confirming all the alibis and checking the financial and phone records of people working on the ship. Something will come up. It's just a process of elimination. A ship is a self-contained space so the killer can't just disappear. At least not without arousing suspicion.'

'I . . . don't mean to interrupt,' said Errol. 'But actually, I didn't come here expecting you to investigate what happened to Bryce. I was a bit taken aback that you wanted so much detail . . . I didn't know you did that kind of thing. I thought you were just asking all those questions out of curiosity.'

'Oh,' said Kitt. 'You came just to let me know, about what happened to Bryce?'

'Yeah, kind of felt a duty to, you know. Bryce didn't have any family to speak of when he passed. He didn't have many belongings, full stop. The police seized what was useful as part of the investigation, for DNA samples and such. The cruise company were going to dispose of the rest but I rescued them and fished out a few things. Your letters among them. So far as I could tell, you were the only person named in any of his effects, so I thought you might want to have these letters back.'

Errol reached into the long, black shoulder bag he had been carrying, pulled out a stack of twenty yellowing letters and handed them over to Kitt. She looked at them on her lap for a moment with tears in her eyes and then slowly began to flick through them. 'I didn't realize I'd written quite so many letters over the years,' she said.

'If you're the only person named in his effects, why didn't the police get in touch with you when they found Bryce's body?' said Grace.

'It doesn't quite work that way,' said Halloran. 'When a person dies like this, we locate and contact next of kin. A person's death is private information, even if it does then end up on the local news. Kitt wouldn't have been listed as a next of kin. And if the pair of them were sending letters to each other, then it's sort of obvious she wasn't on board the ship when the killing happened so she wouldn't be a suspect.'

'I hadn't heard from him in over a year so I'm probably yet to become an investigative priority when they've got a list of crew members to work through,' said Kitt. 'I was getting a bit worried after going so long without hearing from him but just assumed he was taking his time in replying to my last letter. I didn't think—' But then she paused, her hand hovering over one of the envelopes.

'What is it?' said Rebecca.

'This one isn't a letter from me. It's addressed to me. It's been opened, but I don't recognize it.'

'The police will have opened it to check there's nothing in there pertinent to their investigation,' said Halloran. 'Must be a letter he never got around to sending.'

'Must be . . .' said Kitt, unfolding the letter and giving it a quick scan. 'That's . . . weird. There's a poem in here. I've never known Bryce write poetry before.'

'What kind of poem?' said Rebecca.

'See for yourself,' said Kitt, handing her sister the paper. Rebecca quickly read it to herself.

Dear Kitt,

You're always talking about how much poetry stirs your soul. I've never been that interested in it personally but I happened to witness a particularly spectacular sunset on the ship one evening and found myself, for the first time in fifty-seven years, pushing words together in my head. When I finally got back to my cabin that night I thought I'd try my hand at a little poetry. After all these years of writing to you I think your literary influence might actually be rubbing off on me. What do you think? Will I go down in history as the John Keats of the Border City?

Silently, I flick through antique ephemera,
faster and faster until the lonely words merge.
Time hasn't touched these tokens of a journey
buried in a sea chest in a long-forgotten grotto.
Xanthos of Greece knew more fame in two
thousand years than these thirty-
three trinkets no hands have touched in a century.

Do write back when you have a chance and let me know what you think of my humble verse. Given the frankly ridiculous number of books you've read in your lifetime, I'm not sure that anyone else's opinion matters to me.

Stay alert, Red,

Bryce

Rebecca handed the letter over to Halloran, who was already trying to reach for it.

'Red?' Halloran said once he'd given it a quick look over.

'A silly and obvious pet name,' Kitt said, instinctively toying with the ends of her long, copper-red hair.

Halloran's eyes narrowed as he read the letter again. 'The letter is dated from six months ago. It seems strange he didn't get a chance to send it in six months.'

'The whole thing is strange,' said Kitt, reaching for the letter again. 'The police dismissed this because it just seemed like a letter to a friend. But what if it's more than that?'

'Like a clue to who his murderer was?' said Grace, a note of excitement in her voice.

'Possibly,' said Kitt. 'But unlikely given it was written six months ago. If he knew someone was going to kill him six months ahead of time, he'd probably have gone to the authorities.'

'Unless going to the authorities would incriminate him,' said Halloran.

Kitt shook her head. 'You're underestimating Bryce's

survival instinct. He was no angel by any stretch of the imagination but his crimes were petty and, unlike so many people, he didn't have a pristine reputation to protect. If he thought his life was in jeopardy, he would have gone to the police.'

'So what do you think the poem means?' said Evie. 'Some kind of cry for help?'

'I don't know,' Kitt said. 'I'll have to sit down with it and have a think. He mentions the Border City in the letter portion. I think he was from Carlisle originally, but maybe it's a significant location for reasons we don't yet understand. There's also a chance there's some kind of code or message in there that the police have missed. Perhaps some of the words relate to something untoward that was happening on board? Whatever the case, something very odd is going on here. Maybe something that only I can untangle. It seems I might be the only one who knew Bryce well enough to find out what really happened to him on that boat.'

'Kitt, I know you're upset, but no,' Halloran said, standing from his perch on the arm of the sofa.

'But Mal—'

'No. You can't seriously be considering going on that cruise ship when you'll be trapped on board with no back-up?'

'But you said yourself that the police don't have the resources to prioritize a matter like this. The crime scene won't have been protected as it should have been so it's going to take some serious work to root out the true culprit.'

'I am sure the police can handle the matter,' said Halloran. 'There's only so many suspects to work through if it was one of the staff members on board when the ship was docking.'

'And what if it wasn't? You want me to just stand back and risk someone who murdered my friend getting away with it when I have resources and contacts through the agency?'

'It's just too risky. You're going into an enclosed space with a killer without any means of escape. That's nobody's idea of common sense,' Halloran said. 'Look, I'm an understanding man on the whole, even if you have been secretly receiving letters from pirates who have pet names for you, but I'm sorry, I'm going to have to put my foot down here. You're not going on that boat, and that is final.'

CHAPTER THREE

Two days after Errol Jackson's unexpected and somewhat startling visit to York, the horn on the *Northern Spirit* cruise ship blasted out into the North Sea, signalling its departure from Tynemouth harbour. The vibrations from the low, dull siren seemed to reverberate off every surface in the narrow corridor that Rebecca, Kitt, Grace and Evie were meandering down. As the metal panelling rattled all around her, a peculiar sensation stirred in the pit of Rebecca's stomach that was difficult to quantify. A strange mix of excitement and foreboding perhaps?

Though she was still far from convinced that launching an investigation into Bryce Griffin's death was the best thing for her sister's health, even she admitted to being swept up in the general cruise atmosphere from the very moment she set eyes on the ship. She still hadn't completely digested, nor was sure she ever would, the unspeakable grandeur of the *Northern Spirit* which, at sixteen decks high, was quite the spectacle even from the outside. Judging by the giddy shrieks and raucous cackling that had echoed down the gangway from other passengers as they had boarded, Rebecca wasn't the only one to be awed by the ship's magnificence. Even being pulled out of the queue by security for a 'random search' hadn't dampened her enthusiasm for the voyage ahead of them. Rebecca was always, *always* selected for a random search by security guards. She suspected it was because of her tattoos. None of them depicted anything intimidating – one was a fairy, for heaven's sake – but between that and her pink hair perhaps she looked strange enough to warrant further inspection. Still, people had paid a lot of money for this cruise – if Errol hadn't let Kitt use his friends and family discount when she booked their cabins, there would have been no way they could have afforded it – so though thorough, Timothy, the steward who had waved a detector over her, had been the perfect picture of politeness.

Once on board, Rebecca discovered that the interior of the ship, or at least what they'd seen before Kitt had frogmarched them to the scene of Bryce's untimely death, was just as breathtaking as the ship's exterior, if not more so. Opulent in every imaginable detail. The main piazza was connected to the upper floors by an imperial staircase lined with deep red carpet. Giant chandeliers hung overhead, designed to set the mood at the numerous formal gatherings the crew had scheduled for the passengers.

As if all this luxury wasn't enough, the reception area

seemed to smell of bubbling champagne. Until that moment, Rebecca wasn't convinced she'd been aware that champagne had an especially distinctive smell, but there was no missing the hint of that particular fragrance on entry. Neither could anyone miss the way the network of brass railings that ran around the various ledges and walls of all the open spaces sparkled as though they'd been freshly polished that very morning. Which, based on a few comments Errol had made about the crew's schedule, they probably had.

Despite Halloran's insistence that she should leave this case be, Kitt had, true to form, wasted no time in arguing vehemently about the importance of following up on Bryce Griffin's death for herself. So passionate was her appeal that she'd swiftly convinced Evie and Grace to ditch the trip to Scotland in favour of a seven-night cruise to Oslo. Eventually, she even managed to talk Halloran down from his prior objections, though it was unclear if he truly acquiesced or just recognized he'd never hear the end of the matter until he at least pretended to. By the time Kitt was done, Rebecca had been the sole member of the resistance left standing. Given that she was outnumbered, her reluctance to go along with the change of plan mattered little.

'Worry not,' Kitt had said in a bid to placate her sister. 'I can promise you I'll be doing my fair share of relaxing on this trip.' Though Rebecca had had little choice but to at least superficially take her sister at her word, deep down she knew Kitt too well to believe that. Moreover, she couldn't help but wonder what impact any unsavoury discovery about her deceased friend might have.

Led by Errol, the small group came to an abrupt halt when it became apparent they'd reached the door to the staff area, where a sign hung with tall letters that clearly stated: CREW MEMBERS ONLY. According to Errol, beyond this door lay the exact point where Bryce Griffin was shot.

'Can we get into trouble for this?' said Grace, with what sounded like more of a hopeful note in her voice than one of caution or wariness. Prior to making arrangements for this trip, Rebecca had only chatted with Grace briefly on Zoom or over the phone when she'd rung the agency to get hold of Kitt. As such, she only knew three concrete things about her: she was of Indian heritage, she lived in Leeds and Kitt thought she was a livewire. This trip would be a good opportunity to find out if Kitt was exaggerating. Grace's next sentence, however, left Rebecca with the distinct impression that her sister might have been quite fair in her assessment after all.

'The risk of getting into trouble isn't going to stop us going in or anything, it's just good to know the stakes,' Grace explained, with what could only be described as a devilish grin on her face and a mischievous sparkle in her deep brown eyes.

'No,' said Errol. 'There won't be any trouble. I've let the security team know about your investigation and they've informed key members of staff: the bridge – including the captain – and the helpdesk workers in the main reception. Just in case you need their assistance at any point. It would be more than my job's worth to sneak you in here. I want to help and everything but I've got a hungry mouth to feed. Two if you count Skittles.'

'Where is Skittles?' said Evie. 'I was sort of hoping to see him again.'

'He's sleeping in my cabin,' said Errol. 'He doesn't take well to me interrupting his afternoon nap. He can be a real curmudgeon if he doesn't get forty winks in the afternoon.'

'As we've been permitted to board, I assume the security team didn't have any objections to us looking into Bryce's death?' said Kitt, ignoring Evie's interjection about the parrot.

Oh yeah, she was really in the mindset to take it easy . . .

'None at all,' said Errol. 'The people on this ship work night and day to provide an unforgettable experience for the passengers. It's a source of frustration to all of us that crime isn't investigated as well as it could be. As to this particular crime, there isn't anyone on this ship who doesn't want to see Bryce's killer pay.'

'Except the killer himself,' said Kitt.

'Yeah,' said Errol with a frown. 'To be honest, I still quite haven't got my head around the fact that it's a member of staff behind it. We have our ups and downs like any colleagues do but when you're out at sea together for anything between six and nine months of the year, unless you want it to be miserable, you pretty much have to learn to get along.'

'Unless you're Bryce, of course, who, from what you've mentioned previously, seems to have managed to rub quite a few people up the wrong way,' said Grace.

They watched Errol shield the staff area keypad with one hand and input the code with the other.

'Any more thoughts on that strange poem we found?' said Kitt.

'No, not yet,' said Errol. 'Poetry's fun to recite but I can't say I've always understood it. One thing I did wonder is if it would be worth talking to our on-board drag queen, Wendy Lostbuoy.'

'Oooh, that's a quality stage name!' said Evie.

'Who doesn't appreciate a good literary pun?' said Kitt. 'But any particular reason why you think we should talk to them about the poem? Do you think something in the poem relates to Wendy particularly?'

'No, it's just I didn't know much about Bryce as a person. I got on well enough with him for work, but he didn't chat about anything private. Nothing that might have hinted at what that poem was really about, for example.'

'But he did to Wendy?'

'Far as I can tell, she was his only real friend on the ship. Her evening show starts at seven p.m. I can take you backstage just after the six o'clock mark between my afternoon show and early evening performance to introduce you. Though she will be getting ready for her own show at that time so I can't guarantee she'll talk to you.'

'Worth a try,' said Kitt. 'In the meantime, let's see where the murder took place and take it from there.'

'Will this take long?' asked Evie who, in her vintage denim shorts and Hawaiian print shirt, was definitely already embracing the holiday spirit. 'I want to go and find out more about that 1960s dance night I read about on the website.'

'You don't have to hang around if you don't want to,' Kitt said. 'But I need to get the investigative basics sorted before I do anything else.'

'No . . . it's all right, I'll stay,' said Evie. 'It's just you promised that we would have some fun on this trip.'

'What's that in your hand?' Kitt said.

'A . . . cocktail,' said Evie, glancing at the glass she was carrying filled with luminous blue liquid and topped with a pink umbrella.

'Who bought it for you?'

'You did, but—'

'See, fun,' Kitt interjected, before following Errol through the door to the staff lounge.

Rebecca exchanged a look with Evie confirming what they had both suspected, that this trip was going to be a lot more business than pleasure.

'Crime scenes and cocktails wasn't really what I had in mind,' Evie muttered under her breath as she followed Grace through the door Errol was holding open for them. Rebecca was last through and closed the door behind them.

It was evident at once that the staff area was markedly different from the other parts of the ship they had passed on the way here. The walls in the recreation room had been painted the dreariest shade of grey Rebecca had ever seen. There were various sofas arranged around the room, some of which were occupied with weary-looking crew members and all of which had seen better days. Other than a small kitchenette area and a TV, there was little else of note.

'Doesn't seem like particularly grand facilities for staff of more than a thousand,' Rebecca said.

Errol flashed her a smile which was a lot more becoming now that he was wearing jeans and a white T-shirt instead of a pirate costume. With his sandy hair tied up in a man-bun he looked almost normal in comparison to the peculiar and diverting guise he'd been wearing when he showed up on Kitt's doorstep. 'This isn't the only staff area. There's a rec room on every other deck and because everyone is on shift at different times, it just about works out that there's enough space for us all when we need it. But you're right to point out it's not exactly a luxurious life.'

'I didn't mean ...' She tried but was unable to find a non-awkward way of finishing that sentence. Rebecca felt a heat rising in her cheeks. She had just been quite disparaging about the place this man called his home for most of the year. Errol had taken it in good humour but she must think twice before making any such comments in future. She forced a smile, trying to make it clear she was quite a nice, friendly person when she wasn't putting her foot in her mouth. 'I actually think living on this ship must be fairly exciting, having adventures at sea every day.'

'If by adventures you mean helping drunk guests find their cabins and sweeping up their litter after one of our little sideshows, well then, you'd be right.'

Rebecca chuckled at Errol's joke and only stopped when she heard her sister clear her throat. She glanced over to see Kitt, Evie and Grace all watching her and Errol's little interaction. Kitt had crossed her arms and Rebecca could tell by the slight crinkling of Kitt's nose that she didn't appreciate her investigation being interrupted with small talk.

'Crime scene this way, is it?' Kitt said, pointing towards a sliding glass door at the back of the room that led outside.

'Yeah, I'll show you, follow me,' Errol said, seeming not to have noticed the looks the other lasses had been shooting their way or, alternatively, he was just polite enough to ignore them.

Honestly, Rebecca thought to herself as she followed the others out through the glass door. It's not as if she had taken up more than a few moments of Errol's time. Kitt's promises of taking this cruise easy were already out the window if that was how she reacted to her having a little joke with Errol. That said, Evie and Grace had both flashed her a knowing smirk too, as though she had been flirting or something. Surely quite the opposite was true? She had only been busy making the world's worst second impression on the man. This after making the world's worst first impression by referring to Errol as a pirate on their first meeting.

But then again, so what if she had been flirting? She worked ridiculous hours at the hospital and though the work was rewarding, it wasn't easy. Why shouldn't she enjoy herself if the opportunity presented? If Kitt and the gang really wanted to see flirting, she'd show them some. Granted, she wasn't very good at flirting but she couldn't very well make a bigger fool out of herself in front of Errol than she already had and who knew? In the process of embracing the care-free holiday spirit for herself, maybe she'd get Kitt to lighten up a bit.

Walking out to the modest balcony area, where everyone else was now standing, Rebecca sucked in a deep breath as the bracing salt air hit her.

'So, Errol,' Rebecca said, her voice pointedly softer than usual so that the shift in tone couldn't be missed by the others. 'What made you decide on a life at sea?'

As she sauntered past Evie, Grace and Kitt to move closer to Errol, she turned momentarily to flash them a devious grin. Evie and Grace at once returned her grin while Kitt merely narrowed her eyes in a manner that gave Rebecca more satisfaction than it should have.

Errol paused before responding, seemingly caught off guard by the question. 'I . . . er, I used to be a stage actor, down in London. But I got a bit tired of the irregularity of the work. So, when I noticed this job going, I saw an opportunity to use my theatrical skills for a steadier wage packet, and I took it.'

'Hmm,' said Rebecca. 'Yes, with a strong jawline like yours it's no surprise you were once an actor.'

Errol smiled at the compliment and to Rebecca's surprise, as he did so, she felt a strange little flutter inside. Maybe there would be scope to combine business with pleasure on this cruise after all.

'It's true, and a genuine burden, you have to believe me, that I am ruggedly handsome,' Errol said with a sparkle in his sea-green eyes.

'And modest too, I see,' said Rebecca. 'An irresistible combination if ever there was one.'

'Can you continue this conversation at the bar later?' said Kitt.

Rebecca stared over at her sister, raising her eyebrows to indicate she was waiting for something. Rebecca was confident Kitt would know exactly what she was counting on.

And then she saw it. A little smile surfaced on Kitt's lips. A signal that her usual good humour had at last returned.

'Please?' Kitt said.

Rebecca gave her sister a nod. The flirting game was over, for now.

Errol flashed Rebecca another smile before returning his attentions to Kitt. 'I know you were keen to see the crime scene but I don't think you're going to glean much from this area now it's been swept by the police.'

'It never hurts to see where a crime you're investigating took place,' said Kitt.

'Sometimes it's the smallest details that are relevant. For example, the fact that this is the lowest balcony overlooking the sea at the back of the ship makes it more evident why nobody spotted what happened. If he'd fallen from a higher balcony, someone would have been more likely to have noticed. Was this the only place the police swept?'

'Far as I know, the police carried out tests on all the outside areas,' said Errol. 'To wind up drifting by the light-house, they believed Bryce was most likely shot in the open air where he might easily fall into the ocean and be swept along by a strong current.'

'So they likely presumed the killer, before shooting him, lured Bryce to a place where he could easily be cast over-board,' said Kitt. 'Are there other rec rooms that overlook the sea?'

'Yeah, there is one other, but it's higher up. And now that you say it, it's obvious the killer must have chosen this one deliberately to minimize the risk of being seen. They found blood out here on the ledge that matched the blood they found in Skittles' feathers.'

'Bryce's blood,' said Kitt.

Grace patted Kitt's arm. 'I know you don't like to give up on a case and you know I don't like to speak seriously about anything if I can avoid it, but if it gets too much, we don't have to work this one. He was your friend, and it's not like we've got a client paying us.'

'I'm all right,' said Kitt, offering a reassuring smile. 'In a way I'm the client on this one. I don't want to think that Bryce's death will go unanswered for.'

'None of us do,' said Errol.

Without another word, Kitt began pacing up and down the length of the balcony, stopping at various points and squinting here and there, making unspoken calculations.

'Poor Skittles being caught up in something like this,' said Evie. 'I do feel sorry for him.'

'You're welcome to come and visit him, he's a total attention-seeker so I'm sure he'd like that – or you could come and watch him perform.'

Errol's eyes roamed from Evie to Rebecca as he offered this invitation. Was it her imagination or was he requesting her company specifically?

'I'm not sure I'll have time,' said Kitt. Errol wasn't even looking at her but she hadn't noticed, she was too preoccupied with running her hands along the ledge of the balcony and looking overboard at the height of the drop Bryce must have fallen.

'I'll definitely be stopping by to watch,' said Evie.

'Me too,' said Grace.

Errol kept his eyes on Rebecca, seemingly waiting for her response.

'Sounds like fun,' she said.

'Good. It'll be nice to see some friendly faces in the audience. We haven't replaced Bryce yet obviously so Skittles is my only partner now.'

'Where is that camera you mentioned?' said Kitt, apparently disinterested in any talk that wasn't related to Bryce's demise.

'Over in that far left corner,' said Errol, pointing back into the rec room.

'And it really didn't catch the killer on camera from that vantage point?' said Grace. ''Ard to know how it could miss them from that angle.'

'I know what you mean,' said Errol. 'I haven't seen any of the footage so I don't know exactly what happened there.'

'Is there anyone on board who might be able to explain it? Someone we could talk to?' said Kitt.

'Your best bet is to talk to the ship's head of security, Georgia Rhames. She's the one most likely to know what happened with the footage that night. She was pleased to hear about your investigation but I can't be sure she'll talk to you directly. There's a good chance she might send you packing. There wasn't any love lost between her and Bryce.'

Kitt rolled her eyes. 'What did he do this time?'

'I don't know. But the two definitely had an argument a few weeks before Bryce died, and according to hearsay amongst the staff, it got pretty heated,' said Errol.

'What was the argument about?' said Grace.

'I don't know,' said Errol. 'But Georgia's not the one who killed Bryce, if that's what you're thinking. She had an alibi for the murder window.'

Kitt exchanged a look with her assistant that at once put Rebecca on edge. She could guess what the pair were thinking. The absence of security footage was odd given how small the room was. If Georgia Rhames had had some issue with Bryce, not to mention a heated argument with him in public, then she would be well placed to ensure there wasn't any footage of his murder. Meaning she might be at least partly responsible for what happened to Bryce, even if she didn't pull the trigger herself.

CHAPTER FOUR

To everyone's surprise, Georgia Rhames got back to Errol within the hour to say she was only too willing to discuss what had happened with the CCTV footage on the night Bryce had been murdered. Thus, with Grace's notorious travel-sickness at last kicking in and Evie making her excuses to go and confirm the details of the vintage dance party due to take place on the fifth night of the cruise, Errol escorted Kitt and Rebecca to the ship's safety command centre via a series of maze-like corridors that smelled heavily of motor oil and sweat.

Pausing, Errol knocked three times on a heavy steel door. It opened a moment later and he greeted the woman behind it as Georgia.

'In you come,' Georgia said, offering them a brief smile. Her words had a subtly sharp edge to them that Rebecca interpreted as a polite reminder that she wouldn't stand for any nonsense. In Georgia's defence, according to Errol there were about six thousand passengers on board and when you were in charge of so many other people's wellbeing, perhaps it was understandable that you didn't have either the luxury or the inclination to suffer fools.

Taking a deep breath, Rebecca did as instructed and entered the security command centre while running through the instructions Kitt had given her before they'd left their cabin. Rebecca had been given the easier job of 'good cop' while Kitt was going to put up a more reserved front. Kitt had explained that wherever possible they should avoid interrupting Georgia: the more she talked, the more she might let something slip if she was involved. And lastly, Rebecca wasn't to ask any questions that implied Georgia was on their suspect list. As head of security, she could make their investigation very difficult if she chose not to cooperate, or worse, hinder them. Thus, right now, it served to keep Georgia on side at all costs, even if they weren't entirely sure that Bryce's murder had been missed by that CCTV camera by accident.

'Though I don't wish seasickness on Grace, I'm sort of glad she's not here – she's my assistant,' Kitt clarified for Georgia, while she scanned the rows of monitors, dials and buttons that were lit up like a light show in a glow of green and yellow. 'She'd want to press every button in here.'

Rebecca tried not to let the dazzle of the lights stop her from paying keen attention to who else was in the room and what they were up to. Kitt had asked her to be vigilant.

45

In fact, she hadn't been that concise, she had underlined at some length how any minor detail might be of the greatest importance. Consequently, Rebecca was doing her best to harness her doctor's attention to detail.

Gleaning anything substantial about the other people in the room, however, was no easy task. There were several other officers in attendance, monitoring the machines, but they all had their backs turned, paying close attention to the job at hand. They were also all wearing a crisp, white uniform, just like Georgia, so their clothing wasn't much help in differentiating one person from another. She'd have to focus on more subtle details. There were two fairly broad men, one of whom had a tattoo of an anchor on the back of his neck, which Rebecca took a moment to admire. There was also a woman who, when she turned her face in profile to speak to another colleague, looked to be of Chinese heritage. Her short, bluntly chopped hair had a streak of electric blue down one side. But those were the only striking details Rebecca could distinguish at present. Everyone else was either too far away or was facing the wrong direction for her to make a mental note of their appearance.

'An urge to push all the buttons is quite a natural reaction for most people who come to visit us, to be honest. In fact, I was just the same the first time I walked in here,' said Georgia, reestablishing Rebecca's attention. It was subtle, but there was something about Georgia's accent, just in the way some of her vowel sounds landed, that hinted she might not have spent all of her life in the UK. Rebecca couldn't be sure but she wondered if Georgia had spent time in South Africa. Given her job title, it wasn't surprising that some influence of far-flung shores was evident in her speech pattern. Rebecca noticed a little shimmer in Georgia's hazel eyes at Kitt's comment that hinted at good humour lying somewhere deep beneath the no-nonsense exterior. 'It's not dissimilar to being invited up to the bridge with the captain,' Georgia added. 'Few people get to see this side of life on board the ship.'

'Which makes us doubly grateful you made an exception for us,' said Kitt.

'Yes, well,' Georgia said, glancing to the floor for just a moment before meeting Kitt's eyes once again. 'Your friend Mr Griffin died on my watch so I felt duty-bound to do what I could to try and find out who was responsible for his murder. I am . . . so very sorry for your loss, by the way. The crew has felt it keenly and, of course, with suspicion ongoing, it's put us all on edge. What happened to Bryce, it shouldn't have been possible. Don't think I'll ever quite forgive myself.'

'I hardly think you can be blamed for something like this happening,' said Rebecca. 'From what we understand, you've got a lot of sheep to herd. The only one to blame for this is the person who pulled the trigger.'

'Intellectually I understand that,' Georgia said. The way in which she'd tied every last strand of her blonde hair back in a bun made her face look quite severe, but there was no mistaking the small wobble in her lips before she spoke again. 'When security's your job, though, it's hard not to take something like this personally. Mr Griffin should have been safe on this ship. It was my job to see to it. And . . . I failed.' Georgia swallowed hard, her voice almost breaking when she spoke again. 'To make it worse, the last words I ever said to him were not the right side of polite.'

'If you had some kind of falling-out with Bryce, you wouldn't be the first,' said Kitt, feigning innocence despite what Errol had told them earlier. Rebecca glanced over at Errol as casually as she could to see if it looked like he would give the game away, but he didn't react to Kitt's mild deception. Perhaps he was as curious as they were to find out what had passed between Georgia and Bryce.

'Oh, I'm well aware of that. Who do you think had to break up the other fights he started? He was always getting himself into scrapes.'

'And I'm sure if you were less than polite the last time you spoke to him, you had good cause,' said Kitt.

'I . . . I,' Georgia faltered but then recovered herself. 'I don't mind telling you what we argued about on the condition it doesn't leave this room, agreed?' Georgia looked around the trio each in turn.

Rebecca, Kitt and Errol nodded their agreement.

'I turned forty last year and as a special present to mark

the occasion, my parents gave me a watch. A very expensive one, worth about a thousand pounds. Not something I would ever buy for myself given just how many unfortunate things could befall it at sea.'

'Go on,' Kitt nudged, though from the look on her face, it seemed to Rebecca that she had a sense of where this story was going.

'About two weeks before Bryce died, I woke up and the watch was missing. I'd been drinking with him in one of the bars the night before. I had the night off, I hasten to add. I wasn't drinking on the job. He'd been insistent on buying the drinks. I didn't think anything of it at the time. I wasn't good friends with him. He just happened to be in the bar when I was, or so it seemed. We had shared a couple of drinks in the past so it wasn't completely unusual. But when I woke up after that particular night I couldn't remember anything, and the watch was missing.'

'So you think Bryce got you drunk and took it?' said Kitt.

'It was the only explanation I could think of at the time, though he denied it when we argued. He denied it so strongly that it made me think twice about my accusations. I'm still trying to find out if someone else had a hand in it. That's why I don't want you to mention it to anyone. That, and I don't want anyone to know that I was arguing with a soon-to-be-dead man over something as trivial as a piece of jewellery.'

'I wouldn't say it was trivial,' Rebecca said. 'It wasn't just any piece of jewellery, it was a gift from your parents, for a special occasion. It had sentimental value.'

'Thanks,' said Georgia. 'My parents are ex-pats, they live in Spain. I don't see them very often which, I think, is why they went a bit overboard with the present and why I was particularly upset when it went missing. But I've still felt lousy about my altercation with Bryce after what happened to him.'

'Don't feel too lousy,' said Kitt. 'Bryce wasn't much for taking things like that to heart. How can you when you live like he did? He was a bit of a scoundrel and he knew it. I doubt he gave your argument much thought after the fact.'

'I hope you're right,' Georgia said.

'I'm quite sure of it,' said Kitt. 'And there is a good chance Bryce did, in fact, steal your watch.'

'What makes you say that?' said Georgia. 'The police didn't find it in his belongings.'

'No, they wouldn't,' said Kitt. 'If he stole it from you, it was likely to sell it on because he was having money trouble. He mentioned money problems more than once in his letters over the years.'

Georgia frowned. 'He was getting paid his regular salary from Crown Cruises. It's not enough for a lavish lifestyle, I'll grant you, but it's enough to live on with few worries.'

Kitt shook her head. 'In the time I've known him, Bryce Griffin had more money and treasure slip through his fingers than all of the rest of my friends put together. I know for a fact that he uncovered priceless artefacts, precious coins, and was paid handsomely for various smuggling jobs. None of it has ever resulted in financial security.'

'So, you think maybe he was into something that cost him a lot of money and he got in over his head?' said Georgia. 'Like drugs or something?'

'It's a possibility,' said Kitt.

'There were only a few bits and pieces in his belongings when I found Kitt's letters,' said Errol. 'It definitely didn't look like the remnants of a rich life.'

'Were there any other thefts reported between when your watch went missing and Bryce's murder?' Kitt asked.

'Hmm. Around that time there was a bit of an uptick in a situation we've been dealing with for a while now. Or should I say, trying to deal with. Let me check the details first and make sure the dates are a match before we go any further.' Georgia moved over to a computer at the side of the room. 'Despite the amount of security we've got in place, theft is quite common on these cruises.'

'Well, you are trying to monitor a lot of people,' said Rebecca. 'You can't possibly keep track of everything that goes on.'

'We do better when people report the theft because we can examine security footage. Usually, it's just a case of someone playing finders keepers when a guest leaves something in a public space. The people on board aren't short of a bob or two so they often leave high-value items just lying around. But we've also caught several professional thieves at work in the five years I've been with Crown Cruises. Ah, yes, here we go. Over the last three years we've had intermittent reports from guests saying they had large amounts of money stolen from them on their way back to their cabins at night. Six weeks ago the reports picked up in frequency but . . . no, there haven't been any reports since Bryce died.'

'So there's a chance Bryce was part of some kind of on-board crime ring,' said Kitt. 'Although, don't most people pay by card now? Do people really still bring large amounts of cash on holiday with them?'

'Don't get me started,' said Georgia, her face at once flushing. 'With a stolen card we can report it in a matter of minutes and the banks usually reimburse the customer if the thief has managed to use it. But with cash, well, it takes quite a bit of investigating to find out who took it and even when we are able to narrow down a suspect, getting the cash back is usually a matter for a small claims court. It'd be a lot easier if people brought just a few notes with them in case of emergency but a lot of our customers are of older generations, so prefer to have a little something in their pockets. And in quite a few cases you've got people trying to keep up with the Joneses, you know, bringing a wad of fifties with them just to flash it around. Like it isn't already obvious that you're doing all right for yourself if you can afford a holiday on one of these boats. The way they go on, it's like catnip for thieves.'

'And you said these reports were made over the last few

years and were particularly rife in the month before Bryce died?' said Kitt.

'It's not just this ship, otherwise I'd have long since suspected one of the crew,' said Georgia with a nod. 'We've had reports from other ships in the Crown Cruise family and I suspect there have been incidents on cruises run by other companies. My theory was that someone, or a small network of people, were boarding numerous vessels and taking advantage of drunken guests on the way back to their rooms. We've had reports like this every six months for the past few years but yes, there were a few more in the weeks preceding Bryce's death. We've still yet to get an identifiable shot of the culprit on camera.'

'Ah, so you have caught some of the thefts on camera?' said Kitt.

Georgia nodded. 'Once or twice. Most of the time the guests, and the thief, were a bit too far away from the camera for the quality to be much good and often they were turned away so there was just a shot from behind. Even when we did catch a view of them, they were always wearing a hat big enough to obscure their face and a long coat over their clothes. Which I presume they shrugged off when they left the scene so that they couldn't be tracked from one area to the next via CCTV.'

'A common tactic,' said Kitt. 'Change your whole silhouette so you don't look like the same person who was at the scene of the crime.'

'With the thefts being sporadic up until quite recently, I assumed the perps were hopping on and off at different points in the network. And, of course, there'll be some thefts that weren't even reported, which makes it more difficult still to piece together any patterns,' said Georgia. 'Perhaps we only saw an increase in these incidents prior to Bryce's murder because the people who've been targeted have chosen to come forward. Judging by the footage I have seen of them, I think the attackers are male. Certainly they look broad enough and tall enough to make that assumption. The victims who have come forward have also reported that their attackers are strong. They haven't had to work hard to overpower their targets. Another factor that implies a male thief – or a band of them.'

'You . . . said Bryce used to be a smuggler?' said Rebecca.

'That was years ago,' said Kitt. 'Though, I admit, I can't rule out the notion that he might be embroiled in something like this.'

'Were there any unusual items of clothing in Bryce's belongings?' Rebecca asked Errol.

Errol nodded. 'There were one or two interesting pieces but it was mostly costumes we use for the show. There were a couple of long jackets and hats.'

'It's only been a couple of weeks, granted. But there haven't been any reports of theft since Bryce died . . . But . . . I mean, could Bryce really have been committing these thefts all along?' said Georgia.

'Admittedly, I've not dealt with many cases of theft since I started the agency,' said Kitt. 'But there have been times while I've been investigating where less serious crimes like theft have been linked to murders, and looking at the evidence gathered so far, a picture is starting to build here. Your watch goes missing after a heavy night on the drink with Bryce, you experience an increasing number of thefts across the ship as a whole and within two weeks, Bryce is dead.' Kitt paused, pursing her lips before speaking again. 'It seems to me that's highly unlikely to be a coincidence.'

CHAPTER FIVE

'Now I feel even worse,' said Georgia, letting out a big, heavy sigh. 'If it was Bryce, and the problem was right under my nose all that time, then several of our guests have suffered needlessly because of my oversight and, what's worse, if I had realized what was going on sooner, well, Bryce would have been fired but he would also still be alive. How could I have missed this?'

'You can't know any of that for sure,' said Rebecca. 'We've no hard proof as yet that he was even behind the thefts. Or, even if he was, that they were directly related to his death.'

'My sister's right,' said Kitt. 'I have a suspicion that they are related, but I don't have any proof and even if I find some, I don't think there's much you could have done. Bryce had a history as a petty criminal. He'd know how to cover his tracks well enough. And being a member of staff, he'd know that he'd be afforded a certain level of trust. Whether he's directly involved with the thefts you've been experiencing or his death is related to some other issue we've yet to uncover, it's clear he got himself in over his head, and not for the first time.'

'I didn't realize Bryce had a criminal past,' said Georgia. 'When I accused him of stealing my watch, I thought it was a bout of opportunism. I had no idea I was dealing with a professional.'

'It was all a long time ago,' said Kitt. 'I am certainly not here to drag my friend's name through the mud. But it wouldn't be right to paint him as a saint either. He did spend a lot of his early life engaging in activities that would be frowned upon by most members of law enforcement but he did clean up his act eventually. Or so he told me. I have to say, so far this isn't looking good for him.'

'I wonder how he got hired if he had a criminal record?' said Georgia.

'Oh, I don't think he did have a criminal record,' said Kitt. 'I suspect he was invited to spend the night in a police cell on a few occasions but from the stories he's told me in his letters over the years, I'm not sure if anyone ever managed to book him for anything. He might have received the odd warning here and there.'

'Ah, well, those are spent in six years and wouldn't appear on his criminal record check if the crimes were committed a long time ago,' said Georgia. 'Still, if Bryce is connected to the robberies we've been experiencing, I feel a little less foolish for not spotting it if he was once a professional thief.'

'His line of business, as was, is a bit unclear, I'm afraid,' said Kitt. 'But I don't think he was any stranger to pulling the wool over people's eyes. At any rate, the big question we wanted to ask you was how the killer managed to evade the CCTV in the rec room before they got out on to the balcony? Did they somehow manage to disable the camera in there?'

'Not quite what happened,' said Georgia. 'Here, gather round a bit closer and I'll bring up the footage and you'll see what we were left with. But prepare to be infuriated. I can barely stand to watch it another time.'

As instructed, Rebecca, Errol and Kitt huddled around the computer monitor and watched as Georgia tapped a few buttons and brought up a video clip dated two weeks ago, on the twentieth of April. As she watched the tape, something struck Rebecca that she hadn't fully processed before. The video showed the rec room in broad daylight. She knew that the murder had happened just before docking so intellectually understood that it had happened at some point during the day, but in her head somehow she had pictured the scene under the cover of darkness. Having now seen how big the ship was for herself, she had to wonder: how on earth had the killer got away with this on a boat teeming with six thousand passengers and a thousand crew members? With so many witnesses, how was it that nobody noticed a thing?

After a few moments, Bryce could be seen walking into the rec room. Or at least, Rebecca presumed it was Bryce, as Skittles was perched on his left shoulder. Bryce was talking with someone off-screen, occasionally turning his head to the right as he chatted with them.

'The murderer never steps into view?' said Kitt.

'No such luck,' said Georgia. 'I've done everything I can think of with the footage. Enlarged it, enhanced it, run it in slow motion. There are no leads at all.'

'And there's no audio track?' said Kitt.

Georgia shook her head. 'The mics just aren't good enough to pick anything up. On the odd occasion we have employed a professional lip-reader if a major theft has taken place but the police said that the angles weren't good enough on this footage to even try that.'

Digesting Georgia's words, the group returned their attentions to the small screen. Together, they continued to watch Bryce take what were, unbeknownst to him, his final steps.

So this was the pirate friend Kitt had kept secret all these years? Looking at him, even from behind, Rebecca could understand why Kitt hadn't invited him round to Mam and Dad's for tea at any point. His long, tangled grey hair fell down the black leather jacket he was wearing. It was difficult to make out the finer details of his appearance given their limited vantage point, but in the few moments his face was in profile, Rebecca noticed how sharp the man's features were. His chin in particular seemed peculiarly pointed and yet it was an intriguing face. Marked with various lines and scars that were perhaps tokens of previous adventures, such as the one Kitt had shared with him.

A strange, sharp feeling sliced through Rebecca at that thought. Adventure may have proven deadly for Bryce but she wagered those who knew him would have some tales to tell about him. Stories that would keep him alive, if only in the memories and hearts of the people he double-crossed or partnered with.

Rebecca winced at the thought of stories people might tell about her when she was no longer here. On present showing they were likely to be quite dull. It's not that she didn't contribute. Through her job at the hospital she had helped so many people, but it was also all-consuming. When was the last time she'd had an adventure? She wasn't completely sure she'd ever had one. She'd be forty in a couple of years. Hadn't most people had at least one adventure by that point in their lives? Perhaps this unexpected trip to Oslo could count as her first proper adventure. Certainly, it was a welcome change from patient charts and filling in forms. Though she perhaps would have preferred an adventure in the Scottish Highlands away from death and murder and drama, she'd just have to make the most of whatever this adventure brought.

Focusing hard on the remaining footage, Rebecca watched Bryce, and whoever it was who had been with him in the rec room, step outside through the same door they had used earlier. Bryce was still the only person in view, due to the angle at which the camera was pointed.

They disappeared a few seconds afterwards and Georgia paused the footage.

'That's all there is, I'm afraid, barely worth the tape it's recorded on,' she said. 'Whoever it is, that person sticks to the same route on the way out so they're not caught on camera. I scrolled the footage right to the end of the day and nobody else comes back through the door. Much later, some of the company cleaners can be seen entering the room, unaware of what happened on the outside balcony deck just a few hours before.'

'And nobody saw Bryce's body fall from the deck?' said Kitt.

Georgia shook her head. 'That balcony is at the stern end of the ship. There aren't any other balconies below it. At any rate, when you're that close to docking there are very few people out on the upper decks. Most passengers, if not all, have gone to their cabins to collect their luggage or are at the bar having one last drink before they go off and continue their journey on land. It's a very quiet time security-wise so I always use that window to nip down to the casino and speak to Noah Davies who is chief dealer. Sometimes you get people arguing over what they have won or lost before they get off the ship and also, there is a safe nearby where any cash received for bets is kept so it's no bad thing to keep an eye on things as people are disembarking. Of course, that was the one day when there were no argumentative punters. I could have been above deck and if I had been, I might have seen something.'

'Or heard the gunshot,' said Rebecca. 'Your ears are

probably better trained than most to pick up something like that.'

Georgia nodded. 'I like to think my training would have kicked in but, to be honest, I can't really kid myself too hard on that front. I'd bet everything I own that the killer waited for the ship's horn to sound before pulling the trigger. I don't think I'd have had much more chance of realizing something suspicious was going on than anyone else under those circumstances. Ugh.' Georgia groaned, slamming her fist down on the table, and tried to steady her breath which had considerably quickened.

Rebecca jumped at the unexpected gesture.

'I'm sorry,' Georgia said, rubbing her eyes. 'Oh, I didn't mean to startle you but watching that footage just riles me up. I've been going over and over it, and all the other cameras from that day, trying to catch out the culprit. Or even just to generate a plausible suspect. This should never have happened. With all the equipment I've got in here, a killing like this, it just shouldn't be possible. It almost feels like someone is taunting me.'

'Would anyone have any reason to do that?' said Kitt. 'You haven't fired anyone recently, have you? Disgruntled employees can be a force to be reckoned with.'

'No, nothing like that,' said Georgia. 'I've not had any problems with the crew. It just gets to me, I suppose. That someone was able to pull this off.'

'I know it's frustrating,' said Kitt, her tone a bit warmer

than it had been throughout their time in the security command centre. 'But we do have a finite number of people to work through. The access code on the door to that rec room is known only to the crew members, right?'

Georgia nodded. 'It's a disciplinary offence to share the code because we've got to keep security tight. So yes, I think it is almost certainly a crew member.'

'And nobody has resigned or been fired for other reasons since Bryce's death?' said Kitt.

'No, that was something we kept more than a keen eye on directly after Bryce was murdered. Anyone who was leaving the ship for a different rotation had to give a forwarding address, phone number and next of kin information which was all double-checked straight away to make sure they were contactable if anything untoward came to light. I told my superiors that once the investigation into Bryce's death had been closed to the police's satisfaction, one way or another, I would tender my resignation if they wanted me to. As head of security, the buck stops with me when it comes to people's safety. But they wouldn't hear of it.'

'Probably because you've given five years of loyal service,' said Rebecca. 'I'd rather not think about it while on board but I imagine all sorts could go wrong every time you set sail. Yes, a murder is a terrible thing to happen but it doesn't erase all the other times you've kept people safe.'

'That's the argument they gave,' Georgia said, her words coupled with a weak smile.

'And it's a fair one,' said Kitt. 'We will find out who did this, don't you worry. I've never failed to bring a killer to justice once I've started on a case. It's just a matter of cross-referencing the people who have access to that code with people who had motive to murder Bryce.'

Errol and Georgia exchanged a dubious look and then turned back to Kitt.

'I wish you all the luck in the world, don't get me wrong,' said Georgia. 'But as you've probably gathered from all I've said, that list isn't going to be a short one.'

CHAPTER SIX

'Ey up,' said Grace, 'Kitt's packed handcuffs.'

'Feeling better after your seasickness, are you, Grace?' said Kitt, marching back over to her suitcase, which was lying open on her bed in the cabin she and Rebecca were sharing, and snatching the handcuffs dangling from Grace's fingers. Though Kitt might have preferred to share a room with her assistant so she could focus solely on the investigation, Rebecca had ensured that didn't happen. If she shared the room with Kitt, she could keep a close eye on the work-to-play ratio and try to persuade Kitt to take things a bit easier when it swung out of balance.

'My travel sickness comes and goes,' said Grace. 'But don't worry, I'd never let it get in the way of ridiculing you.'

'Oooh, you're like a kinky Mary Poppins,' said Evie. 'What else are you going to pull out of that bag.'

'The handcuffs are in case we need to make a citizen's arrest, thank you very much,' said Kitt, before adding with a cheeky smile, 'As Halloran isn't with us, I don't have any other use for them.'

At this, Grace and Evie hooted at Kitt as though she were a celebrity on an American chat show who had just revealed she had a boyfriend.

'Call the *Times*, pronto!' Evie said. 'I do believe that Kitt Hartley just admitted to having fun.'

'All right, all right, you two,' Kitt said with a chuckle. 'You do get overexcited about the silliest thing.'

'This isn't the silliest thing, this is a Dear Diary moment,' said Grace. 'Dear Diary, I thought this day would never come . . .'

'Will you give over?' said Kitt, shaking her head.

Rebecca laughed along at their little show while lounging on her bed and drinking from a miniature bottle of schnapps she'd found in the mini-fridge. Though they had hardly been able to book the most lavish rooms on the ship, this was still one of the most luxurious suites Rebecca had ever had the good fortune to stay in. The bed was so soft it seemed to hug you. Long windows lined the end of the room, offering a view out to the endless blue ocean, and in case you ever tired of that, there was a massive flatscreen hung on the wall, a mahogany writing desk and a couple of armchairs upholstered in the richest crimson fabric Rebecca had ever seen. She just knew they'd be the perfect place to sit with a book and she planned to lure Kitt there at some point for some much-needed relaxation.

'As for what else I'm going to pull out the bag, I've packed numerous items that I think will be of use to us if we have to inspect any areas of the ship for forensic details. Gloves, evidence bags, fingerprint powder, just the essential items. And, though I know this will come as a disappointment to some of you' – Kitt paused, eyeing Grace – 'I'm afraid that even at sea we are still sailing under the British flag and are therefore subject to UK laws. So I have not packed pepper spray, a taser or any other defensive weapon. And there will be no GPS tracking of any kind.'

'Awwww,' said Grace, looking genuinely put out.

'Don't give me that,' said Kitt. 'You're not the one who'd have to explain to Halloran that we were due in court for violating UK privacy laws.'

'Do you not think it'd be worth it, though? Just to see the look on his face when you told him, like,' said Grace.

'A bit of a risky ruse considering it would be highly likely to induce a heart attack. Now, moving on, I've seen from some reviews online that roaming signal can be a little bit hit and miss on board these ships. Given that we don't yet know what we're up against, we can't really afford a communications black hole, so I did bring four walkie-talkies along that are to be used only for important communications to do with the case. Did that last bit sink in, Grace?' Kitt said, handing one to each of them.

'Yes, I heard you,' said Grace.

'That means no rapping the lyrics to the "Thong Song" over it.'

'Well, I need to do something for entertainment. The cinema's out. Have you seen what they're playing? A *Sharknado* marathon. On a ship sailing through waters where there are very likely to be sharks. I'm usually the first to suggest watching a scary movie under any ordinary circumstances but I think even I draw the line there.'

'That is a bit of a rum choice,' said Evie. 'If you're really trying to scare the hell out of people on a boat, why not just play *The Poseidon Adventure* and have done with it?'

'I'm sure you can find other ways to amuse yourself on a ship of this size without going to see a movie marathon about man-eating sharks, or misusing the walkie-talkies,' Kitt said.

'These are a bit old-school, aren't they?' said Grace, tossing the device lightly from hand to hand to get used to the weight of it. 'Is this how you used to communicate with your friends in the olden days?'

Kitt didn't dignify Grace's teasing with a verbal response. She simply glared at her.

'Hey, don't knock it. Nothing wrong with old-school, jelly bean,' Evie said with a wink.

'Yes, well, there is a little something wrong with old-school in this case, I'm afraid,' said Kitt. 'It's much more difficult for us to keep our communications private than it is with the tech we use on land. Even when we're not talking into them, it's fairly obvious we're carrying them. We're probably all going to need to use larger handbags this week. If we can keep them out of sight, that would be better. If the killer sees us using them, they might start trying to listen in to our conversations. To keep things doubly secure, we'll also need a list of code names for everything in case the killer, or anyone else on the ship, is already tuned into our frequency. I thought it might be fun if we used characters from books.'

'Makes sense,' Rebecca said, whilst picking up the walkie-talkie and figuring out the buttons. It didn't really make sense, of course. Not unless you knew Kitt well, who, shall we say, was rather fond of books to put it mildly. Still, she had worked in libraries for more than a decade so perhaps that wasn't so surprising.

'I'll be Jane, from Jane Eyre, of course,' said Kitt. 'Evie?'

'I'll be . . . Holly Golightly. Vintage glamour at its finest.'

'Just Holly, it will be more covert,' said Kitt.

'It's not really the same without the Golightly bit,' Evie started to complain, but Kitt was uninterested in minor qualms and moved straight on.

'Rebecca?'

'I'll be . . . Buttercup.'

'William Goldman?'

'Who else?'

'Good choice,' Kitt said approvingly. 'Dare I ask . . . Grace?'

'Hmmmm. How about, the Reverend Roger Thwackum?'

Rebecca bit her lip in a bid not to burst out laughing while Kitt crinkled her nose the way she always did when something irked her.

'Grace, in case you missed it, we're trying to stay inconspicuous here. Dear me, you are in an even more ridiculous mood than usual.'

'But Rebecca is allowed Buttercup and that's an unusual name.'

'More unusual than Reverend Roger Thwackum? I think not.'

'All right, how about Natty Bumppo?' Grace said. It was clear from the grin stretched from ear to ear that she was enjoying baiting Kitt just a little bit too much.

'James Fenimore Cooper's books are a gripping historical quadrilogy if ever there was one, but there's a reason that particular character had several aliases. Roll again?'

'Fine,' Grace said. 'I guess I'll be Lyra.'

'Lovely,' Kitt said. 'And I suppose we should come up with some code names for the suspects. Now, we've obviously interviewed Georgia and ascertained where she was during the murder window but we've yet to verify that alibi. There's a strong likelihood we will as the odds are the police verified it for themselves and, to be frank, there was nothing about her manner in the interview that suggested she had a hand in Bryce's death.'

'I did look her up online, whenever I could stand to look at a screen,' said Grace. 'All her social media profiles are pictures of the fantastic places she's sailed to. Pictures of her with crew members hugging on beaches and stuff. The kind of thing that'd make you right jealous if you were sat back in Leeds on a rainy day. But I couldn't find any immediate online connections between her and Bryce.'

'She did say she wasn't close with him. It doesn't seem like many people were, which might put a bit of a spanner in the works.'

'How so?' asked Rebecca. Though she was mostly concerned with making sure Kitt took a break from the investigation as needed, she knew this wasn't a game. She had to make sure she was up to speed with what was expected during an investigation. Justice for Kitt's friend was on the line here, not to mention Kitt's peace of mind.

'With each suspect we need to consider means, motive and opportunity,' Kitt explained. 'From the way people have been speaking about Bryce, and indeed from what I know about him, quite a few people had motive to harm him, which might make it difficult to narrow down the true culprit,' said Kitt. 'Georgia may not be connected to Bryce online but she definitely had an altercation with him about an expensive item of sentimental value so there is a motive there. She also had opportunity to make sure nobody saw who the shooter was. As such, during the investigation, we may need to communicate about her over the radio until we're able to confirm her alibi and rule her out. If she happens across our channel, however, and finds out we suspect her, that could be game over for the investigation. There's no way she'd help us after that. So I thought when it came to suspects we'd go for an Oz theme. Georgia can be Dorothy. Her alibi, Noah Davies, he can be the Scarecrow.'

'Oooh, I like this!' said Evie.

'Yes, I thought you might,' Kitt said with a grudging smile. 'We'll refer to any public areas on the ship as Kansas. Employee-only areas will be Oz and so on. We'll add more characters to the list as we go. Now, we'll still need to keep our communication over radio limited. Even with codes, it wouldn't take a genius to work out what we're up to. It would likely only delay someone figuring it out. Bide us a bit of time. So my advice would be only to use the radios when we absolutely need to.'

'All right, all right,' said Grace. 'I'm not going to use them to rap the "Thong Song".'

'I wasn't having a dig at you,' said Kitt. 'I was just making a general observation. Though your defensiveness is some-what suspicious, I have to say. Anyway, we don't have time for that now.' Kitt paused to look at her watch. 'We'd better get ourselves organized. Errol will likely be here any minute to introduce us to Wendy.'

'Oh, yes . . . about that, I had an important message from Errol,' said Evie.

Kitt shook her head. 'So important you've been here half an hour and you're only remembering to tell me now.'

'I got distracted by the handcuffs. So really, it's your fault.'

Kitt closed her eyes for a moment as though recharging her own personal patience battery. 'What was the message?' she said, once her eyes were open again. 'Without any silly quips thrown in, if you don't mind.'

'I had no plans to throw in any silly quips, actually,' Evie said, her tone betraying the fact that her plan had been just that. 'Grace thought she was feeling momentarily better this afternoon so we swung by Errol's show and he apologized but one of the stage hands was off sick so he would have to help re-set the stage for his early evening show. So he won't be able to escort us to see Wendy personally but he's asked one of the stewards at reception to show us there. He said we just had to ask for Timothy Perkins.'

'Right, howay then,' said Kitt, picking up several papers from the writing desk. 'We'd best not be late. From what Errol said, Wendy could be our best chance of understanding what on earth this strange poem from Bryce means. The more I think about it, the more it makes sense that he was trying to send me some kind of message. A message that, for all we know, may provide an integral clue in the case.'

CHAPTER SEVEN

'I'm sorry, but this little ditty doesn't mean anything to me,' Wendy Lostbuoy said in her American accent, her wig of bleached wavelets undulating lightly as she gave a slow shake of her head and handed Bryce's letter back to Kitt. Although Rebecca was by no means an expert on transatlantic intonation, given the way Wendy's sentences went up at the end, as though she was asking a question rather than answering one, she guessed she might hail from somewhere near Los Angeles. Though Rebecca had spent most of the afternoon in the cabin with Kitt, cataloguing the details Georgia had conveyed about the slew of on-board robberies, she had briefly glimpsed several other areas of the ship and had been struck by the diversity of the staff. It seemed people from all corners of the globe were drawn to working on cruise ships, perhaps hoping they could sail to a better life somewhere new. In Wendy's case, Rebecca reasoned that the glamour of the Hollywood hills might not have been all she'd hoped.

That said, their surroundings just now could hardly be described as glittering. When the steward Errol had referred them to, Timothy Perkins, had delivered them to the stage door he'd made a joke about how they should try not to be too overcome when they discovered the glitz of behind-the-scenes life at the on-board theatre. It was the same steward who had been so jolly and cordial while sweeping Rebecca during the random search. It was clear that Tim had a good sense of humour but the moment she stepped through into the backstage area, Rebecca had understood why he felt justified in making this particular joke. The cabaret theatre dressing room was little more than a long, thin cubbyhole at the side of the stage that smelled strongly of acetone and hairspray. There was a line of mirrors that were likely fought over with some ferocity when one of the major productions was taking place on stage. But Wendy's show was a solo act and thus only Wendy, Kitt, Rebecca, Evie and Grace were currently in attendance. Even so, it felt like a bit of a squeeze and Rebecca was grateful for the fact that Evie had spent most of her time slightly separated from the group trying on various costumes and headdresses that were lying around. This had, at least, offered a little bit of room to breathe.

Even though the surroundings might be less than opulent, Wendy's outfit was nothing short of dazzling. She was draped head to toe in a purple taffeta fishtail dress which showed off her bare, bronzed shoulders. Her false eyelashes were encrusted with a purple glitter that was a perfect match to the fabric of her outfit and her nails were painstakingly manicured and painted silver. Her look was everything a person could hope for from showbiz glamour.

'I appreciate you taking a look anyway,' Kitt said, accepting the letter back from Wendy and placing it in her satchel. Rebecca could tell from the flatness in Kitt's voice that this was a disappointing blow. 'I knew it was a bit of a long shot but I thought I'd ask. He's never done anything like that before. Written a poem, I mean. I've no idea why he would but I can't think it is a coincidence that he wrote it and then a few months later was dead.'

'If there's something in it, I'm afraid I don't know what it is,' said Wendy, turning briefly to the mirror to apply a thick layer of red lipstick. Just watching her make-up-artist-calibre technique gave Rebecca a hankering for glamming herself up a bit more. Given the long – and usually sweaty – nature of her hospital shifts, an opportunity to apply lipstick was rare.

'Perhaps you can help us in another respect,' said Kitt. 'We need to start narrowing down who had a motive, a real motive, for killing Bryce.'

Wendy flashed a similar look to the one Georgia and Errol had given Kitt earlier.

'I know, I know,' Kitt said, raising her hands in the air, 'he wasn't a popular man. But there's annoying somebody and then there's doing something that somebody might kill over – in broad daylight no less.'

'I take your point,' said Wendy. 'Bryce might have rubbed people up the wrong way but this is obviously much more than that. I can only really tell you what I told the police. That there's just one person I could think of who had genuine cause to be angry at Bryce. And that's ...' Wendy paused, looking over her shoulder before hissing, 'Captain Ortega.'

'Wait, Bryce was on the wrong side of the captain?' said Grace.

Wendy waved her hands to indicate they needed to keep their voices down and duly, when she spoke, it was barely a whisper. 'Yes, got to be careful what we say, though. The captain pulls all the strings around here. One wrong word and you don't have a job any more. I only told the police about my suspicions on the promise that they wouldn't reveal I was the one who'd told them, even though I knew the captain couldn't have done it. Not when the ship was so close to docking.'

'He'd be on the bridge, navigating the ship,' Kitt said with a nod.

'Right,' Wendy confirmed. 'But even so, I had to be honest with the police and let them know that he was the only person I could think of who had a significant issue with Bryce. One that might cause a more violent reaction, I mean.'

'What issue did the captain have with Bryce, dare I ask?' said Kitt.

'Well, remember, I only heard this story from Bryce's

77

point of view. But the way he told it, he was the innocent party in it all.'

'Amazing how many times Bryce was innocently involved in a great deal of trouble,' Kitt said, shaking her head.

Wendy chuckled but kept her voice low. 'Yes, he had quite an impressive hit rate on that score, I'll give him that. It was all to do with the captain's wife. She had joined her husband on the voyage before the one where Bryce was killed. Like I say, I don't know exactly what happened. Bryce had a habit of embellishing stories for dramatic effect or leaving out important details that might get him into trouble, you know? But somehow Bryce got chatting to the captain's wife in one of the bars. She took quite a shine to him, and the captain discovered them looking a bit too cosy and didn't hide his distaste over Bryce's advances on his spouse.'

'Things got physical?' said Rebecca.

Wendy nodded. 'I should say so. Bryce had a black eye when I spoke to him the day after all this went down, so I can vouch for that much.'

'Do you think the captain will speak to us about it?' said Kitt. It seemed Kitt still hadn't ruled out that he'd played some part in the killing, even if he was on the bridge during the murder window.

'I don't think he's going to volunteer himself for an interview after he's already pacified the police, no,' said Wendy. 'And at any rate, despite the fact that they had a bit of a blowout before Bryce was killed, it might not be the best use of your time.'

'What makes you say that?' said Grace.

Wendy looked between Rebecca, Kitt and Grace before speaking again. 'What do you know about the Gulf of Aden?'

'Nothing really,' said Kitt.

'Wait a second,' said Grace, taking a step backwards in surprise. 'Nothing? *Nothing?*'

'I think you heard me,' said Kitt, shooting her assistant a look that sat somewhere between annoyance and confusion.

'Ey up, I need to sit down,' said Grace. 'At the very least I am going to need a moment to process this shocking development. I think we've just found a gap in Kitt's never-ending non-fiction knowledge.'

'Oh, Grace, really,' said Kitt. 'Will you give over – it's not the time.'

But it was too late. Grace was off and Rebecca got to witness yet more of her 'livewire' antics for herself.

'You've never visited the Gulf of Aden? Or read a book? Or listened to a podcast? Or attended a lecture just for the fun of it, really?'

'For goodness' sake Grace,' said Kitt, while Rebecca was again left biting her lip in an attempt not to laugh. 'I have never claimed to know everything about everything, that's impossible. Sorry, Wendy, please do excuse Grace. She's excitable at the best of times. Why do you bring it up?'

Wendy smiled at Grace's shtick but just as quickly her

smile faded. 'About six months ago, Bryce took a trip to the Gulf of Aden. I suppose if you live mostly on land, there's not much reason to know about that place but those of us who live at sea are quite familiar with the most infamous stretches of the ocean and that one, well, it is still one of the most notorious places for smuggling, trafficking and pirating.'

'I thought you said Bryce had gone legit?' said Rebecca.

'He said he had,' replied Kitt. 'So why did he go there?'

'He never said . . . Well, that's not quite accurate, I suppose. He wouldn't say,' Wendy explained. 'When I joined the company a few years ago, me and Bryce just hit it off, you know? I thought he told me most things but this thing with the Gulf of Aden, whatever it was, it's the first time he ever held back with me when we were talking. I did ask him straight, several times in fact, and he wouldn't be drawn on that subject. I told the police this, of course, and they said that they'd look into it but I don't know if they did. When . . .' Wendy lowered her eyes.

'When . . . ?' Kitt nudged, gently.

'When you're someone like me, the police don't always take what you say seriously. And frankly, they're not alone in that.'

Rebecca swallowed hard. In her years at the hospital she'd witnessed, and intervened in, some outrageous treatment of minority groups. If there was one thing guaranteed to boil her blood, it was discrimination. What a terrible way for Wendy to feel. As though her voice wasn't heard. As though she didn't count. She must feel especially helpless in this instance, when it was one of her closest friends who had been murdered. From the way she described it, she and Bryce had really connected.

Kitt's posture had turned rigid in a way that suggested she was just as angered by Wendy's experience as Rebecca felt. 'I can assure you that all voices will be listened to without bias in this investigation,' she said.

Wendy offered a weak smile to Kitt, Grace and Rebecca. It wasn't clear that she really believed that and Rebecca couldn't blame her for being sceptical. Wendy had probably endured her fair share of lip service over the years.

At that juncture Evie, completely oblivious to the sensitive nature of the moment, called over from the cupboard she'd been raiding. 'Oooh! Boffo! I really want one of these!'

When the four companions turned to see what Evie was referring to, they saw her waving around a pair of oversized fans decorated with pink ostrich feathers.

'What on earth could you possibly need those for?' said Kitt. 'It's not like there're many places in York where you'd have use for an accessory like that. Unless you're planning to make a real entrance at The Exhibition on a Friday night.'

'Maybe I'll find a use for them behind closed doors,' Evie said, playfully hiding her face behind one of the fans until only her eyes peeked over the top. 'You and Halloran aren't the only ones with an exotic love life, you know? Me and Charley might even be classed as deviants.'

'And I'm sure she'll be so glad you've shared that fact with us all, Evie,' Kitt said. Evie was dating Halloran's partner, a sergeant. From what Kitt said, she was a pretty closed book so perhaps Kitt was right about Evie casually broadcasting details about the flavour of their sex life.

'What's the matter,' Evie purred as she waved the fans around with a flourish, 'worried you and Halloran might have some competition?'

Rebecca couldn't help but laugh at Evie's goading. One of the most entertaining elements of her sister dating Halloran was that he didn't much care what people thought and would, on occasion, make the odd reference to their elicit activities just to see the blush rise in Kitt's face. Although Rebecca was happy not knowing the finer details of her sister's sex life, anything that offered Kitt an opportunity to have fun and take things a bit more lightly was welcome. Her heart was always in the right place but given half a chance, she could be somewhat intense. Of the two of them, Rebecca had definitely been gifted with the more easy-going temperament.

'I am not being lured into a conversation about that again,' Kitt said, though there was no mistaking the cheeky little smile that had surfaced on her lips at the mention of Halloran. 'And I'm fairly sure Wendy doesn't want you playing around with all her stuff.'

'It's all right, I don't mind,' Wendy said with a chuckle, and went to join Evie so she might better instruct her on how to hold the fans in the most striking poses.

'So,' said Grace, 'if I'm getting the timeline right, Bryce took that trip to the Gulf of Aden six months before he died, around the time he wrote that letter he never sent to you.'

'I know he told you he'd gone legitimate,' said Rebecca, 'but Wendy says he had a habit of leaving out details that would incriminate him. So, sad as it is to think about it, he might not have been completely honest with you. What if his pirating days weren't over? And what if he'd got himself into some hot water on that trip? Too hot even for him to handle? There's also a chance that his trip was related to the robberies that were taking place on the ship somehow.'

'It is a strong possibility that he got himself in over his head with some kind of criminal activity, given my previous dealings with him,' said Kitt. 'He was always an act-first-think-later sort of a fellow. But to be honest, I'm also wondering why Errol never mentioned this trip.'

Rebecca shrugged. 'He did say Bryce didn't tell him much. That Wendy was the one he confided in. Maybe he didn't know about it. If Bryce was up to no good on that trip, he might not have told anyone else he was going.'

'Maybe,' said Grace. 'But that is a pretty big trip to hide from a person who is essentially your business partner. What if he'd been delayed and was unable to make it back for the next voyage? It feels as though he must have told Errol something about it.'

'Agreed,' said Kitt. 'I'm not about to jump to any conclusions but somehow it seems unlikely that Errol wouldn't know anything about this.'

Rebecca shook her head. 'I don't know, Kitt. Errol has done nothing but help us. He was the one who suggested we talk to Wendy. If he knew about Bryce's trip to the Gulf of Aden, he must have guessed she would too, in which case, why wouldn't he just tell us about it?'

'I don't know, maybe he was hoping we wouldn't find out about it?' said Kitt. 'It's just a hunch. Maybe there's nothing to it. All I can say is that, based on past experience, we need to be very careful who we trust.'

CHAPTER EIGHT

After all of the morbid chat about Bryce's untimely demise, Wendy had been insistent that Rebecca, Kitt, Evie and Grace stay and watch her perform her show to the packed-out cabaret theatre on board the *Northern Spirit*. To Rebecca's surprise, Kitt had agreed. But then, even though it had been a bit of a knock that Wendy didn't know anything about Bryce's mysterious poem, she had provided them with some very useful information so it had hardly been a waste of time.

In fact, the first day on the case had been a long one but at the same time incredibly fruitful.

In the space of an afternoon they had already uncovered a significant amount of detail about Bryce's dealings before he met an unfortunate, and rather brutal, end, with the visit to the safety command centre proving particularly helpful. Between the revelation that there had been a long-term issue with theft on board the *Northern Spirit*, and discovering that Bryce was on particularly sour terms with the captain – a figure of formidable power, at least as far as the crew were concerned – and the fact that he had taken a trip to the Gulf of Aden around the same time that he wrote that strange note to Kitt, the pieces of some bigger mystery were beginning to jigsaw together. Granted, they had no real idea as yet what that grander puzzle might centre around but it was, after all, only day one of the investigation so to get this far this quickly didn't seem like bad going. Perhaps this progress was, in part, why Kitt had felt justified in giving the investigation a rest for a couple of hours.

After the nigh on relentless chatter about possible suspects and motives for the last eight hours, Rebecca felt more than justified to be blithely reclining in the plush, royal blue seating in the cabaret theatre. Wendy's show was immensely popular and empty spaces were few but Wendy had managed to pull in a favour and get Rebecca and the girls settled together just a few rows back in the raked seating. Seated around some circular tables, between the girls and the stage, were, judging from their fine evening gowns and sharp tuxedos, some quite well-to-do passengers. Rebecca guessed they had likely paid over the odds to be installed in that particular spot. So much about cruises seemed to be about exclusivity and expense – a fine way to live if you could afford it!

On the stage, Wendy stood in front of a thick curtain, cut from the same blue fabric as the seating. The way in which the spotlight rippled over the pleats created a watery effect that made Wendy look like a sultry, purple mermaid. The harsh glare of the spotlight didn't seem to bother her. In fact, she appeared to bathe in it as naturally as anyone else would sunlight, while she sang a cover of 'Since I Fell for You' by Lenny Welch in a voice that was smoother than warm caramel. The second Wendy opened her mouth to sing, Rebecca understood why the theatre was so full. She had one of those voices that sent goosebumps along your arms and had the hairs on the back of your neck standing on end. It was so long since Rebecca had had a chance to relax like this, she closed her eyes just for a moment to savour those rich, velvetine tones.

Rebecca was not alone in her admiration for Wendy's performance.

Various whistles and hoots rose up from the audience as she sang. When Rebecca opened her eyes again she realized that the bulk of them were coming from Evie and Grace. Wendy smiled at the encouragement and gave them a little wave as she put every ounce of breath available into the concluding high note. It was so bold and audacious a sound, it almost seemed to Rebecca like she could feel the force of it hitting her, even though she was sitting some distance from the stage.

Applause roared as Wendy unhooked the microphone from its stand and stepped down from the spotlight to mingle amongst the circular tables arranged near the foot of the stage. Despite the fact Wendy was wearing the highest silver heels Rebecca had ever seen, she floated effortlessly amongst the well-to-do, strutting with a confidence Rebecca could only dream of. Perhaps it was because in that particular outfit, Wendy was able to indulge her true self without any fear of judgement or dismissal. Such authenticity was a rare and spectacular sight.

As she flounced around the tables, Wendy proceeded to ask audience members their name and where they came from until she at last reached a table at which a tanned couple, who looked like they might be in their early seventies, were seated.

'I hear we've got some ship celebrities in the house this evening,' Wendy purred before tilting the microphone towards the lady who was wearing a powder-blue skirt suit and pearls.

'That's right,' the lady said, clamping her hands over Wendy's so that she had better control of the microphone and there was no chance of it being whipped away anytime soon. 'I'm Joan Miller and this is Ted Miller and this month marks our twelfth consecutive month at sea. Nothing but ocean cruising for a whole year! We've never been so happy, I can tell you.'

'My my,' said Wendy, with a knowing eyebrow raise to the rest of the room. 'Will you ever see dry land again?'

'Not if we can help it,' Ted Miller chipped in, leaning across his wife so he could be heard over the mic. 'We'd much rather be here eating the five-star meals and brushing shoulders with the captain. We're part of the captain's circle, you know. We've been cruising almost non-stop for the last eight years. In that time we've taken dance classes on every ship. You should see our tango.'

'Would I live to tell the tale if I did?' Wendy said, just about managing to get the mic close enough to her mouth for everyone to hear her. In less than thirty seconds, however, Ted Miller had well and truly regained control.

'Only one way to find out,' Ted replied with a light chuckle. 'We only wish we'd started cruising in our younger years. I don't mind telling you all that we are hoping to get our hands on the most-travelled passenger award this trip. We think we deserve it,' he said.

'That's right, that's right,' Joan said, shoving Ted away from the microphone with impressive force and adding, with a surprising amount of bitterness, 'We missed out on the last trip: someone on that ship had been sailing for the last fifteen years. Well, how is anyone this side of eighty-five going to compete with that? We had no chance at all with that kind of competition. But we've got a good feeling about this trip. We're hoping to win out this time.'

'Certainly are, this is our time. We just know it. That trophy will mean our luggage weighs in a little heavier but it'll be worth it, I can tell you,' Ted said. 'Nothing on earth like being a winner.'

'I wish I could speak from experience on that,' Wendy

said, after at last managing to grapple the microphone off them. The crowd laughed at her dryly mocking tone and Wendy sashayed back to the stage. 'But I can't pretend I don't understand the desire to take it all,' she added while singing the opening lines to 'The Winner Takes It All' by Abba. The pianist, who had accompanied Wendy's earlier ditty, jumped to attention and started to fill the spaces with the familiar but haunting melody. Wendy's voice became stronger, bolder as she approached the chorus – so well known that many an audience member chose to join in. None of them, sadly, had quite the same vocal mastery as Wendy. But they had all, by the cut of them, had enough wine to believe they did.

Rebecca looked over at Kitt expecting to see her enjoying the show. She usually loved stuff like this. Half a glass of wine and she was all over the karaoke mic herself. Instead of revelling in the dry wit and sumptuous voice of Wendy Lostbuoy, however, her sister was wearing the most peculiar expression.

'What is it?' Rebecca said, just loud enough so Kitt could hear her over the music. Evie and Grace, who had been engrossed in Wendy's performance, turned and leaned in to listen.

'Errol said that he can't really imagine Bryce's murderer being a staff member. And Georgia has been trying to solve a series of thefts for several years,' said Kitt.

Rebecca, Evie and Grace exchanged a look.

'Yeah . . .' said Evie. 'I know you're going somewhere with this but we're going to need a little more direction than that.'

'The Millers have just made it quite clear that they are not the only passengers to spend long periods of their life at sea. Hopping from one boat to the next. Never staying in any one port for any time at all. They've been sailing for twelve consecutive months and I bet they're not the only ones if there's a trophy for the most miles travelled at sea.'

'Oh!' said Grace. 'You think that the person carrying out all of these crimes might be one of the top passengers? Part of the captain's circle, or whatever it was Mrs Miller called it. I suppose someone like that would really know their way around ships considering how much time they spend on cruises.'

'But Errol also said handing out the code to the staff area was a sackable offence,' Rebecca said. 'Would a crew member really give it out knowing that? Even to someone who was a regular passenger? It seems like a pretty risky thing to do. I think positions like this, where you get to travel the world as part of your day job, are pretty coveted. Would someone throw that all away?'

'They might not have given the code out at all,' said Kitt. 'If such a scheme was in operation amongst passengers who spent large chunks of time at sea, it's likely these people would be used to keeping a sharp eye out for any useful information about the behind-the-scenes life on board. They may, for example, have just waited outside the rec room and watched people key in the code as they went in and out.'

'Wouldn't that have been a bit obvious?' said Evie. 'Standing outside the room like that, watching people enter?'

'I don't know,' said Kitt. 'I think you could come up with any number of excuses to be hanging around there if you had a clear sense of how the ship worked. You could claim you got lost, or that one of the crew members had asked to meet you there. That's just a couple of ideas off the top of my head. I'm sure seasoned thieves, part of some kind of crime ring, would have much better ideas than that.'

'So, if we're to include passengers as well as staff in our investigation, how do we go about following that up?' said Rebecca. 'Is it even possible to get hold of the information we'd need to draw up a list of suspects?'

'It's highly unlikely that the staff will hand over the names of their most valuable passengers from the voyage on which Bryce was shot,' said Kitt. 'But, since she feels so guilty about what happened to Bryce, maybe I could encourage Georgia to see if she can whittle down any passengers who were on the last voyage and are also on this one, who might have come into contact with Bryce. I could also message Halloran and ask him to approach the North East police service and see if they'll share any information about passengers on board the ship when the murder took place. But those are both long shots. Going through that amount of information – given the number of passengers – would take a significant chunk of time and nobody's likely to sign up for that based on a hunch alone. The swiftest route to getting some idea about the plausibility of a theory is probably to get ourselves invited into a special event with the captain's circle and see what we can find out through casual conversation. Those kinds of events are always flowing with free champagne. It wouldn't be difficult to get the information we were looking for after they'd had a few glasses of fizz.'

'But if the person who killed Bryce was a passenger rather than a crew member, they might not even be on this ship. In fact, they could be anywhere by now,' said Rebecca.

'I know,' said Kitt. 'And I don't relish the thought that we might be wasting our time here. But if we have stumbled on to a wild goose chase, better to find out sooner rather than later.'

CHAPTER NINE

The sun had long since set over the ocean and the golden lanterns strewn about the Top Deck Bar were eating into the starry darkness as Rebecca sipped on her cocktail and listened to Kitt continue her analysis of the information they had gathered so far. The pair were perched on stools situated at the edge of the ship, allowing them an uninterrupted view across the rippling, dark expanse below. The bar was fitted with some outdoor heaters which were keeping the edge off the night-time chill, while still enabling them to breathe in the fresh, salty air. As Rebecca looked up at the moon which hung pale and full above them, she let out a contented sigh and congratulated herself on striking this compromise with her sister. Especially since striking any compromise with Kitt was always a nigh on epic battle.

Rebecca had hoped that after Wendy's show they would be officially 'off duty' but the second they left the theatre Kitt was making a list of all the things she needed to check into about the captain's circle. Evie and Grace had both looked shattered by the time the curtain fell on Wendy's early evening show so Rebecca had sent them off back to their cabin and dragged her sister to the bar. If Kitt insisted on talking about the investigation long into the night, Rebecca wanted a drink in her hand. Of course, she could have just come to the bar by herself and left Kitt to her own devices but, given that the whole point of their getaway had originally been to give Kitt a break, Rebecca didn't like the idea of her sister sitting alone in her cabin getting ever more embroiled in her friend's death.

Her doctor's sense of self-sacrifice always kicked in when it came to a choice between her merriment and the well-being of others.

'We'll need to make some time tomorrow to stop by the casino and check in with Georgia's alibi,' said Kitt.

'I think that will be a quick job,' said Rebecca. 'I know they had that altercation but I thought she seemed quite remorseful about Bryce's passing.'

'Yes, that's how it appeared to me too but, well, in my experience, people can seem a lot of things when they're trying to cover up their ill deeds,' said Kitt. 'They can seem helpful, remorseful, devastated, outraged, friendly. I have seen it all in the time I have been investigating and, trust me, there is no mask a killer isn't willing to wear if it gives them even a small chance of covering up what they've done.'

Rebecca took a deep breath and looked into her sister's

ice-blue eyes, identical to her own. 'You do worry me when you talk like that. I don't think it's healthy to go around second-guessing the dark side of everyone you meet. You never used to say these kinds of things before you got into investigating.'

Kitt gave a little shrug as if she didn't much mind being turned into a cynic but that gesture didn't fool Rebecca even a little bit. 'I know, but I'm not some moon-eyed twenty-one-year-old any more.'

'Not by some margin!'

'A bit rich given we're the same age almost to the minute, don't you think?' Kitt said, smirking at her sister. 'Anyway, I still look for the best in people whenever I can. Cynicism is . . . well, it's just part of the job I didn't anticipate. I admit there are prices to pay for this line of work that I never imagined.'

'I'm sorry,' said Rebecca. 'Obviously, I can identify with that.'

'Oh, of course you can,' said Kitt, with a dismissive wave. 'Here's me wittering on about my lack of faith in humanity while you're sitting there grappling with the momentous task of keeping humanity going.'

'Suppose we at least both chose our burdens,' said Rebecca, raising her glass and taking another gulp of the deliciously fruity concoction.

'Indeed, and as such, there is no point wallowing. It's too late for me to give this up now. If I wasn't out working these cases, I'd just be lying awake wondering if the people who were doing it were finding the justice that the victims deserve.'

'Speaking of which,' said Rebecca, 'I think you might be the only person on the ship who really wants justice for Bryce. Well, besides Wendy.'

'Based on what the others have said about how unpopular a crew member he was, you might be right,' said Kitt. 'He couldn't even ingratiate himself with the most important people on the ship, like the ship's head of security and the captain. You'd think of all people he'd want to stay on their good side at least. Honestly, he did baffle me,' Kitt said, but she couldn't help but smile as she spoke of her lost friend.

'On that note, you don't really think that the ship's captain is involved in this, do you? Someone like him has a lot to lose by committing a crime like that. Would Bryce really have been worth all that trouble for him? Even if he had been getting cosy with his wife?'

'You're right that it would be a big risk for someone with so much to lose, which is why if he is involved, he won't have done the dirty work himself. Just because he was on the bridge during Bryce's death window doesn't mean that in a fit of passion he didn't pay someone or order someone to kill Bryce and then went to great pains to cover it up. Georgia also may have an alibi for the murder itself but if the ship's captain is responsible for the death, she may yet be in his pocket. Bribed into making sure there wasn't any video evidence.'

'But the camera didn't move suddenly in that footage when Bryce entered. That just seemed to be the angle the camera was usually pointed in,' Rebecca argued.

'Maybe,' said Kitt. 'Or maybe Georgia got plenty of notice that something was going to happen on that balcony and was told to make sure as little could be seen as possible.'

'If you're going down that road,' said Rebecca, 'then Georgia might not have covered it up because she was paid, she might have been threatened or coerced in some other way. I know that's not much of an upgrade in the faith in humanity stakes but we shouldn't assume, even if she's in on it, that she wants to be. You're the professional investigator, of course, but after speaking to her at some length, I find it easier to believe that if there is any connection between her and this murder, it's because someone is manipulating her. The woman I spoke to today seemed trustworthy to me, that's all I'm saying.'

'Noted,' Kitt said with a smirk before picking up her own cocktail and taking a quick sip.

'I just think the theory that the captain's behind all this, and Georgia is helping him to cover it up, falls flat, on one particular point anyway,' said Rebecca.

'How's that?'

'It's not a proportional response to what Bryce did. And there were easier ways of fixing the problem if the captain wanted him out of the picture. If he hated Bryce, he wouldn't have to kill him. You saw how keen Wendy was to keep her voice down when she mentioned the captain. I'm betting that if he wanted to, he could get anyone fired. Probably wouldn't have to even give much of a reason and from what we know of Bryce, finding a legitimate reason for dismissal wouldn't have been very hard. When he could get rid of Bryce so easily, why would he even risk something as elaborate as murder – a shooting in broad daylight no less?'

'It's a point well made but it still doesn't get Captain Ortega off the hook. If we're willing to believe the best in Georgia, then we have to do the same for him. He might not have meant for Bryce to die,' said Kitt. 'Murders aren't always premeditated. There are many possible scenarios that may have started off fairly innocently – well, as innocently as any situation involving a gun can start out – and led to Bryce being killed accidentally.'

'But we know the killer lured Bryce outside to the balcony. We've already established that the murder was premeditated.'

'We can't know that for sure and it's important that we do our best to keep an open mind on that point. Yes, the balcony was the ideal place for the killer to murder Bryce in the way they did. But it's also the ideal location for a quiet conversation. To threaten or coerce someone without there being any witnesses. The killer may only have brought the gun to make it clear to Bryce that they meant business, in a bid to compel him into doing something that he then refused to do.'

'And you think, what? That they struggled, things got out of hand and the gun fired?' said Rebecca, trying to figure out if that seemed like a plausible thing to happen. Did you really carry a gun unless you were going to use it? Or at the very least were willing to use it. 'And there's still the question of how the killer smuggled a gun on to the ship, of course.'

'At this stage, the idea of a struggle and an accidental killing makes more sense than a premeditated murder in broad daylight with a weapon that might easily be heard,' said Kitt. 'And yes, I wanted to ask Georgia about how a gun might find its way aboard the ship but I didn't want her to think I was questioning her ability to keep the ship secure – or to accidentally imply that she might have had something to do with it. We really need to keep her on side.'

'When you describe the killing like that, I suppose it does make more sense that it was an accident,' said Rebecca. 'And that means if we make it to an event with the captain's circle, it's not just the passengers we're going to need to keep an eye on. We'll have to watch the captain carefully too.'

'It's far too early to rule anyone out, so yes. Given that the captain could have her fired for even making such an accusation, I don't think Wendy would have mentioned his name unless she thought he might be capable of something like that. And if he did pay someone or coerce someone into threatening Bryce, only for it to go badly wrong, then there might not even be any coercion involved. Georgia could be covering up what really happened to Bryce out of loyalty to her captain. You heard what Errol said, the staff on this ship are like a family. They may not all see eye-to-eye – Bryce's death is surely proof of that – but maybe when the going is really tough they pull together, and that could be what's happening here. Perhaps the police haven't found a suspect because everyone is covering for everyone else.'

Rebecca offered a light nod. She couldn't argue with her sister's reasoning. That was a real possibility. But, of course, it wasn't the only explanation Wendy had offered. And to Rebecca's mind, the other possible theory about what was behind Bryce's demise seemed much more likely – the theory that he never really did go legit.

'What about what Wendy said, about the Gulf of Aden?' Rebecca said in the gentlest tone she could. Even if Bryce had gone back to his old smuggling ways, he didn't deserve to die in such a violent manner and she didn't want Kitt to think that she was in any way insinuating that. 'Maybe his death didn't have anything to do with his brush with the captain's wife – maybe there is a link between the letter he failed to send you and his trip there and his death.'

'Be that as it may, until I understand what the poem in that letter is all about I don't think I will easily be able to investigate that strand unless somebody on board was with him during his trip. And I have a vague theory that Bryce might have gone away sailing with your boyfriend.'

Rebecca was about to ask who Kitt was talking about when she put two and two together. 'Give over, will you? Errol is not my boyfriend.'

'Not yet but he obviously wouldn't mind the job,' Kitt said, raising her eyebrows and taking another sip of her drink.

'You really think he went to the Gulf of Aden with Bryce, and has tried to cover that fact up?' Rebecca replied in an attempt to change the subject. 'Would that even be possible?'

'Oh yes, quite straightforward actually. Especially out here where people are perhaps freer to move around. Just pay for everything on the trip in cash. Don't take any mobile devices with you. Nobody would know where you'd been unless you told them.'

'And . . . you think they got up to something they shouldn't have out there that resulted in Bryce's death?' Rebecca shifted in her seat. She had to admit that the way people behaved at sea differed to that on land. People seemed a lot more free and easy with what they wore, how they spoke and what they spoke about. Granted, she'd only been on board the ship for a short time. But she'd overheard quite a few conversations in that time and it was clear that, once they'd boarded a ship, people could zip all over the globe doing pretty much as they pleased, provided they had the right documentation. Of course, it probably helped that everyone on the ship – except the crew members themselves – were wealthy folk. When you had that much money few people would stand in the way of you doing whatever you wanted.

'I don't have any evidence for thinking it. But, as I said earlier, I've learned the hard way on previous investigations that the nicest person in the room usually knows more than they're letting on.'

'So the fact that Errol seems a genuinely nice guy makes him more suspicious to you?'

'That's right.'

'You need help,' Rebecca said, shaking her head.

Kitt took another mouthful of her cocktail before responding. 'I've worked with Grace for almost five years, Becca. Of course I need help.'

Rebecca laughed. Grace did rather seem to live up to her giddy reputation.

'Regardless of any involvement he may or may not have in what happened to Bryce, I think you're our best chance of persuading Errol to get us an invite to one of the captain's circle events, and of finding out if there's anything to the idea that Errol isn't telling us the whole story.'

Rebecca frowned. 'Me?'

'He's taken a shine to you. Must be your shameless flirting.'

'That's so unfair,' Rebecca said through a chuckle. 'You know I was just trying to get you to smile.'

'Maybe, or maybe you were just using that as the perfect cover so you had an excuse to flirt with him.'

'There you go again with your cynicism! Anyway, he's probably not that interested. I think he was only playing along for a bit of fun.'

'Not from where I was standing. But, as it happens, we can probably play this to our advantage.'

'What do you mean?' Rebecca narrowed her eyes and looked at her sister side-long.

'So long as he is, albeit loosely, on the suspect list (I've decided his code name is Professor Marvel, by the way), I don't want you going anywhere with him where there won't be any witnesses, and I definitely don't want you to spend lengthy amounts of time with him without checking in. But . . . if you can arrange a drink, that would be a start. See what you can get out of him.'

'Kitt, wait, I don't know about this,' said Rebecca, but Kitt wasn't interested in her sister's protests.

'Nothing could be simpler. You just make sure you don't drink anywhere near as much as him and get him talking. You never know what might slip out.'

Rebecca shook her head. She'd agreed to come along on this ridiculous mission to find Bryce's killer but she wasn't sure that signing up for undercover work was the best idea. 'But I'm terrible at lying. I don't know if I can do that. Or if I want to do that.'

'Do what?' said a deep voice that Rebecca at once recognized as Errol's.

CHAPTER TEN

Swallowing hard, Rebecca paused for about ten seconds longer than she would have liked before answering that question and when she at last found the words, she could feel the burn in her cheeks. 'St-stay for another drink,' she stuttered out.

'Actually, you're morally obliged to stay for another drink,' Errol said with a grin.

'Am I indeed?' Before she could stop herself Rebecca felt a smile surfacing. There was just something about Errol's demeanour that tickled her. Perhaps it was his easy confidence. There was nothing overbearing or intimidating about him. 'And why is that exactly?'

'Well, I know Kitt's been busy with the investigation so she's excused from sitting through my show. But Evie made it to my afternoon performance and I saw Grace – though she did rush out at one point unexpectedly.'

'Seasickness,' Kitt clarified.

'I hope she's feeling better and I must admit I'm relieved to hear it wasn't my show that caused that reaction.'

Rebecca and Kitt chuckled at the idea.

'But I didn't see you there and you promised you'd come. Left me broken-hearted, you did.'

'I didn't promise a thing!' Rebecca said. 'And besides, I have the same excuse as Kitt. I've been helping with the case.'

'And very helpful you've been too,' said Kitt. 'But I need to get back to the cabin now and compile everything we've learned so far – not to mention take another look at that cryptic letter Bryce sent which is still a complete mystery. But I'm sure that Rebecca would love to join you for another one.'

Rebecca opened her mouth to protest. Not because she didn't want to spend time with Errol per se but because she knew what Kitt was up to. She was damn near pushing Rebecca into an impromptu undercover operation. Before Rebecca got two words out of her mouth, however, Kitt had slipped off her stool and thrown her satchel over her shoulder.

'Surely you can stay for one more?' said Rebecca, widening her eyes for a moment to make it clear she wasn't comfortable surreptitiously interrogating Errol. Just because her sister was in the habit of sly observation didn't mean that Rebecca was interested in taking up that particular hobby for herself.

'Don't worry, sis,' Kitt said. She really was laying it on thick. Kitt had never called her 'sis' in her life. 'I'll still be awake when you get back so we can discuss important topics such as the best nail varnish to suit our skin tones.'

And with that Kitt was off.

Ugh, Kitt was so bull-headed. There's no way she'd be in the least bit interested in discussing nail varnish when Rebecca got back to their cabin. She'd be expecting to hear about one thing only: any and all intelligence collected on Errol. Who, for all Rebecca knew, was a completely innocent party.

'What are you drinking?' he asked.

'Oh no, let me buy you one,' said Rebecca, wondering what on earth Errol thought of Kitt's sharp exit. Most likely he thought that she was leaving so that they could be alone together, which was in itself an embarrassing prospect. 'Not that I'd really be buying anything since all of this is being paid for out of Kitt's account and she bought us all-inclusive hospitality passes.'

Oh great. She was babbling. Which not only meant that she looked like an idiot but also must mean that she had taken a genuine shine to Errol. She was articulate in every situation except in the presence of someone she fancied. Mercifully, either Errol hadn't noticed or was far too polite to let it show that he had.

'Just a bottle of any beer they've got going will do me fine, thanks. Good of Kitt to stump up for that. Those passes are not particularly cheap.'

'I think she understood it was the only way of getting us all to agree to come on this cruise,' Rebecca said with a forced little chuckle. It wouldn't have done her much good but she should have protested harder when Kitt had convinced the other girls to change their plans. They still would have ended up on the boat, of that Rebecca had no doubt. But perhaps her sister would have thought twice about asking her to manipulate Errol like this.

She waved at one of the waiters and ordered him a beer but, in the space of time it took her to do so, her companion was taken into the arms of another woman who spotted him on her way past their table.

'Errrrol,' the woman cooed as she hooked her arms around his neck. She was wearing a short, silky red dress that made Rebecca wish she'd actually had time to change out of her jeans and jumper into something more fitting for evening cocktails on a five-star cruise ship.

'Jemima . . .' Errol said, a slight catch in his voice betraying the fact that he hadn't expected to see her. Taking hold of Jemima's hands, he managed to gently release himself from her grip. 'You're back on another cruise so soon?'

'Don't look so surprised,' she said, pressing a tapered fingernail to the end of his nose before running her fingers through her long black hair. 'I had such a good time on the last cruise I couldn't wait to come back. I am in cabin 213C this time,' she said, putting a hand to the side of his jaw and holding his eye. 'I do hope you find your way there tonight.' Someone, another woman, called Jemima's name loud enough to get her attention over the gentle reggae music that had been playing in the background. She smiled back at Errol and blew him a kiss before sashaying off into the crowds.

'You . . . all right? You look like you've seen a ghost,' Rebecca said as the waiter set a bottle of beer on the table.

'Well, I suppose they do say mistakes come back to haunt you,' he replied with a light sigh.

'I'm sure it didn't feel like much of a mistake at the time,' Rebecca said, doing her best not to make it sound like a dig. From Jemima's display of affections and Errol's mention of a 'mistake' it was clear what had passed between them on the last cruise. Perhaps Errol's self-assured charm wasn't a byproduct of a naturally easy-going outlook after all. Perhaps it had developed due to the number of women he had falling at his feet. After that little show Rebecca was quite sure he must have a different woman at his disposal on every voyage. Perhaps more than one.

Part of her was slightly put out that the little bit of attention she had got from him was just part of a routine he used on women he met on the ship. Perhaps it had been naive of her to think she was special in some way. She had so little time for dating she wasn't exactly an expert in gauging these things. Such a shame. It would have been nice to have some fun with a man who had eyes as strangely tempestuous as his were, but she was not in the market to be the latest in a long line of women he would come to view as mistakes should they ever dare to re-board the ship and come looking for his attention a second time.

On the plus side, this revelation would make extracting information from Errol much more palatable. So she would be able to please her sister, even if she couldn't please herself.

'No, you're right. At the time it didn't seem like a mistake but I'm not exactly making the best relationship decisions right now,' said Errol.

All right, she had to admit it, that was a tantalizing line. It took all of Rebecca's self-control to resist asking what he meant by that statement. She told herself that was likely a practised sentiment he used with the women on the ship he wanted to bed. Perhaps in a bid to make himself seem more gentlemanly after Jemima's behaviour. Though she had limited experience, she had had men play games like that with her before. Pretend to be very cut up about something that had happened to them so they might seem sensitive and emotionally available. In every case, the morning after, Rebecca hadn't seen them for dust. She wasn't going to bite. Best to just do what her sister wanted and get this silly undercover business over with.

'I am sorry to hear that, and I'm sorry to have missed your show,' she said, skipping over his prior statement as best she could. 'We've been very busy with the case.'

'Any dazzling new leads?'

At the word 'dazzling' Rebecca did all she could not to notice how his eyes sparkled in the glow of the nearby lanterns. She looked out to the blackness of the ocean for a moment before replying. 'I'm not sure yet, to be honest. There is one thing we might have hit on. But we're going to need your help to look into it. It's a can of worms to say the least.'

'I'll help any way I can,' Errol said. 'What do you need?'

'I know this is a big ask, huge really, but we would appreciate any help you can give us in getting into one of the captain's circle events.'

Errol nodded. 'I can't promise anything but I'll definitely ask for you. Why do you need access to the captain's circle? You suspect someone from that group?'

'Suspect is a bit strong at this point in the investigation. But Kitt wants to rule out the possibility that a long-term passenger didn't kill Bryce.'

'But Kitt doesn't have any evidence pointing at a passenger?'

'No, I think it's just a theory for now. Really it came about because of something you said. That you found it unbelievable that a crew member was responsible for what happened to Bryce. And then we found out that there were some people who spend months and years at sea, which we thought might put them in a position to know the ship's protocol pretty well.'

'So Kitt thinks a long-term passenger somehow infiltrated our secure staff area?'

'It's one of the possibilities she's exploring in the spirit of not ruling anything out. Until your friend Jemima appeared, I didn't think it was that plausible that someone on the last voyage might be on this one but it seems like there is some overlap in passengers between one crossing and another.'

At the mention of Jemima's name Errol shuffled in his seat. 'There isn't usually lots of overlap between one voyage and the next but it's true that you do get some.'

'And such people are likely to be members of the captain's circle, right?'

'Not guaranteed, but likely. I'll see what I can do to help you get into one of their upcoming events. I think there might even be one happening tomorrow night. I know some people in hospitality who might do me a favour.'

'I appreciate it. But please don't go to any ridiculous lengths on our account. I really don't know if there's anything to it. Kitt . . . well, she is naturally suspicious given the business she's in and these days that business is sort of taking over her life. It's hard to get her to do anything that isn't work-related.'

'And is her twin the same?' Errol said, smirking before taking a sip of his beer.

'I . . . suppose you could say that, to some extent,' Rebecca said, unable to keep a straight face at having been caught out as the pot calling the kettle black. 'I am a doctor so it is pretty intense. But I've had training to deal with a lot of the fallout. Kitt started this investigation thing independently, so I sometimes worry about her.'

'That's understandable,' said Errol. 'She does seem fairly robust, though.'

Rebecca couldn't help but laugh at that. 'You've chosen a more polite expression than most to describe my sister.' But then her smiled faded. 'It's like with most people, though, they seem a certain way on the outside. Inside is another matter. Like this case, I mean. It's about the death of someone who was her friend, you know, and she's finding out things about him that maybe she doesn't want to find out.'

'Given the kind of person Bryce was, I'm probably going to regret asking this but, like what?'

Rebecca paused, reminding herself to pay close attention to Errol's reaction to what she was about to say. 'Talking to Wendy was really useful, and thanks for that recommendation by the way, but one of the things she mentioned was that Bryce visited the Gulf of Aden six months ago.'

Errol frowned. 'What? Are you sure?'

'We only have Wendy's word for it but she has no reason to lie to us as far as we can see.'

'Hmm. Six months ago,' Errol said, rubbing the salt and pepper stubble on his chin. 'Bryce did take a couple of weeks off but he didn't say he was going to the Gulf of Aden, he said he was going to Bermuda to relax. That seemed unlike him at the time but not strange enough to question it, to be honest. I just thought all the time at sea was finally catching up with him.'

'According to Wendy, he may have lied to you but what we don't understand is why. I know you weren't close but you were business partners in a way. It just seems odd he wouldn't give you some kind of heads-up. You really had no idea that's where he went?'

Errol stared at Rebecca for a moment before answering. 'If I'd known he'd gone off somewhere other than the place he said he was going, I'd have mentioned it from the outset.'

Rebecca nodded. 'Sorry, I didn't mean to insinuate anything, if that's how that came off. There's just a lot to make sense of. Trying to put together the pieces. You don't know why he might have taken a trip there?'

'No, I suppose it doesn't mean anything necessarily but it is not an area with a good reputation. Not long after he came back from that trip, he did seem shorter tempered but I didn't think that had anything to do with the time off he'd taken. I put that down to the woman trouble he was having.'

'You mean with the captain's wife?'

'Oh, no. I did hear about that, though. God, I don't mean to speak ill of the dead but Bryce could be a bloody nuisance at times,' Errol said with a shake of his head. 'I'm talking about his girlfriend. Bryce decided, in his wisdom, to date a co-worker and it didn't end well.'

'Yeah, not usually the best move,' Rebecca said with an involuntary cringe. Over the years she'd made that mistake of dating colleagues who were more understanding of the odd hours and work patterns but in every case it had proven disastrous. In many cases she'd been relieved when either she or they had been transferred to a placement at a different hospital. 'Who was this co-worker?' she said, trying to forget the other doctors who had seemed like such good prospects on date one.

'Her stage name is Miss Ocean Blue, she's a burlesque dancer. Her real name is Carla . . . not sure of her surname, sorry. They broke up about six months ago.'

'Six months?' Rebecca repeated. 'Was this before or after the trip he made?'

'Hmm. I think it was just after. But don't quote me on that. The thing is, she wouldn't really let it go. She got pretty obsessed with Bryce when they were together and didn't take his decision to end their relationship well.'

Rebecca tilted her head. 'Pretty obsessed like how?'

'From what I saw, she was following him around the ship at one point. Wherever he'd go, she'd show up as if it was some kind of coincidence. She'd sneak into his cabin. All kinds of stuff like that. Bryce wasn't the kind to appreciate clinginess. I think he wound up being quite firm with her.'

'Did the police talk to her? That seems like the kind of thing they need to know about.'

'Oh yes, she was definitely on their list – just as I was – but she had an alibi for Bryce's death window. I think she was with Wendy actually.' Errol paused for a moment, thinking.

'That's the weird thing about Bryce's death. Everyone on the staff seems to have an alibi. The police weren't able to take any lines of enquiry any further because there was no evidence linking anyone on board to the killing and everyone had someone who could corroborate where they were. I was in one of the on-board cafés at the time, and I've never been so glad that someone could vouch for my whereabouts, I can tell you.'

'I'll bet,' said Rebecca. 'Can't think of many things scarier than not being able to provide an alibi when you're a suspect for a crime you know you didn't commit.'

'Me neither. But the fact that everyone on the police's original suspect list has an alibi does get me wondering if somebody who wasn't on staff somehow got hold of that code for the rec room like Kitt thinks. And nobody would be in a better position to do that than a long-term passenger. If a passenger did somehow get hold of that information, and they knew how to avoid the CCTV camera, they would be able to use it to make sure only staff members would ever be suspected. Leaving them free to get away with murder.'

CHAPTER ELEVEN

It was one of those moments so full of dread you can't really believe that it's happening. Rebecca was in one of the dingier stairwells that led up to the cabin she and Kitt shared when she felt it. A gloved hand quickly and silently closed over her mouth, establishing an iron grip on her head, making it impossible to pull away. Her first instinct was to at least try to call out, or struggle, but almost at once she felt a sharp sensation in her side. Piercing enough for her to naturally arch her body away from it as far as she could.

Was it a knife?

She couldn't be sure but it was definitely a blade of some nature. She had barely had a moment to process what was happening when she was shunted backwards into one of the deep fire-door alcoves and an impatient hiss sounded out in her ear.

'Don't you dare scream,' came the hiss. 'Drawing attention to yourself in any way would not be a wise move right now.

I'm a person of importance on this ship. Nobody is ever going to suspect me of doing something like this so leaving you for dead will be easy if you don't cooperate. Nod if you understand.'

Slowly, with tears in her eyes, Rebecca nodded. Out of the haze of disbelief some questions that she both did and didn't want the answer to started to form in her mind. Like, what the hell was this guy going to do with her? Was it a guy? It was impossible to tell from the voice and the attacker was behind her so she couldn't get a good look.

Maybe that was for the best.

If she was able to identify them, whoever they were, she probably wouldn't be long for this world, especially if they were a 'person of importance' and had a reputation at stake. Given the strength of her attacker's grip, she would guess they were male. The most likely scenario here was that she was being attacked by the on-board thief Georgia had mentioned – and she had said they were most likely to be male. On the plus side, the thief hadn't killed anybody. If they had, she was pretty sure Georgia would have mentioned that. Unless . . . the thief had been the one who killed Bryce. Rebecca swallowed hard, trying to stay calm. The likelihood was, she would see the other side of this experience if she just did what he said. At least, that's what she had to tell herself.

And it's not like she had much of a choice but to do what her attacker asked of her at any rate. She could tell by the force of his grip that this guy was strong. From the direction of the hisses she would also guess he was a little bit taller than her.

Yes, that's it, Rebecca thought to herself. She had to try not to focus on how scared she was. Even though she could feel every muscle in her body had tightened. Even though she could barely breathe through the hand over her mouth. She had to focus on something, *anything* that might help her identify this guy when she got out of this alive.

And she had to get out of this alive.

If she didn't, she knew that Kitt would never forgive herself.

Strength, girl, courage, metal. Breathing through her nose as best she could, she recited that old family motto through her mind. The phrase their parents always used when they wanted her or Kitt to be brave about something. The pun on mettle – because they were born in Middlesbrough known across the world for its iron and steel – had always brought a smile to both Kitt and Rebecca's face, no matter the dilemma. And it was a reminder that they were hardy, northern lasses not prone to taking any challenge, no matter how distressing, lying down. She took a breath, and realized there was at least one salient feature that might later be of help in identifying this attacker.

His smell.

Not an aftershave or a cologne but the attacker's natural scent. A blend of nicotine and sweat. He was a smoker. That might help to narrow things down. The number of smokers in the world was ever decreasing. A figure Rebecca had to keep a keen eye on given that she was often treating people who had for one reason or another been unable to give up.

'I've . . .' the voice began but then trailed off.

Her attacker had heard the same sound Rebecca had.

The sound of hope.

Footsteps echoing down the corridor leading to the stairway.

Someone was about to walk by.

She was just about to convince herself this was her chance of escape when her assailant repositioned the blade and pressed it hard into her chest. She could see the weapon now. It was long, thin and silver. It looked like a skewer of some kind and there was no mistaking how sharp it was. She could feel it stabbing into her skin. She couldn't be sure if it had drawn blood, but even if it hadn't, he wouldn't have to press much harder for the blade to go straight through her heart. She wouldn't stand a chance.

'Make even a squeak and I'll kill you. And then I'll kill whoever's walking down this corridor.'

Rebecca's breath quivered out of her and a single tear trickled down her cheek as she watched a man walk past the alcove without even looking. Even if he had looked, he might not have seen them. The alcove was deep enough and dark enough that the minimal light from the corridor would hardly reach them.

Rebecca listened to the footsteps getting further and further away until a door swung shut and then there was nothing except silence, and the thunder of her own heart in her ears. Panic filled her chest as she realized she wasn't carrying any cash and she really didn't want to find out what the thief would do if he was left disappointed.

'I've got a message for your sister,' said the voice.

Rebecca's eyes widened at this. So, this wasn't a random attack. She wasn't being robbed. The voice knew who she was. And knew who Kitt was too. Had they been watching? Or was Rebecca currently being held hostage by one of the people they had already spoken to today?

But she was ninety-nine per cent sure the person holding her was a man. And they hadn't spoken to any men ... except Errol.

Rebecca tried to push that thought out of her mind. Surely he wouldn't do this? Surely she hadn't misjudged him so badly? Kitt's words about the nicest person in the room always being the true deceiver rang in her ears. She'd only said goodbye to Errol about ten minutes ago. Once he'd told her about Miss Ocean Blue she'd made her excuses, saying that she needed to let Kitt know about it straight away. And now she was being held by a shadowy figure who had a message for her sister. Could that really be a coincidence?

Rebecca decided not. But then, the attacker had said they were a person of importance and even if he was a little on the over-confident side it seemed unlikely Errol would describe himself in that manner. He did however know, by his own admission, that Bryce had had trouble with the captain. Perhaps he was trying to throw her off the scent, merely pretending to be high ranking personnel. But what about the smell of nicotine? Errol wasn't a smoker, or certainly didn't smell like one from close range. So it couldn't be him . . . unless he was a secret smoker and had just had a cigarette while he was biding his time. Waiting for her to enter one of the lonelier areas of the ship. Either Errol was the one holding her right now or it was someone who had been at the bar, surveilling their conversation. Listening in.

'Tell your sister,' the voice hissed, 'her little investigation ends here and now. Georgia Rhames has been a thorn in my side for three years. I don't need anyone giving her a helping hand in figuring out my true identity. I don't know who you think you are. Coming on to my ship. Sticking your faces in my business. But it stops now. If it doesn't, I'll come after you and next time I won't leave you alive. So, unless she wants her sister's blood on her hands, she'll forget about Bryce Griffin, understood?'

Rebecca's attacker gave her a firm shake.

All she could do in response was emit a quiet little whine and nod. And in that moment she had never felt so small, so helpless.

'Get down on your hands and knees and put your head against the floor,' the voice hissed. 'Hands behind your head. Eyes on the ground. Get down, I said.'

Rebecca felt a shove from behind that left her on her knees.

'Count to one hundred in your head,' the voice hissed again. 'If you even look like you're going to turn your head while I can still see you, you won't make it back to your cabin alive so don't try anything funny.'

Praying her attacker was a man of his word – that she might actually get out of this situation in one piece – Rebecca did as instructed. She put her forehead to the cold lino and with hot tears of fear and disbelief dropping to the floor, she started to count.

CHAPTER TWELVE

Twenty minutes or so later, Rebecca was sitting on the bed in the cabin surrounded by three anxious faces. Rebecca wasn't quite sure precisely how long she had knelt there, on the floor, in the dark, alone. But it was quite some time after she'd finished counting to one hundred before she was able to stand. Even once she did pull herself upright, leaning against the nearest wall for support, she couldn't stop shaking and felt utterly disconnected from her body as she walked. Intellectually, she knew she was putting one foot in front of the other but the feet didn't feel like they belonged to her.

The moment Rebecca had returned and relayed what had happened to her, Kitt had knocked on Evie and Grace's cabin next door and all four of them were now formulating their next step. If indeed there should even be one.

'What are we going to do?' said Evie at last once they had all asked Rebecca at least three times apiece if she was all right.

'I can tell you what I'm not doing. I'm not putting my sister's life at risk, obviously,' said Kitt. 'I'm so sorry I got you into this. If continuing the investigation is going to put any of us in danger, it has to stop here and now. I promised Mal as much before we left but even if I hadn't, it is, of course, the right decision.'

'It's not your fault,' Rebecca said. 'We were working on the assumption that the killer – and their accomplice if they had one – would keep a low profile. Hoping to evade the investigation until we disembarked.'

'Yes, but it's clear we've underestimated them, and that's on me. I should have at least considered that the killer might be on the offence rather than the defence but I must admit, I never quite anticipated this. Given his knack for rubbing people up the wrong way, I thought Bryce's killing was a one-off event. A specific targeting of him. The worst I imagined happening was if we didn't catch them now, they might lie low so long that the suspicion around the crew dissipated, allowing them to murder again at some far-off point in the future. An immediate and physical assault to intimidate us into ending the investigation ... well, if I'd known that was a real possibility, I wouldn't have brought you all along, and may not have even come myself.'

'There's no getting off the ride now,' said Evie. 'Sadly.'

'I know, but you needn't worry. We won't take the investigation any further, not after this. At the end of the day, no matter how much I might want justice for Bryce, he's ...

he's gone now and nothing more can hurt him. The same can't be said for us.'

'Damn right,' said Grace, bringing a hand dramatically to her forehead. 'And I'm too young to wind up sleeping with the fishes.'

Rebecca could tell by the way in which Grace was glancing at her out the corner of her eye that she was trying to use her whimsical streak to cheer her up. Though she appreciated the kindness, she wasn't in the market for cracking a smile just yet. Kitt had wrapped a blanket around her but she still felt cold. A sure sign that she was in shock.

'Yes, well, I'm not sure it would quite come to that,' said Kitt, 'but the attacker said themselves that they are a person of importance on this ship, which likely means they are not someone to be messed with. After the warning Rebecca was given, we've got to assume that the person who attacked her is either the killer themselves or an accomplice, and if they can kill someone as streetwise as Bryce, I'd rather avoid finding out what they are capable of doing to us.'

'Me too,' said Evie.

'Me three,' said Grace.

Rebecca swallowed hard and thought for a moment. 'I don't know if the idea of keeping the investigation going scares me more than the idea that if we give up, then we'll have been successfully intimidated. And whoever attacked me tonight will know they got away with it. Will know we're too scared to report it to security. So they might do something else to us. We'd spend the rest of the trip in fear and we've still got another six nights to go after this one.'

'I take your point. But the same would be true if we continued the investigation,' Kitt argued.

'Yes, but at least we'd be closer to finding my attacker's identity. Or getting some leverage over them maybe,' said Rebecca. 'They said that Georgia had been a thorn in their side for three years. That's how long the thefts have been going on.'

'So the odds are the thief and the killer are one and the same and Bryce was somehow mixed up with them,' said Kitt.

'Which means they're an experienced criminal and know what they're doing. Is there any real telling what someone like that will do? Especially if they think nobody's got anything on them. In that respect, giving up the investigation might leave us more vulnerable.'

'Maybe,' said Kitt. 'But I don't know if it's really worth the risk. Six nights of looking over your shoulder might not be anyone's idea of fun but at least we'd have more chance of staying unharmed if we followed the attacker's demands.'

'Don't make any rash decisions just now,' said Rebecca. 'You're probably right to say we should give up, but let's at least sleep on it.'

'What I don't understand is how that person, whoever they were, knew about our investigation,' said Grace. 'We've only spoken to a small number of people and Errol's the only man amongst them.'

'Well, Wendy is a man dressed as a woman,' said Evie. 'But I know for a fact she's on stage right now, her late show started half an hour ago.'

'Which leaves Errol,' said Rebecca. 'He could easily have followed me after our conversation at the bar.'

Rebecca felt a strange churning inside at making this accusation. Perhaps it was because Errol had shown such kindness to them since he'd visited Kitt's house a couple of days ago that on the surface she had no real reason to suspect him. But Kitt seemed to be of the opinion that trusting others while running an investigation wasn't a luxury they could afford. Even if they would like to give someone the benefit of the doubt, right now it wasn't the most sensible course of action.

'But if Errol was behind Bryce's death, and your attack, why would he seek Kitt out in the first place?' said Evie.

'He didn't know she was an investigator,' said Rebecca. 'He admitted that much himself. He said he just came to break the news to Kitt because he found her letters.'

'Yes, but why even do that if you're behind it all?' said Evie. 'Sounds like a fine way to draw attention to yourself if you ask me.'

'And I suppose if anyone knows about drawing attention to themselves in any given situation, it's you,' said Kitt with a knowing smirk.

'That's unfair and you know it,' said Evie, putting her hands on her hips.

'Is it?' said Kitt. 'How many of those feathered fans from Wendy's dressing room are now in your suitcase?'

'Four,' Evie said, shuffling on the spot. 'But they're just old ones Wendy doesn't use for her act any more. I'll probably just use them as decorations somewhere in the house.'

'We'll see,' said Kitt.

'Anyway,' said Rebecca, trying to drag the conversation back on track. 'I suppose Errol might have visited Kitt, even if he was behind it all, in a bid to make himself look more innocent. Like he bore Bryce no ill will and was going out of his way to reach out to people who were acquainted with him, without realizing he was inadvertently inviting a proper investigation into the murder.'

'That's possible,' said Kitt. 'Errol was a close colleague of Bryce's, he had opportunity to lure him somewhere. But the means and the motive, that's a different matter. If it was him, why would he do such a thing? Did he say anything to you about Bryce's trip to the Gulf of Aden?'

After the attack, Rebecca had clean forgotten to update Kitt on all the things Errol had said during their conversation at the bar. 'He flat out denied knowing about it and instead tried to point me in the direction of an ex-girlfriend of Bryce's who's a burlesque dancer on the ship. Miss Ocean Blue she calls herself. He said she was exhibiting obsessive behaviour. Following him around. Turning up in his cabin uninvited.'

'I'll make a note of it, just in case something shakes out later. But to be honest, it's not just the people we've spoken to directly that we need to think about. Errol said this morning that he'd notified several factions of the crew. Any one of them could have got chatting with the wrong person and told them about our investigation.'

'That's true,' said Grace. 'He said the bridge team, the security team and the reception team all knew about it. Isn't it more logical that rather than being the attacker himself, Errol unknowingly spoke to someone who was involved? Or that the people he told passed information on? Word might have spread quite quickly about what we're up to.'

'Wait, the security team as a whole probably know about our investigation and the attacker mentioned Georgia by name,' said Rebecca. 'Implied she'd got in his way. I've been wondering, sitting here just now, if my attacker might have been one of the other members of the security team. If one of them is into some kind of shady business, such as covering up Bryce's death, for example, and given that Georgia runs a tight ship, she might have made things very difficult for them.'

'Georgia was elsewhere when Bryce was killed – or so she says,' said Kitt. 'In that case, if there was somebody corrupt on the security team, they would have been able to angle that camera away from the crime scene and Georgia wouldn't have been any the wiser until she looked through the footage.'

'I would much rather believe it was one of the security team than Errol,' said Rebecca. 'Although, remember, it wasn't just us and Georgia's crew in the safety command centre. Errol was with us, and he knew exactly where I was because he'd just spent time with me in the bar, so I still feel we need to keep an eye on him.' Rebecca lowered her eyes to the laminate flooring. She knew the attack was clouding her judgement but right now she couldn't take the risk that Errol was all he seemed to be.

'Nobody will be given the benefit of the doubt, especially when it comes to keeping you safe,' said Kitt.

'Probably a wise idea,' said Grace.

'But we can't also discount the idea that we might be being watched very closely by a member of staff with eyes all over the ship,' said Kitt. 'If one of the security officers overheard our conversation with Georgia, and one of them is the person who attacked you tonight, they would easily be able to monitor us and see if we're adhering to their demand. Check whether we were meeting regularly with Errol or following up on any other leads like Georgia's alibi or Miss Ocean Blue. It's clear that we're being watched somehow. And with that in mind I don't think we can now just go traipsing up to another likely suspect without the person who threatened you getting suspicious. Given the threats made, there's a strong likelihood they'll be watching our next move very closely. We could try and continue the investigation in secret but personally, I think it's too great a risk and that we should just hand all this over to the police.'

And with that, as though to show her commitment to giving up the case, Kitt began collecting up a pile of papers that were lying on her bed.

'So, I suppose that's it then?' said Grace, her voice as flat as Rebecca felt. 'I suppose at least we tried. Yes, we've got that to hang on to. It is a real shame, though. I was so sure we could crack this one.'

'No need to sound so down,' said Kitt. 'There'll be other investigations. You win some, you lose some. That's just the way these things shake out sometimes.'

Rebecca knew her sister too well to believe she could let go of an investigation that easily but appreciated her insistence on putting their collective safety before her search for justice.

'I know,' said Grace. 'It's just, I've never caught a killer on a cruise ship before.'

Kitt frowned at her assistant. 'I can hardly believe your bucket list is that specific, Grace.'

'Maybe it should be,' said Grace. 'Maybe that's what's wrong with our society: vague bucket lists.'

Kitt shook her head and then looked back again at the papers in her hands. Then she brought the paper on top very close to her face, staring at it as though it was the most fascinating object she'd ever seen.

'Safety box – two, zero, zero, zero, three, three, one, zero, zero.'

Rebecca, Grace and Evie all looked at Kitt.

'What's that about?' said Evie.

'Look, Bryce's letter – his poem. There's a code in there. The first and last letter of each line form the word "safety box". And then each line after that ends with a number. Of course, I should have thought of that sooner. Back in Seaton Carew, when he was hunting for those silver dollars, the map I deciphered, that involved some basic cryptography.'

'What?' said Rebecca. 'Are you sure you're not just seeing things?'

'Take another look for yourself,' said Kitt, handing Rebecca the letter. Quickly, she re-skimmed the poem. Concentrating on the first and last letters of every line.

> Silently, I flick through antique ephemera,
> faster and faster until the lonely words merge.
> Time hasn't touched these tokens of a journey
> buried in a sea chest in a long-forgotten grotto.
> Xanthos of Greece knew more fame in two
> thousand years than these thirty-
> three trinkets no hands have touched in a century.

'All right,' Rebecca conceded, 'you're not just seeing things. But why would he do this?'

'When you say safety box,' said Grace, taking the letter from Kitt and confirming what she'd said, 'do you mean, like, a deposit box at a bank or something?'

'I don't know,' said Kitt. 'But that's the identifying number of the box and whatever's in it, wherever that box may be, it could very well be the reason Bryce was killed.'

CHAPTER THIRTEEN

Chewing on an almond croissant, Rebecca did her best to swallow what would usually be a scrumptious treat for her. After last night's attack, however, she had rather lost her appetite and the thick, sweet pastry stuck to the roof of her mouth in a manner that left her feeling somewhat nauseated.

Her companions had not been affected so.

There were several breakfast restaurants throughout the ship but this one, serving a range of continental and American options, was the nearest to their cabin and Kitt, Evie and Grace had almost fallen over themselves to get down here. She watched them chomping down on a mix of pancakes, waffles and continental breads while wishing she could better appreciate the ordinarily mouthwatering scent of sizzling bacon wafting through the air. As it turns out, having your life threatened rather takes the kick out of the five-star atmosphere.

'Still can't believe Ruby sent you a telegram,' Evie said to Kitt, while giggling into her orange juice. 'You know, I think there might actually be some truth to her magical prowess. At least, she always seems to find you wherever you go. That's a sort of magic.'

Ruby was a friend of Kitt's who, from what Rebecca understood, was deeply involved in the occult and kept trying to convince Kitt she had 'psychic powers'. As yet, according to her sister, these psychic powers had been no help whatsoever to any of Kitt's investigations.

'The only magic abilities Ruby possesses is the knack of wearing my loved ones down to the point that they tell her where I am just so she leaves them alone,' said Kitt.

'Oooh, you can't really mean that,' said Grace.

'I might be being tart,' said Kitt.

'You? Never!' said Evie, before surrendering to yet more giggles.

'I'm glad you find it funny,' said Kitt. 'I am, of course, very fond of her, but my goodness, it's getting a bit much when there's no escape from that woman's wild theories, even at sea. And when I get back I'm going to give Mal a piece of my mind for letting her know where I was and what I was up to. He knows better than that. It only encourages her and I do worry about how excitable she gets.'

'Maybe Halloran's getting a little bit of revenge for you insisting on coming on this trip in the first place,' said Grace.

'Hmm, yes, you might be on to something there. I had a patchy Zoom call with him last night and after he heard about what happened to Rebecca he was even less enthused about this trip than he had been before,' said Kitt.

'I can imagine,' said Grace. 'I hope you didn't part on angry terms; I was just kidding about him using Ruby as revenge.'

'Difficult to say what his mood was at the end of the call,' said Kitt. 'The screen froze so we had to give it up. But the last facial expression I saw from him wasn't a look of gentle encouragement and understanding. I haven't had the signal to email him back yet but I will do and hopefully he'll have settled down a bit.'

'Still, after what happened last night, you can't blame him for being worried,' said Evie. 'Charley was hardly thrilled about the news.'

'No, and I must make a point of apologizing to her too when we make it back home. I never meant to put you all in such jeopardy,' said Kitt.

Evie smiled. 'It'll turn up roses, don't worry.'

'What exactly did Ruby's telegram say?' asked Rebecca, keen to keep the conversation away from what had taken place the night before. Anything to take her mind off the memory of that gloved hand, and the stench of nicotine and sweat that still seemed to fill her lungs.

'Oh, it was one of her most ridiculous theories yet. Apparently, I shouldn't rule out that a kraken may have been involved in Bryce's demise.'

'From what I know about them, krakens do have very long tentacles,' said Grace with an impish smile on her face.

'Oh, yes,' said Evie. 'It's not impossible that poor Bryce was whipped off the deck by one of those tentacles.'

'Thank you for making light of the death of my friend.'

'You know we don't mean it that way,' said Evie, reaching across the table and squeezing Kitt's hand.

'No, we were just saying,' said Grace, 'it could happen.'

'Oh, good grief,' Kitt said, 'perhaps I do need my head read for thinking seven nights in an enclosed space with you two was a good idea. Let alone arranging for you to stay in the same cabin. It's like criminals in prison, learning the worst tricks off each other.'

'That's one way to look at it,' said Evie. 'Another is to see it as a creative collaboration between me and Grace to keep your life more interesting.'

Rebecca had almost managed a smile when a familiar voice said, 'Ah, there you are, thought I might find you here.'

Everyone at the table stopped and stared at Errol.

He was in casual wear again, rather than his pirate costume, but did have Skittles with him. The bird cocked his head from side to side in a manner that suggested he was as uncomfortable with the sudden silence as his master was.

Frowning, Errol looked around the group of faces. 'Is something wrong? Skittles is allowed in here if that's what you're worried about.'

And then, in a move that smacked of suspicious behaviour, Rebecca, Kitt, Evie and Grace overcompensated by falling on top of each other to answer that nothing was wrong.

'Sorry,' said Kitt, once their overly casual clamour had died down. 'We're just all still waking up. Some of us didn't sleep well last night and decided that since they were awake, the rest of us should be too.'

'Not my fault I get seasickness,' said Grace. 'It's bad enough suffering it without suffering through it alone.'

'Yes, and we were all so pleased to be invited to that show,' said Kitt, her voice arid.

Errol let out a light, easy chuckle. Previously, Rebecca had found that laugh of his gently charming. After everything that had transpired the night before, however, she couldn't help but wonder if it was all part of an act. The man was a trained actor after all. He knew how to make people believe whatever he wanted to make them believe.

Is that what he had done with her?

'Oh Skittles, it is good to see you again,' Evie said.

At this, Skittles began to hop from one leg to the other, swishing his long crimson tail left to right as he did so.

'I think he's pleased to see you too by the look of things,' Errol said. 'He was cut out for this line of work, he's always happy to be in the limelight.'

'Mechanic,' Skittles said. And with that, Errol's smile faded. As did everybody else's at the table.

'I didn't mean to interrupt your morning caffeine hit,' said Errol, trying to move the conversation on. 'I knocked on your cabin door and when I didn't get any response I decided you were likely at breakfast so thought I'd take a bit of a wander and see if I could find you.'

'Hunger waits for no woman,' said Grace, shovelling in another forkful of pancakes with what seemed to Rebecca like impressive zeal considering she had spent the first twenty-four hours at sea under the weather.

'Yes, it seemed a shame not to make the most of all this glorious food while it's on offer,' said Kitt.

'Too right,' said Errol. 'I just wanted you to know that there's been a couple of leaps forward. I caught up with Georgia last night after my drink with Rebecca.'

'Oh, really?' I hope you weren't up too late on our account?' said Kitt. Rebecca could see what she was driving at. She wanted Errol to say how long there had been between his drink with Rebecca and his chat with Georgia. If he stated a time, it might give them a greater sense of whether he had been Rebecca's anonymous attacker or whether he had simply let slip about the investigation to the wrong person and they had taken matters into their own hands.

Unfortunately, Kitt's comment hadn't been quite pointed enough as he breezed over that piece of information. It seemed casual enough but there was, of course, a chance that he was actively avoiding giving any specific details in case he got caught out.

'No, no, don't you worry,' Errol continued. 'I told her about your concerns about the captain's circle and she brought up some passenger lists. There's only one couple in that group who were both on this voyage and the last: Francisco and Julia Perez. If something was going on in the captain's circle, they might have overheard something or seen something suspicious. I thought you'd want to speak to them so I had a word with the hospitality staff first thing this morning and told them you were friends of Bryce. I didn't say you were running an investigation. I thought I'd give you the option of staying undercover. In light of Bryce's death they agreed to give me these extra tickets to a special champagne gala dinner event this evening. It starts at seven. The captain will be in attendance, alongside members of the captain's circle. The event is black tie, just so you know.'

'Though we did come prepared for black tie given the five-star nature of the cruise, and though I'm grateful to you for speaking further with Georgia and securing the tickets, really I am,' said Kitt, 'I'm afraid I don't think we'll be attending.'

Errol frowned. 'What do you mean?' He lowered his voice. 'You no longer suspect it's someone in the captain's circle?'

'It's not that,' said Kitt. 'I'm sorry to tell you because I know you'd also like to see Bryce's killer brought to justice – and we would too – but we've decided not to take the investigation any further.'

Errol looked around the group in disbelief. 'What? But

you went to all this effort. Booked on to the cruise. Spent all that money. Why are you giving up now?'

'It comes down to an error of judgement on my part, I'm afraid,' said Kitt. 'I thought I could do this. Investigate the murder of a friend but, as it turns out, I was wrong. I am so sorry you went to the trouble of getting us those tickets but being on this ship has affected me more than I expected. I keep imagining it, you see, what happened to him. Those final moments. And on top of that I keep finding out things about Bryce that I'd rather not know.'

'I'm so sorry,' said Errol, a mixture of confusion and sympathy flaring in those sea-green eyes.

Kitt gave a dismissive wave. 'It's silly really . . . but I'd just rather think of him as the rascally man I used to write to. Mal was right, I shouldn't have started this investigation . . . Just don't ever tell him I said that because I'll never hear the end of it.'

'Your dark secret's safe with me,' Errol said, flashing a roguish smile at Rebecca. She looked down at the table for a moment. When she looked up again, she could see that his frown had deepened. As though he had no idea why she might have a new-found wariness of him. She would like to believe that was true but, after yesterday, she was beginning to understand just why Kitt was so cautious about who she trusted. Suspicion was such a cold, empty feeling; she really didn't want to succumb to it. But how could she take any chances? It could mean her life.

'So, is the plan to just relax between here and Oslo?' Errol said, trying to rouse some reaction from the group who were a lot more reticent in his presence than they had been this time yesterday.

'That's the plan,' replied Grace.

'I see,' Errol said with a nod. 'Well, I suppose that's understandable. It's just ... I did pull a big favour with hospitality to get you these tickets. Even if you're not going to follow through with the investigation, I think you should go. Otherwise they'll probably never let me ask another favour ever again and, to be honest, you'll probably really enjoy it. You'll get to meet the captain, and the food and drink is supposed to be out of this world. Very few people get into these kinds of events so perhaps you'll make some interesting memories.'

'Well,' Kitt said, pondering. 'I suppose there's no harm in going just for the fun of it, and, like you say, it's a pretty exclusive event so when else will we get a chance like that?'

Errol held out the tickets for Kitt and she accepted them. 'I appreciate it,' she said.

Errol tried to make eye contact with Rebecca a second time but again she lowered her eyes to the table, not sure of what else to do.

'Well, I suppose I should leave you to your breakfast,' Errol said. Though she wasn't looking at him directly she could hear the wounded note in his voice.

'Thanks again for the tickets,' said Kitt. 'It really was very kind of you to get that organized for us.'

'No problem.'

Seemingly at last grasping that he wasn't particularly welcome, Errol didn't hang around to ask any more questions. When Rebecca looked up again, he had already begun walking away.

Only then did Rebecca, Kitt, Grace and Evie all exchange a look.

'What did you think of that?' said Rebecca, once she was sure he was out of earshot.

'I don't know what to think about him,' said Kitt. 'It's too soon to say whether he's masking his misdeeds behind a friendly face or just happens to have a bit of a loose tongue.'

'But do you think he believed us? That the investigation was off?' said Rebecca.

Kitt nodded. 'I think he did. So now it's time to move on to the next phase.'

CHAPTER FOURTEEN

The plan was simple, or so it had seemed when Rebecca, Kitt, Evie and Grace had thrashed it out that morning in the cabin. Last night's attack had been pretty much the most frightening moment of Rebecca's life to date, but it had also told them something very important: Bryce's killer was on this ship.

Not only that, but they had described themselves as a person of importance. Which meant it was someone who thought themselves beyond reproach, perhaps not that surprising given they'd been bold enough first to shoot someone in broad daylight and second to attack Rebecca when anyone might have discovered them. Not to mention the thefts that had been committed over the last three years. Whoever the perpetrator was, they were well used to getting away with their criminal activities. Rebecca admitted that it was hard to believe Errol was such a person, but there was a chance that even if he hadn't attacked her directly, he worked for whoever did and had tipped them off as to her whereabouts.

In terms of those considered a person of importance, there were only a few potential suspects who might be described in this light: Georgia, as head of security, surely held a substantial amount of power on board (or perhaps someone working with her who had overheard their discussion about Bryce's demise the day before). Then there were the passengers in the captain's circle who, given the Millers' display at Wendy's show last night, thought themselves significant members of the cruise community. Whether or not the other members of said community agreed with their self-assessment remained to be seen. Either way, Francisco and Julia Perez were definitely on their list of people to talk to. After them, there was just the captain himself.

On waking that morning Rebecca had still been trying to manage a great deal of residual shock and fear after a fitful night's sleep. But something else had surfaced alongside all that: blind fury that anyone had the gall to attack her, and in such a blatant manner. Almost in plain view of any passers-by. To make her feel small and helpless and unsafe in her own skin. She had, like most people, endured frightening experiences. Working the night shift at a hospital, you never quite knew who was going to walk in, or how aggressive they might be towards you just for trying to keep them pain-free. But all of that had paled against the way she had felt during that attack.

If she had been alone on the ship, she would have curled

up into a ball in her cabin and probably not come out again until the boat docked at Oslo. But she wasn't alone. She had the support of three caring and courageous companions. With them by her side, she was confident she could root out and face down her attacker to make sure what happened to her never happened to anyone else.

Kitt, who wasn't known for keeping her temper at the best of times, had needed little encouragement to agree to continue the investigation covertly to figure out who had threatened her sister and report them.

But, of course, they had to be careful.

For one thing, they weren't going to leave any member of the group alone at any point. Just in case the attacker sussed out what they were up to and took it upon themselves to strike again. Moreover, if they went straight after Georgia's alibi, or even Bryce's ex-girlfriend who was, after the attack from someone who was believed to be male, further down their list of suspects, then whoever was watching them would surely know they had not really given up the investigation. If they were careful, however, if they spaced out any activities related to the investigation between spa treatments, poolside cream teas and Kitt's inevitable visit to the on-board library, they would likely ascertain some key information that would lead to the unmasking of Bryce's killer and Rebecca's assailant.

It was in this spirit that Rebecca and Kitt were sitting at a table in the casino bar, listening to scratchy audio over the set of family radios Kitt had brought along to aid communication between the group while they were at sea.

As they couldn't be sure who was listening into that particular channel, Kitt and Rebecca were not going to say anything to Evie and Grace who were currently sitting at the blackjack table in front of Noah Davies, the man Georgia had claimed she was speaking to when the ship was docking the day that Bryce was killed. Given that this was the riskiest interview they were likely to undertake in terms of potentially alerting the killer to their true agenda, it had been decided that it was best if the Hartley sisters monitored the conversation rather than engaged with Davies directly. If one of the security team was behind all this and they were monitoring their movements on CCTV, then it would just look as if Rebecca and Kitt were enjoying a drink while Evie and Grace played a little blackjack. Hundreds of other people around them – in varying degrees of inebriation – were doing just that so it seemed a perfectly reasonable way of blending in.

Rebecca glanced over to where Evie and Grace were sitting, trying to get another surreptitious look at Davies. He was quite a stocky man. The lines of the casino uniform – which comprised a black waistcoat, black chinos and dark green shirt – made him look very smart, suave almost. It was difficult to make out the finer details of his face from this distance but Rebecca could see he wore thick-rimmed glasses, and had styled his dark brown hair neatly with gel.

She couldn't be sure, given the fact that Errol's uniform was a costume and he was the main point of reference she had for the experience of staff on the boat, but she assumed that Crown Cruises liked their staff in the hospitality areas to look as smart as possible. These cruises cost a pretty penny and, looking around at the other dealers and servers, it was clear that each and every one of them had taken care to make themselves as presentable as they could.

There was something about that fact that made Rebecca shuffle in her seat. The *Northern Spirit* looked, on the surface, like a glittering paradise of surf, sunsets and sirloin steaks but between the information Georgia had shared with them about the robberies and Bryce's shooting, it was clear that there was something darker going on aboard this ship and not all was as it seemed. Rebecca's eyes roamed the crowds, hopping from a suited man with broad shoulders and silver hair to a woman with the biggest collagen-enhanced lips Rebecca had ever seen, and several others in between. How many of these people were good people? How many were up to things behind closed doors that they never had to take responsibility for because they happened to be in the one per cent? Rebecca didn't have an answer and frankly wasn't sure she wanted to know.

A slight scratching sound drew Rebecca's attention back to the task in hand. She and Kitt were using earphones so that nobody around them could hear the conversation Evie and Grace were striking up with Davies. Right now, the pair of them were giggling. They were hoping to lure Davies into a false sense of security by pretending they had had a little bit too much to drink, and so far they were pretty convincing.

'Right, I've put my chips in. How do you play blackjack again?' Grace said.

'Something about twenty-one,' Evie fake-slurred back.

'That's right, madam,' Davies said in a warm, friendly voice. 'The aim is to either reach the total of twenty-one with the cards you've been dealt or, if that's not possible, get as close to twenty-one as you can.'

'Any tips on how to win big?' Grace said, coupling it with a hiccup.

'I'm afraid I just deal the cards, madam. I have to keep a very neutral stance to keep things fair,' Davies explained.

'Call me Grace.'

'Grace,' Davies repeated.

'You're a bit naughty, aren't you?' There was a pause then and Rebecca glanced over to see Grace leaning towards Davies, presumably to get a glimpse of his name tag. 'Noah,' she continued. 'Pretending that a casino is about fairness.'

Davies chuckled. 'It's all in the luck of the draw, I can promise you that.'

'Do you have a fairness monitor?' Evie said.

'Sort of,' said Noah. 'If you look up, you'll see lots of security cameras. Our security team makes sure there's no cheating, or any other bad behaviour of any kind.'

Excellent. Davies had given them an in to ask some casual questions about Georgia.

'I've heard security people at casinos are scary,' said Grace.

'Well, you'd have to be a bit scary,' said Evie, 'to keep everyone in line. Keeping that number of people safe is no easy thing to do. I wouldn't switch places with whoever's heading that up, I can tell you. Life and death it is . . . Just look at what happened to poor Bryce.'

Kitt and Rebecca looked at each other at this point. They both knew that staring over at the blackjack table to gauge Davies' physical reaction for themselves wasn't a good idea. If he noticed them looking at him, he might suspect something and refuse to say any more on the subject. Besides that, the security team may not be monitoring their movements now but someone – perhaps even Georgia herself – may review this footage later. Looking over at Evie and Grace too often, especially given they were talking to her alibi, might rouse her suspicions that they were still on the case, if indeed she was involved in Bryce's death.

'You . . . knew Bryce?' said Davies.

'No, not personally,' said Evie. 'We're travelling with someone who knew him. They were going to try and investigate what happened to him but they've given that up now. Decided to leave it to the police.'

'Probably for the best,' said Davies. 'The whole thing was a nasty business. If you can avoid getting involved with something like that, I'd steer well clear. The police are used to dealing with difficult situations. They can probably handle it better than the rest of us.'

Kitt and Rebecca looked at each other again. This was another prong to their plan. Conduct covert interviews while also explicitly stating that the investigation was closed. If the killer – whoever they were – came asking any of their interviewees questions, the message would be relayed that they hadn't been there on official business. That, as far as they were concerned, the investigation was over.

'Sorry to bring up depressing topics,' said Evie. 'For all we know you were close to him too.'

'Not really. But it still shakes you when someone you know goes out like that.'

'Of course it does,' said Grace. 'I hope you didn't see anything, you know, witness anything when it happened. That'd be enough to traumatize anyone.'

'No, no, no,' said Davies. 'In a way, I wish I had seen something, though. We might have tracked down the person responsible. But I was here – like I always am – talking to our head of security at the time the police said it happened.'

'I understand you wanting to catch the person responsible,' said Grace. 'Our companions had the same idea, until they decided it was too dangerous, but I think it's a lucky thing you didn't witness it. There's just no telling how something like that might affect you.'

'You're right, of course. Crown Cruises have been very vigilant about any possible effect on the health of the crew, though, in case you were worried. We've all had counselling made available to us.'

'I'm glad to hear it,' said Grace. 'It is the least they can do under the circumstances.'

'Well, you're probably right about that,' said Davies. 'I think—'

At that point, Davies was cut off as he had to excuse himself and answer a question from another passenger. It looked as though the conversation was likely at a close and there wouldn't really be much point in talking to him any further when he'd already confirmed what they wanted him to.

Rebecca unhooked her earphones and looked at Kitt.

'Georgia's alibi checks out,' she said, making sure to keep her voice low in case anyone in the bar was listening in.

'It would seem so,' said Kitt. 'I'm satisfied that she didn't have a part in it. Between the way your attacker talked about her, her demeanour in the interview and the alibi being confirmed, I think we can rule her out for now. But I'm still not convinced the camera failed to record Bryce's killing by accident. The best course of action is to pursue the other suspects on our list. If they draw a blank, we'll circle back to the security team and feel out Georgia. See if we can subtly find out if she's noticed any odd behaviour from any of her crew members.'

'We're going to have to be really careful about that,' said Rebecca. 'With the investigation being called off, we don't have a legitimate reason for talking to Georgia or to be invited back to the safety command centre to suss out any potential suspects. I agree that we should make sure there aren't any red flags with our other suspects first. If we hit a dead end, we'll try and reach out to Georgia. If the killer is on her team, she might be able to help us flush them out.'

'Agreed on all counts,' said Kitt. 'So for now that leaves us with the Perez couple, Miss Ocean Blue and the captain himself.'

'I'm sort of hoping it's anyone but the captain,' said Rebecca. 'If it is him and he realizes we're on to him before we can apprehend him, I dread to think about what he might do to protect himself and his reputation.' She paused to look around at the other passengers who were blithely playing at the roulette table or trying their luck on the slot machines. 'When it comes down to it, every last one of us is at his mercy.'

CHAPTER FIFTEEN

Back at their cabin, Rebecca and Kitt were just putting the finishing touches to their outfits for the captain's circle event when there was a sharp knock at the door. Rebecca looked over at Kitt, her eyes widening. She knew it wasn't rational to react so nervously to something so trivial. Intellectually she understood it was unlikely her attacker would just come merrily knocking on their door if they were going to try and target her again, but at the moment every sudden noise startled her.

'Who is it?' Kitt called through the door.

'It's Errol.'

Rebecca's posture tensed and she held her breath. What could he want? They were off the case now, they'd told him as much. He knew they were going to the gala tonight. So why would he call now?

'I'll deal with it,' said Kitt, walking over to the door and opening it.

'Yes, Errol, what can we do for you?'

'I . . . wow. You two are going to fit in very well at the captain's circle,' Errol said, his eyes flitting between the two sisters before finally landing on Rebecca.

Ordinarily she would be flattered by the attentions of a man like Errol. To know that the silky, rose-pink evening gown she'd picked out – the same pink as her hair – had the desired effect. But even though Errol was not considered a person of importance on the ship, he'd had opportunity to come after her last night once she left the bar – or tip off whoever the person of importance really was. He hadn't liked the way she'd asked him so directly if he knew why Bryce had visited the Gulf of Aden. If she'd hit a nerve, that would also mean he had motive to find a way of stopping the investigation in its track while masquerading as a person of importance in an attempt to divert their suspicions elsewhere. In a bid not to give the game away, she offered him a measured smile in return for his compliment.

'We are just about to make our way to the gala now,' said Kitt with a somewhat pointed note in her voice. 'We want to make the most of every minute since you took such pains to secure the tickets for us.'

'Yeah, I obviously know you have plans, I don't want to hold you up but I was just wondering if I could talk to Rebecca for a minute alone . . . just out here? It won't take long.'

Kitt turned to her sister to gauge her response. This was, of course, the last thing Rebecca wanted, but there was no doubting it was also an opportunity. Perhaps Errol would tell her something in confidence if he thought no one else was listening. Maybe one-to-one she could find a way to get him to confess any role he had in her attack, if he was indeed involved. So long as she left the cabin door ajar she would feel safe enough. God help him if he attempted anything when Kitt was in arm's reach. If he tried to hurt Rebecca in any way, she didn't like his chances of coming out on top once Kitt got hold of him.

'Just for a minute then, we don't want to be late for the big event,' Rebecca said, giving Kitt a quick nod and stepping out into the corridor.

Once alone with her, Errol looked her up and down again. 'You really do look beautiful. But there are mirrors in your cabin so you're probably already aware of that.'

'Thank you. Now, what was it you wanted to talk about?' Rebecca leaned back against the wall, trying to find a position that looked nonchalant, quite difficult in evening wear.

'I . . .' He faltered and looked into her eyes as if an answer might lie there that would negate the need to talk about whatever he was going to say next. He must not have found what he was looking for, as he continued: 'This might sound silly but I'm a believer in just being forthright. Have I done something wrong? Something to upset you?'

Rebecca frowned and shook her head. 'Why on earth would you think that? You've done nothing but help us since the moment we met you.'

'When I saw you at breakfast you seemed, I don't know, different. I don't know you very well, of course, but yesterday when we first boarded it seemed like, maybe, like you might want to spend some time with me. Have a drink, maybe have some fun. But now you've stopped the investigation and . . . Look, I'm not the kind of person who pushes if a woman wants nothing to do with me. If that's the case, just say so. But I also didn't like the idea that I could have done something to offend you without at least getting the chance to apologize for it. Especially if it was something I did that made you stop the investigation. I can just stay out of your way if it's a problem.'

'You didn't offend me,' Rebecca said, folding her arms. 'I'm fine and Kitt explained why she had to stop the investigation. I've got to respect her wishes on this.'

Errol took a step closer to Rebecca. She breathed in deeply. She'd never stood quite this close to him before and wanted to know, could she smell nicotine? But there wasn't even the faintest hint of it. Unlike her attacker, Errol wore aftershave that had heavy notes of cedarwood. The kind of scent that reminded her of October walks in Newton Dale when the trees were damp with rain.

'And from where I'm standing her reasoning doesn't really ring true,' Errol said, trying on a gentle smile for size. 'Truth be told, I'm a bit worried about you all. Giving up the investigation, just like that . . . well, it's in complete contrast to the way Kitt was behaving before, back at her house.'

Rebecca paused, thinking. Could this be her chance to try and catch Errol out? The attacker had said to stop the investigation. He hadn't said anything about not telling anyone about the attack. They'd just thought it good common sense to keep it to themselves until they knew who they were dealing with and Rebecca didn't imagine her assailant would be thrilled to know she was going around the ship broadcasting what had happened to her. They were trying to avoid provoking him. But perhaps she could tell Errol in a way that would make him think she had been protecting him by keeping him in the dark? His reaction to the news she'd been attacked would surely tell her something about his possible involvement?

'All right,' she said, looking into his deep green eyes. 'That isn't the real reason we stopped the investigation. I will tell you why but . . . you have to promise me that you will not tell anyone else what I'm about to say. If you do, it might put you in danger and I could never live with myself if anything happened to you, the way it did to Bryce. Promise me and I will tell you.'

'I won't tell a soul, you've got my word on that,' Errol said, his breath quickening, whether at Rebecca's words or at how close he was now standing to her, she couldn't say.

'We didn't tell you the truth because we didn't know what would happen if we did. We didn't know if there'd be consequences.'

'What do you mean, consequences? Consequences to telling me what?' Errol said.

'Last night after our drink I was . . .' Saying the words out loud again was harder than she'd expected. 'I was attacked. On my way back to the cabin.'

Oh, she felt so sick even talking about it. It was almost impossible not to imagine herself back there. At the mercy of that brute. Unable to do a thing to stop him. And perhaps the worst thing was that he knew she couldn't fight back. That he was in control and there was nothing she could do about it.

'What?' Errol's face darkened. 'Attacked how?'

'I'd rather not go into it in detail, if you don't mind,' said Rebecca. 'I probably shouldn't even be telling you this much. But they had a knife . . . or at least a blade of some kind.'

'Who was it?' Errol's voice was deeper than usual. It wasn't quite a snarl but it wasn't far off. 'Who attacked you?'

'I don't know,' Rebecca said, tears forming in her eyes. 'They attacked me from behind in a stairwell.'

'And nobody saw?'

Rebecca shook her head. 'Someone walked by but they didn't see.'

'They didn't . . .' Errol swallowed hard barely able to get the words out. 'They didn't touch you, did they?'

Rebecca shook her head. 'They had a very clear agenda but it wasn't that. They told me if Kitt didn't stop the investigation, they would come after me again, and if they did, I wouldn't survive.'

'Bloody hell,' Errol said, lacing his fingers behind his head for a moment before dropping his hands back down to his side. 'I'm . . . I'm so sorry. If I knew you better, I'd give you a hug but it's probably not appropriate.'

'Probably not,' Rebecca answered quickly before any hesitation crept in. Errol's response to the news of her attack seemed genuine. She could swear she saw true suffering in his eyes at the news of what she had gone through. But maybe his concern only seemed genuine because, right then, she wanted it to be. She shouldn't have let herself stand so close to him, even in the spirit of undercover work, when she was feeling this vulnerable. She had a notion that she would feel much better if he wrapped his arms around her. That somehow that would make her feel safer. Perhaps he was trustworthy, and, as they had theorized, he had just unknowingly told the wrong person about their investigation.

'You should never have had to go through that,' he said. 'You must have been petrified.'

'I still am,' Rebecca admitted, though she looked at the ground as she did so. 'We all are. That's why we're not looking into this any more. We're going to the event tonight because you kindly got us those tickets. But we're just going for fun. To try and take our minds off what happened last night. It's just too risky to push the situation any further.'

'Well, you don't have to be afraid any more,' he said.

'Closing the investigation was probably the right move but I won't let anything else happen to you while you're on the ship.'

'That's sweet but you don't need to worry, the girls aren't about to leave me unattended again in a hurry. Apparently I'm a liability.'

'You didn't do anything wrong,' said Errol. 'You should be able to walk freely around the ship and feel safe. But since someone has targeted you specifically and you wouldn't even be here if it wasn't for me, you'll have to get used to me pitching in to look after you too. I thought I was doing the right thing – just telling Bryce's friend about what happened to him. But I've got all of you into trouble and, by the sound of it, deeper trouble than even I realized when I said I'd help you with the investigation.'

'I think we'll be OK as long as we abide by the demands of the attacker,' Rebecca said with a little shrug, though she felt far from casual about the whole ordeal. 'Once we're clear of the ship we should be safe.'

'Well, obviously I have my job to do but I will spend every spare minute making sure you stay safe. I will escort you all to the captain's circle event tonight.'

'But—'

'No,' Errol said, 'no buts. And I will escort you all back to your cabins afterwards.'

'Oh, you don't have to—'

Errol held up a hand. 'There's no point arguing with me

on this. Don't worry, it will do you good being seen out and about with someone as devilishly handsome as me.'

In spite of herself, Rebecca forced out a little chuckle. 'Is there a shortage of mirrors in your cabin?'

'Oooh,' Errol said, clutching his chest. 'Straight through the heart. A comment as piercing as that is a good sign you're feeling better. And you've no need to worry any more. Until you're safely docked in Oslo you can expect me to be checking in on a regular basis.'

Rebecca smiled the easiest smile she could manage just then. A suspicious thought lingered. She secretly wondered if his concern was simply a good excuse to keep tabs on them. Was he going to follow her everywhere they went for the next few days? If he did, that was going to make their covert operation a lot more difficult. And perhaps that was his plan to ensure they didn't restart the investigation without his knowledge. But then Rebecca looked into his eyes again and her suspicions began to crumble. He may be an actor, but she was a good judge of character. His concern for her seemed genuine and they didn't have any concrete evidence that Errol was involved. If she was going to waltz around the place thinking the worst of everyone she crossed paths with, she was going to end up just like Kitt. And the whole idea of this trip was for Rebecca's optimism to rub off on Kitt. Not for Kitt's cynicism to rub off on her.

Rebecca felt the smile that had surfaced sag, however, as she realized that even if Errol was innocent, as she now believed him to be, she still couldn't tell him the truth about the investigation. He seemed nice enough but it wasn't clear whether or not he could keep a secret. If he blabbed to anyone about her attack, or let something slip by accident, and it got back to the killer, then they would likely just be pleased that the attack had had its desired effect. If Errol accidentally mentioned their investigation to someone after too many drinks, however, that could be the end of all of them.

As much as it pained her, given how kind he seemed, Errol would have to remain in the dark. He stared back into her eyes with an almost dreamy intensity that at once filled Rebecca with guilt. No wonder Kitt wasn't sleeping. It seemed the road to justice was paved with lies, distrust and deceit. Walk it long enough and that would take its toll on anyone.

CHAPTER SIXTEEN

The gala for members of the captain's circle was held in a ballroom on the top deck of the ship which offered guests jaw-dropping views across an uninterrupted sunset sky filled with oranges and pinks and reds. For the first twenty minutes on entering, it was all Rebecca, Kitt, Evie and Grace could look at. Despite everything that had befallen them over the past twenty-four hours, that vista went a long way to taking the edge off all the fear and suspicion.

Once they'd become more accustomed to the dazzling sights across the horizon, however, they had begun circulating amongst the other guests. Rebecca teamed up with Grace to give Kitt and Evie a bit of quality time together and she almost spat out her champagne more than once over the wild cover stories Grace came out with as they moved from guest to guest. She managed to convince one couple from the Philippines that she had actually been born at sea, and had only spent longer than a day on dry land on a handful of occasions in her life.

In the few instances in which Rebecca glanced over to see how Kitt and Evie were getting on they looked to be having a quieter time of things. Both pairs took pains to dance around their intended target: Francisco and Julia Perez, who had stationed themselves right next to the platters of prawns and not moved for a good twenty minutes. Every now and then Francisco, a round, jolly man, reached a hand over to the prawns and snatched one off the plate, gobbling it up whilst watching whoever he was speaking to intently with dark, twinkly eyes to make it clear that although his mouth was otherwise engaged, his ears were very much still listening.

The second Francisco and Julia were left without anyone to talk to, Rebecca, Grace, Kitt and Evie swooped from both sides.

But alas, the couple made for very unlikely murderers. When Kitt brought up the topic of Bryce in casual conversation, they both confirmed very quickly that they had never met him. In contrast to her husband, who seemed to laugh even when – so far as Rebecca was concerned – there was no real reason to laugh, not one smile reached Julia's blood-red lips in all the time they were speaking to her. She made a point of explaining that the kind of sideshow Bryce performed was somewhat low rent and she much preferred Crown Cruises' operatic offerings.

Which meant there was only one person of interest to talk to with regards to Bryce's untimely death and that was Captain Dominic Ortega himself. Unfortunately, it had quickly become apparent that they had no hope of getting a quiet word with him tonight. He was surrounded by a small gaggle of passengers, most of whom were either asking to have selfies taken or talking his head off about how many cruises they'd been on where he'd been the captain. Rebecca had never seen such sycophantic behaviour in all her life and she'd once made it backstage at a Nine Inch Nails concert.

Though getting up close and personal with Captain Ortega wasn't an option just now, they had, at least, got a decent look at him earlier when he made a little speech before dinner was served. Though, of course, there were no clear physical markers of a murderer, Kitt had all of them analysing the captain's body language and general demeanour as he spoke. Dominic Ortega was a self-assured man, that much was certain. He held his head high, dignified, as might be expected of a person entrusted with the lives of several thousand passengers and crew during the course of a cruise. His thick black hair was peppered with grey that betrayed his years of experience, and his goatee beard was meticulously trimmed. His welcome speech had been delivered in deep, almost seductive tones that left Rebecca of the opinion that if she ever did get close to him, she would think him most charismatic.

Luckily, Kitt was quite accustomed to working around little hitches like your suspect being surrounded by a bunch of salivating groupies, and in this instance, she had identified a second-best person of interest: his wife was also present. And to say she was not getting anywhere near as much attention as her husband was an understatement. She was sitting at a table quite alone and nursing a large glass of red wine while the passengers bustled around her spouse next to the champagne fountain.

'What's the plan?' said Grace.

'Probably best if you and Evie sit this round out,' said Kitt. 'I'm not sure how welcoming she's going to be here and I might need you to have another crack at her tomorrow on an undercover basis.'

'I'll agree to this only if my cover story involves me adopting some kind of exotic accent,' said Grace. 'I've never had a chance to do that in any of our other cases.'

'Yes, well, although you know I love helping you to fulfil your life's ambitions, Grace, the priority is solving the case, not finding ways to let you play around with silly accents. Just keep an eye on the captain and if it looks at any point like he might come and interrupt us, intercept him and see what you can get out of him for yourselves.'

'Got it,' said Grace.

'As this plan means I can stay standing next to the French bread, I'm all for it,' said Evie, slathering the thickest layer of butter Rebecca had ever seen on a chunky slice of baguette.

'Follow my lead,' said Kitt, setting off towards the table where the captain's wife was seated. Halfway between the buffet and the captain's wife, Kitt began to limp.

'Are you all right?' Rebecca said, taking Kitt's arm.

'Oooh, no, ow, ow, ow. Oh, my giddy aunt!'

'What's wrong?' Rebecca said, wondering how on earth this could be part of her sister's strategy as Kitt half hopped the rest of the way to the table where the captain's wife was seated.

'I'm so sorry,' Kitt said. 'Do you mind if we perch here for a few minutes? These heels are killing my feet. They're supposed to be top of the range. I'll be returning them the second I hit dry land, I can tell you.'

'By all means,' the captain's wife replied, a practised smile gracing her thin lips as she gestured for Kitt and Rebecca to take a seat.

Quite clever, she had to give her sister that. Though Kitt had never been voted most likely to strike up a conversation about shoes, she knew enough about the people she was dealing with here to plot a decent ruse.

Kitt started rubbing her feet. 'Such a shame about the shoes,' said Kitt. 'In all other respects, this is the most wonderful event I've ever been to in my life.' Though this was clearly part of the cover Kitt had decided on, she wasn't having to lay it on too thick since the room was a sight to behold. Everything in it glistened and sparkled, from the glasses on the champagne table to the chandeliers that hung overhead. There was a clear theme of decadence, the likes of which they were unlikely to see again in their lifetime.

'Don't you agree?' Kitt said, staring hard enough at Rebecca to realize she was missing some kind of cue here.

'Oh yes,' Rebecca said, echoing her sister's sentiments. 'Everything is so lavish, an absolute dream.'

Slowly, the smile that was previously on Kitt's face began to fall and for a moment Rebecca wondered if she'd somehow got her part wrong.

'But oh, my only wish is that Bryce was still here to enjoy it with us,' Kitt said with a sniffle. 'I can just see him now, revelling in it all. The two of us, two friends reunited after all these years. I always meant to make that happen. But we never quite got around to it, and now we never will. My heart breaks to think about it.'

Kitt had been sure to place enough emphasis on Bryce's name to ensure that the captain's wife overheard and, sure enough, she started when she did.

'I beg your pardon,' she said. 'I didn't mean to eavesdrop. I'm Yvonne Ortega, the captain's wife.'

'Oh,' Kitt said, the feigned pained expression on her face still very much on display. 'A pleasure to meet you, I'm sure. I'm sorry ... I ... I'm mourning the loss of a friend at the moment. I'm probably not the best conversationalist.'

'I don't mean to intrude,' Yvonne said, tucking a wave of red hair behind her ear. 'But before, were you by chance talking about Bryce Griffin?'

'Why, yes,' said Kitt. 'He was a friend of mine and he died rather tragically – but of course, if you're the captain's wife you probably heard all about it.'

'Yes . . . I did,' Yvonne said. She looked down into her wine for a moment before her eyes flitted back up to Kitt's. 'My husband was captaining the ship when your friend died.'

'Oh, I'm sorry,' said Kitt. 'I didn't realize. Your husband must just feel terrible about what happened to Bryce.'

Yvonne's eyebrow flickered in a manner that was difficult to read. She glared over at him and then looked back at Kitt. When she at last spoke, she didn't provide Kitt with an answer to her question. 'I met Bryce not long before he died and we got on very well.'

'How well?' Rebecca asked, leaning in and flashing a cheeky grin. Not really her natural comportment but she understood the game now. They were luring Yvonne into some girl talk and if they were lucky, she would let something vital slip. Her unwillingness to outright state that her husband felt bad about Bryce's passing was potentially already a worrying sign.

'Perhaps a little bit better than we should have,' said Yvonne, tracing a finger around the top of her wine glass. Her French nails were immaculate. Rebecca instinctively scrunched her own fingers into her palm. She'd put on a nice dress and worn a long-sleeved cardigan to cover her ink but she hadn't gone so far as to get a manicure. Yvonne wasn't alone in the room when it came to having all the time in the world to pamper herself, though. Rebecca hadn't seen anyone else with so much as a hair out of place all evening.

'Oh, goodness me. He didn't overstep, did he?' said Kitt. 'He was a friend but he could be a bit of a rascal.'

A knowing smile surfaced on Yvonne's lips. 'That's one of the things I liked about him actually. A woman shouldn't go too long without a rascal in her life. Don't you agree?'

Kitt chuckled at Yvonne's comment and Rebecca joined in. She stopped short, however, when she realized that for reasons she couldn't quite explain, Errol had leaped into her thoughts. Scrunching her eyes shut for a moment, she tried to push the thought away. She must stop thinking about him in affectionate terms. She didn't have the luxury of trusting him. Not right now anyway.

'Did your husband not mind you having a rascal in your life?' Kitt said, a light note in her voice. 'I only ask because my boyfriend has quite the jealous streak. He didn't even like me receiving letters from Bryce, let alone anything more.'

Yvonne paused for a moment before answering the question. It had been a risk for Kitt to ask something so direct but Rebecca was fairly convinced she'd been casual enough when she'd asked to avoid suspicion. 'Dominic wasn't pleased but Dominic isn't the one waiting at home for months on end for his spouse to return. So when I was talking to Bryce I didn't give his possible reaction much thought. Being lonely is a terrible thing.'

'I agree,' said Kitt. 'We're only human. Anyone would find that difficult.'

Yvonne shrugged. 'I suppose I knew he was a captain when I married him. I was just too young and naive to understand the reality of that. You have all these glittering ideas when you're young and then they all sort of just fade away.'

'I know what you mean but lots of us get into relationships without understanding what the reality will really be like,' said Rebecca, trying not to think about her own similar experiences.

'True,' said Yvonne. 'It's just sometimes difficult to remember that I once thought him as fantastic as everyone else seems to. But Bryce, he made me feel younger than I have done in years. He reminded me of what it was like to expect light and laughter on any given day. And for that, though he is no longer with us, I will always be grateful to him.'

'I'm so glad the two of you felt such a connection to one another,' said Kitt. 'I would love to stay and hear more of your memories but we are leaving very shortly. These shoes really are killing me and I can barely keep my eyes open now after all the champagne. I'll never learn my lesson – the fifth glass is always a mistake. But I wonder if it would be too much of an imposition to visit you at your cabin tomorrow and hear some more about what you remember of Bryce? It's been so many years since I last saw him in person, I feel like there's lots you must know about him that I don't. It would be a great comfort to me during this time of grieving.'

'I would welcome the company,' said Yvonne. 'We're in suite 221B. Dominic will be working. I'll make sure I'm in around three o'clock, if you can make it for then?'

'That would be so kind of you,' said Kitt. 'We'll give you a knock then.'

After that Kitt made their excuses and began to fake-hobble towards the exit with Rebecca, giving Evie and Grace a quick wave as they went to make it clear now was the time to leave.

'You just got us an invite to the captain's cabin,' said Rebecca, in slight disbelief.

'I know,' Kitt said with a smug smile. 'We might not be able to question the captain directly tonight but we'll find a way to search that cabin tomorrow, right under her nose if necessary, and if there's anything suspicious linking the captain to Bryce's death, we'll jolly well find it.'

CHAPTER SEVENTEEN

Though Rebecca had grudgingly agreed for Errol to meet them outside the top deck ballroom at eleven p.m. when the gala finished, it was somehow still a surprise to see him standing there, in a pair of jeans and white shirt and a sandy-coloured blazer, his long hair falling over his shoulders. Did he look more appealing just because her decision to continue the lie that they were off the case made him off limits now – or at the very least not a very sensible prospect? Or was her growing fondness for him a result of how kind he'd been when she told him about the attack?

Though the original plan was for Errol to safely escort them back to the cabin, he suggested that they all go dancing in the Paradise Bar and Club instead. After the general dreariness of the conversations at the gala – Rebecca had at one point got stuck talking to a duke who was only interested in telling stories about his bowls club – Evie and Grace accepted the invitation before either Kitt or Rebecca could politely decline. Grace had finally bounced back from her seasickness and all the signs were that she was more than raring to make up for lost time.

The Paradise Bar and Club was, to Rebecca's mind, little more than a floating cliché decorated with a desert-island theme. She'd visited a hundred clubs that looked pretty similar to this one in the nineties when her increased tolerance for alcohol helped to take the edge off the sticky surfaces and the strobe lighting that did nothing but emphasize your acne. The dance floor was covered in sand to simulate a beach. The walls had been stencilled with ocean wave motifs and potted palm trees had been arranged around the bar – which, of course, only sold the most garish cocktails with the most sexually suggestive names.

She had been rather impressed that Kitt had managed to order 'five Slippery Nipples' without blushing. Her once somewhat conservative sister was clearly a bit more worldly wise than she had been even four years ago now. No doubt Halloran was to thank for that. Though as a doctor Rebecca was hardly scandalized by the mention of a nipple, she had a feeling she might feel a bit different placing that order with Errol standing next to her.

Despite the less-than-inspired choices in decor, on the dance floor, swaying to a blend of eighties and nineties pop classics spun by the resident DJ, Rebecca could feel some of the tension she'd held on to since the attack shaking out of her. It was difficult to tell if it was the club atmosphere or the industrial-strength cocktail that was having this effect, but all of that suspicion and dread and death felt suddenly very far away. Perhaps the fact that Errol was holding her hand, and twirling her round and round to the point that she almost fell over in dizziness, had something to do with it too. Mercifully, he had the reflexes to grab hold of her when she nearly toppled over.

'Graceful as ever,' she chided herself, loud enough for Errol to hear.

'Easy there,' he said, smiling and holding on to her for another moment or two to check she'd regained her balance.

'Well, that's what you get for twirling a woman who's had as much alcohol as I have this evening.'

Errol chuckled. 'It was worth it just to see you smile. And I'd twirl you again, I tell you.'

'You are daft, I hope you know that,' Rebecca said, fighting a smile and failing.

He responded by putting his hands on her hips and swaying her from side to side so they could slow dance together. As he did so, she cast a glance over to Kitt, Evie and Grace who were dancing in a small circle together just a few feet away. So her nerves weren't completely settled after what had happened to her then. She took a deep breath, trying to convince herself she was safe with Errol. And if anything happened she didn't like, her friends were well within shouting distance.

She suddenly realized how close her body had become to Errol's. Was slow dancing with him the best idea given that she was lying to him? Getting romantically attached to someone you were deceiving, even in the name of justice, surely couldn't end well? And yet, for all Rebecca's rationalizing, it was getting increasingly difficult to ignore how strong his arms felt as they guided her across the dance floor.

'I've actually been trying to cut back on daftness lately,' he said at last. 'So you haven't really seen me at full daft capacity.'

'The first time I met you, you were wearing a pirate costume and had a parrot on your shoulder and you're telling me there is a level of daft above that?'

Errol laughed. 'Well, I did a little performance in the main square. Thought I might as well recoup the train fare. Skittles is always a crowd-pleaser. I didn't want to knock too early on a Saturday either. Some people sleep in past midday, you know, after a hard week.'

'And now that you've met my sister, what time do you think she rises on a Saturday?'

'Probably before midday,' said Errol with a nod.

'Do you think it will be difficult to find another partner for your act?' she asked, looking into his distracting sea-green eyes and immediately regretting it.

Errol shook his head. 'Eventually Crown Cruises will find someone else to take Bryce's place, I'd say. They've said they'll let me have final approval on the candidate, which is good of them. I think they, understandably, feel bad about the fact Bryce was killed on one of their ships. If he had any next of kin, they might have ended up paying compensation so making the professional transition easy for those of us who knew him is the least they can do. I'm sure there'll be a lot of applications. It's surprising how many people are eager to give up their life on land and exchange it for a life at sea. Everyone here has a reason. Something they left behind.'

'Even you?'

Errol's eyes lowered.

Rebecca bit her lip. 'Oh, I'm so sorry, I shouldn't pry. It's Kitt's curiosity, it's infectious. It's not my place to be asking such questions.'

Despite her polite apology, just at that moment, Rebecca wanted to know more than anything why Errol had decided on a life at sea. It was obvious from his reaction that there was a story there.

'It's fine,' Errol said with a shrug. 'I just had a messy divorce, that's all. Nothing that a million people haven't been through before me. I need to stop licking my wounds.'

'Just because other people have been through it doesn't mean your pain isn't valid,' said Rebecca. 'I don't think it's healthy for you to try and force yourself to be OK about it when you're not.'

'Thank you, doctor,' Errol said, his grin widening.

Rebecca raised her eyebrows at him to make it clear she had seen comedy used as a self-defence mechanism more times than he would ever know and it didn't wash.

'I hear what you're saying,' he said, his smile fading. 'I'm not denying it was a shock. I don't like to talk about it much, I feel so stupid. Ashamed, I suppose.'

'There's no need to feel stupid,' said Rebecca. 'Lots of people decide to break things off with their spouse and, more often than not, it's for the best – for both parties. What's the point of being in a relationship if your heart's not in it? Making a clean break is surely the much more sensible option?'

'That's just it really. It wasn't a clean break. Not in any sense of that phrase. My wife, she had this whole other life I didn't know about. Separate man. Separate phone. Separate social media accounts. You hear about things like that happening but you never think it's going to happen to you. That's why I feel like a mug.'

Against her better judgement, Rebecca could feel her heart softening at Errol's story. Perhaps that was why he was, in his own words, not making the best relationship decisions just now. And she had judged him as a serial womanizer. Chalked it up as another sign that maybe he couldn't be trusted. When, in truth, he was just hurting and she had completely misread him.

'You weren't a mug. You were trying your hardest to make a relationship work,' said Rebecca. 'There's no shame in that.

And what happened to you, that's . . . a pretty difficult thing to bounce back from. You should make sure you take the time you need to process it all. How long were you together?'

'Six years. Married for two. Thought I'd been smart waiting a good three years before popping the question, and then having a leisurely year-long engagement. Thought I knew her. Thought she loved me back. Maybe she did in her own way. I don't know. How can you ever know with someone like that?'

Rebecca shook her head. 'I can't even imagine the pain.'

'You've never been married?'

'No, my work pattern has seen to that.'

Errol muttered something she couldn't make out over the music. 'Anyone who can't cope with the fact that you work at nights and weekends to save other people's lives definitely isn't worth your time.'

Rebecca chuckled. 'That's probably right but does rather limit the range of potential suitors. Still, it's small fry in comparison to the challenges you've faced relationship-wise.'

'It has taken some getting over.'

'Well, at least you have ladies like Jemima to take your mind off things.'

The moment the words were out of her mouth Rebecca chided herself for them. Why couldn't she just let it lie? Had her increased exposure to Kitt left her incapable of accepting an explanation at face value? Would she have to probe every little detail in future simply to establish basic trust with another human being?

Errol shook his head. 'That was a one-off. I am not into being treated like an accessory after what happened with my ex. And that's how most of the women who board the ship see people like me. Except . . .'

'Except what?'

'Not sure I should say,' Errol said with a knowing grin.

'I don't think you can leave a girl hanging like that.'

'OK, well, when you look at me, I don't feel that.'

'No, well, I'm not in the habit of looking at people as accessories.'

Errol paused and stroked his hand down the side of her face. 'You'd be amazed how rare that is.'

Rebecca swallowed hard. Not just at his words and the heat she felt in his fingertips but because their faces had drawn closer as they'd strained to talk over the music. His lips were well within kissing distance. If only she could have just leaned forward and thrown caution to the wind. But it was no use. Especially after the story about his wife, guilt filled her. He had already been deceived by one woman and now she was deceiving him too. She could kiss him, of course she could, more than happily. But it would be dishonest.

Taking a step back, she released herself from his arms. 'It's late. I really should go back to the cabin with my sister. I didn't sleep that well last night and was hoping to catch up.'

The light in Errol's eyes dimmed. 'If that's what you want, of course.'

Rebecca smiled and took a couple of steps towards Kitt to signal she was ready to leave. Evie and Grace followed them out of the club and Errol insisted on making good on his original promise to escort them back to the cabin. As they walked he occasionally touched the small of Rebecca's back to guide her along the corridors, while she contemplated her terrible luck when it came to romance and how Errol might feel if he ever found out she was lying to him.

CHAPTER EIGHTEEN

Rebecca had never seen a burlesque show live before but that's where their covert investigation began the next day, once they'd all made headway in recovering from everything they'd drunk the previous night.

Miss Ocean Blue had a midday show which they managed to get tickets to, and from the moment the performance began it was very clear indeed why she had a job aboard the *Northern Spirit*. Her act involved various gymnastic contortions on a stepladder while dressed in a blue sequined leotard and fishnet stockings. Her long blue hair had been rollered into silky curls. Her striptease was slow, seductive and punctuated with cheeky winks. A knowing smile remained perpetually on her candy-pink lips as she strutted and twirled in a pair of blue sequined heels that matched her shimmering leotard.

Rebecca wasn't the only one to be mesmerized by this sensual vision. When she glanced over at Grace, Evie and Kitt, their eyes, she saw, were also glued to the stage.

Considering just how dazzling a sight she was, Rebecca decided there and then that if they ever had cause to speak over the radio about Miss Ocean Blue, Glinda would be the only appropriate code name for her.

Once the show was over, they paused at a café in view of the stage-door area, poised to follow Miss Ocean Blue and contrive a coincidental meeting. After what Errol had said about her relationship with Bryce, they had formulated a plan to strike up conversation but before they could execute it, they needed an opportunity to get close to her.

Before long, Miss Ocean Blue exited the stage door. She looked quite different without her make-up and dressed down in a pair of black leggings and a salmon hoodie, but there was no mistaking that blue hair. A marker they followed all the way to the jacuzzi area.

There was much cursing when Kitt realized where she was heading. They hadn't thought to bring their swimwear from the cabin and had to leave Evie and Grace to keep tabs on Miss Ocean Blue while they nipped back for a quick costume change.

When they returned, Grace and Evie confirmed that Miss Ocean Blue was lounging in the jacuzzi, so Kitt and Rebecca seized their moment.

'Do you mind if we sit here?' Kitt asked, sliding into the jacuzzi not far from where their target was sitting.

'Not at all,' Miss Ocean Blue replied, with a gentle Spanish inflection in her voice.

'Thank you,' Kitt said, leaning back on the ledge and waiting for Rebecca to slide in next to her before starting their pre-arranged script. 'Gosh, it's nice to relax.'

The water was warm and frothy and felt nothing short of rejuvenating against Rebecca's skin. At once she was aware of all the tension she'd been holding in her body as the soothing bubbles danced around her every joint and limb. Could the solution to the many doubts and suspicions that filled her mind right now be so simple? She could only hope.

Rebecca glanced for a moment around the other passengers in the jacuzzi, allowing herself to snatch a look at Miss Ocean Blue as she did so. Her face, just like the others, was illuminated by an eerie green light reflecting off the water. Sitting in a large circle like this with their green faces, they looked like a cult performing some kind of demonic ritual to Rebecca's mind.

Kitt cleared her throat.

A signal that Rebecca had taken a moment too long in responding to Kitt's earlier comment.

'I agree, some downtime is long overdue,' Rebecca said, delivering her next line with what she hoped sounded like haughty indignance. 'Besides, you deserve a bit of relaxation after what that pig of a boyfriend did to you.'

'Don't remind me about him,' Kitt said, loud enough for Miss Ocean Blue to overhear. 'All that time I spent making him my priority and then he just walks away. As though I'm disposable or something. I don't even wanna think about him.'

At this point, Kitt glanced over to Miss Ocean Blue who had been listening with keen interest. 'Oh, I'm sorry to spoil your peace and quiet,' Kitt said to her. 'But men really are the worst, aren't they?'

Rebecca noticed a couple of guys, sitting over on the other side of the jacuzzi, frown at each other on hearing this comment. She wished she had a way of letting them know that this was all pretend. That they didn't believe every man they came into contact with was a scoundrel but unfortunately, just then, they had bigger things to worry about than getting on the wrong side of a couple of strangers.

'They can be,' Miss Ocean Blue said, slowly and sadly. She had quite a deep voice and the Spanish lilt to it sounded most exotic to Rebecca's ears.

'I'll admit it,' said Kitt. 'I'm not sure I'm going to get over this one. Or, if I am, right now I don't know how.'

'I . . . understand that feeling,' Miss Ocean Blue said, staring into the bubbling waters. 'I think most people do, yes?'

'You're probably right about that but oh,' said Kitt, pressing a hand to her chest, 'I'm sorry to hear you've been through the same. I wouldn't wish this kind of heartbreak on anyone. I really do need to learn to keep my big mouth shut.'

At this, Miss Ocean Blue shrugged. 'It's all right. I'm sure I'm not the only broken heart on board.'

At these words, Rebecca realized she could think of at

least one other: Errol. She tried to push his face from her mind but he wouldn't budge. Was he telling the truth about the ex-wife with the second, secret life? Or was that a cover for something much darker? Though she wanted to believe him, she still couldn't figure it out and the more she thought about it, the more she realized why her sister was so reluctant to trust anyone when carrying out this kind of work. Trusting the wrong person could be fatal. Literally.

'Was your . . . break-up recent?' Kitt said, snapping Rebecca out of her thoughts.

'Not that recent . . . about . . . five months ago now but' – Miss Ocean Blue tapped her chest – 'I still feel it.'

'Was it someone you met on a cruise?' said Kitt. 'I was rather hoping to meet someone to take my mind off my ex.'

Miss Ocean Blue smiled. She'd removed the rest of her stage make-up but the pink pout remained. 'I wish you luck with that. But no, I work for the ship I . . . I was involved with one of my co-workers.'

'Ah,' Rebecca said. 'I know all about that. Did things get too awkward in the workplace? I hate it when that happens.'

'Not quite our story. It's rather delicate, you see. Before I could convince him to change his mind about being with me, he died.'

Miss Ocean Blue had been trying to convince Bryce to get back together with her for five whole months? That really was commitment, though not the kind most daydream about. Rebecca couldn't help but wonder if Bryce had said no to her one too many times, and that's why he was no longer with them. Miss Ocean Blue would know the code to that rec room. She might have apologized for her previous behaviour. Convinced Bryce that she just wanted a quiet word with him, for old time's sake. And then, out on the balcony, when he wouldn't agree to reuniting, she decided if he wasn't going to be with her, he wasn't going to be with anyone.

That was motive and opportunity but what about means? And what about the man who had attacked Rebecca? She was almost certain it had been a man . . . Did that mean Miss Ocean Blue was working with an accomplice? If she really was the ultimate wronged woman, how did she get hold of a gun? And, more to the point, how did she manage to smuggle it on board . . . smuggle.

Bryce was a seasoned smuggler. Kitt had said so herself. All this time, they had assumed the gun belonged to the killer but what if there had been some kind of altercation, and Bryce had pulled out the gun in self-defence only to be shot by his own firearm? Rebecca had read some statistics a while back. She couldn't remember the numbers now. But it was an article arguing that carrying weapons was actually more dangerous as they can be turned on you. What if the same thing had happened to Bryce?

If this was even close to what had happened, why would Bryce hold Miss Ocean Blue at gunpoint? To warn her off stalking him? Somehow that image, of Bryce waving a gun in Miss Ocean Blue's face, didn't match the picture Kitt had built of Bryce in Rebecca's mind. But then, Kitt was his friend – at a distance. She didn't really know about his day-to-day dealings. He really could have been up to anything and they would have no easy way of knowing it.

'He died? My goodness. I am so very sorry.' Kitt pressed her hand against her chest. 'I may be wrong here, but I have to ask, it wasn't Bryce Griffin, was it?'

Miss Ocean Bloom started and narrowed her eyes. 'You knew Bryce?'

'I am an old friend of his,' Kitt said with a nod. 'When I heard he'd been killed I boarded the ship to try and investigate his death but as it turns out, it was too difficult a case to solve. So we've given up on that and just hope the police are able to figure it out. I am so very sorry for your loss. That must have been so painful, to lose Bryce when you had once had such a close relationship with him.'

Miss Ocean Blue stared into the frothing waters, her voice taking on a wistful note. 'To be honest, I haven't yet truly convinced myself he's gone. I know that he is. I know that in my head. But still, I keep expecting to see him in the bar. Or find him waiting for me outside my cabin door, the way he did once. I don't know if that feeling will ever go away. Not so long as I'm on this ship anyway.'

There was a splashing sound in the periphery as the men who had been sitting opposite them left the jacuzzi. It was just Rebecca, Kitt and and Miss Ocean Blue in there now which was no bad thing. Perhaps she would open up a bit more without an audience.

'Oh, I see. Are you planning to leave your job here?' said Rebecca. If Miss Ocean Blue was keen to put some distance between herself and the *Northern Spirit*, she might have her reasons, and they may not be grief alone.

'Right now I don't know where else I would go,' she replied. 'But . . . I have to say, I don't think it's too difficult to solve this case. I think the police just don't want to get involved with the person who is really behind it.'

'What do you mean?' said Kitt. 'You know something about what happened to Bryce?'

'I have my theories,' Miss Ocean Blue said, glancing back up from the water, looking between Rebecca and Kitt. 'I think the reason Bryce broke up with me is because I got too close to something. A secret.'

'What kind of secret?' said Rebecca, frowning.

'I don't know,' said Miss Ocean Blue, lowering her voice. 'But I do not think he broke up with me because he didn't love me any more. I think he did it to keep me safe. No matter what I tried, he wouldn't take me back even though I could see in his eyes that he wanted to.' She paused before speaking again as though weighing up if she should say any more. When she did speak her voice was barely a whisper. 'He said the name Archippo in his sleep.'

'Archippo? What's that?' Kitt said, keeping her voice low.

'The name of a notorious crime boss. He's been in

operation for about twenty years and apparently he doesn't like being told "no".'

'And you think that Bryce's death is somehow related to this crime boss? Why would he target Bryce?' said Kitt.

'Bryce went on a trip,' Miss Ocean Blue explained. 'He wouldn't tell me where to. When he came back, that's when he began saying that name in his sleep and I knew something was terribly wrong. When I first told him that he had said that name in his sleep his whole face went white. He tried to laugh it off, the way he always tried to laugh everything off, but I could see there was something else going on there. I started asking questions he didn't want me to ask and that's when he broke up with me. I think he was scared of what else he might say in his sleep. That he might let me in on something that would get me into trouble.'

'What kind of crime does this . . . individual do?' Rebecca asked, reluctant to say the name out loud again in case she was overheard. They already had an unknown enemy on board the ship somewhere. If it was Archippo, not letting him know they were on to him was probably a good idea.

'People say he's deep into money laundering, arms smuggling and robbery. And I can only think of one reason why Bryce might mention that name in his sleep. I think he was working for him. And I also think someone else who works for Archippo is behind Bryce's death.'

'And you told the police this?' said Kitt.

'Yes, they laughed at me. They said Archippo was a myth.

That there's never been any evidence that this person even exists and so he couldn't have anything to do with what happened to Bryce. But I think there was some kind of racket going on. I don't know exactly what kind or why on earth Bryce would mix himself up in it but it's too much of a coincidence, for Bryce to say the name Archippo in his sleep almost every night and then be found dead so soon after.'

'I understand why you might come to that conclusion but if the police don't have any evidence that Archippo exists, how can you be sure that Bryce wasn't just mumbling nonsense in his sleep?' said Kitt.

'Bryce was shot in broad daylight,' said Miss Ocean Blue, her voice hardening. 'That's not the work of an angry novice. It would take a professional to get away with something like that. I am certain of it.' Miss Ocean Blue pressed her pink lips together and shook her head. 'No, I'm right about this. I know it. It cannot be a coincidence. You should restart your investigation and look into it.'

'I don't think we can restart the investigation,' said Kitt. 'It was too hard investigating the death of a friend. But I will pass on the information to the police. Maybe if more than one person makes a fuss about this particular line of enquiry, they will take it more seriously.'

'I sincerely hope they do,' Miss Ocean Blue said, her brown eyes watering. 'If they don't, Archippo is going to get away with yet another crime and there is no doubt in my mind that, whoever that man is, he's the one behind it.'

CHAPTER NINETEEN

Despite the seriousness of their prior chat with Miss Ocean Blue, Rebecca couldn't help but chuckle as she watched Evie dig a spoon into a massive banana split at the on-board ice cream parlour.

The ice cream parlour itself was painted in gawdy shades of pink and yellow, giving it a strangely eighties vibe. Though it was a treat for the nose as well as the tongue – the whole place smelled of hot, melted caramel – Rebecca was a bit dubious about some of the serving choices. All of the drinks, for example, were served in oversized cardboard cups – the 'small' would provide enough carbonated drink to last anyone a week – and all the ice cream, even if all you wanted was a single scoop of vanilla, was served in ornate sundae glasses in various sizes. It was flamboyance for the sake of it, no doubt. The sheer range of toppings alone, from chocolate raisins and honeycomb to rainbow sprinkles and fudge chunks, was enough to get your mouth watering and, despite it being a little bit over the top for her personal taste, Rebecca couldn't deny the place had a certain offbeat charm.

There was, however, one feature of this rather quirky little venue that put Rebecca on edge: the waiting staff moved around on roller-skates. A detail Rebecca truly had needed to see to believe. She couldn't quite grasp that such a practice had been signed off from a health and safety perspective, given that, should the boat hit stormy waters, they might all be knocked off balance.

'I don't know where you put it all,' Rebecca said, marvelling at how Evie could even think about eating again after the massive pancake stack she'd devoured, with almost animal enthusiasm, at breakfast.

'Oh, I won't eat for another six months now,' said Evie. 'Gotta make the most of this trip because the calories have got to last me till Christmas.'

'Or,' said Kitt, 'and I'm just throwing this out there, you could enjoy your food all year round.'

A stifled groan came from Grace. 'Oh, here we go. Better change the subject before Kitt starts talking about how eating three square meals a day is a form of feminist protest.'

'Well, it is,' said Kitt.

'I know, I've heard the TED talk,' said Grace. 'But let's move on to the topic of the hour. If what Miss Ocean Blue has just said is accurate, Archippo is on board and operating out of this ship. Which means that I, Grace Edwards, will finally come face to face with a hardened crime boss. Maybe I'll have to go undercover and then halfway through my mission, they'll realize there's a rat and there'll be this big mole hunt and I—'

'Grace!' Kitt said. 'Don't you think you're getting just a little bit ahead of yourself? We don't even know if what Miss Ocean Blue told us *is* accurate. For one thing, she took pains to plant the seed that Archippo is thought of as a mythical figure by law enforcement, that as far as any official is concerned this person doesn't even exist.'

'So?' said Evie, between mouthfuls of ice cream. Rebecca got the impression that she might have liked to say more on the subject but her mouth was otherwise engaged.

'So, what if he is fictional?' said Kitt. 'And she's just trying to push blame on to some imaginary foe? We can't verify that Bryce said anything of the sort in his sleep. She might be trying to throw us off the scent, get us to waste our time investigating a person who doesn't really exist so she can disappear once we reach Oslo. If we played into her hands, we wouldn't give up our search for Archippo just because initial research indicated he didn't exist. We'd keep going, believing there was more to it.'

'So you think she's trying to make us believe there's some deeper truth when it comes to this Archippo chap,' said Grace. 'That other people are dismissing it but if we keep digging, we'll find something even though, in reality, we won't.'

'Right,' said Kitt. 'But it could be a double-bluff. It's quite a clever trick really.'

'So we can't believe anything she told us?' said Rebecca.

'I'm not saying that,' said Kitt. 'I'm just saying it's not a verifiable story. Even if Bryce did say it in his sleep, that doesn't mean that this Archippo fellow is operating out of this ship. Miss Ocean Blue said he didn't start saying his name in his sleep until after he'd been on some mystery trip she knew nothing about. Which has to be the trip to the Gulf of Aden. Bryce might have started to talk about it in his sleep because he met with Archippo out there. So by that reasoning, we can't be sure that Archippo himself is operating from this ship.'

'We can't be sure, not on what Miss Ocean Blue told us alone,' said Rebecca. 'But some pieces of evidence do suggest that organized crime might play a part in this.'

'Like what?' said Grace.

'Apparently Archippo specializes in money laundering, arms smuggling and robbery. Georgia said she's been dealing with a range of thefts for some time now. Whoever's behind them, it's a long-term operation. It's possibly happening on a grander scale than Georgia's even aware of too. She said other ships in the Crown Cruise family had been targeted.'

'Yes, you're right to point out that at least in scale, these robberies do fit the profile of organized crime,' said Kitt.

'But it's not just that,' said Rebecca. 'The way I was accosted, that is the kind of thing an organized crime boss would be able to achieve. And if they've got some crew members in their pocket covering up their activities, getting away with it all becomes a lot easier. That's not even taking into account the fact that Archippo deals in arms and we've not been certain this whole time how a gun was brought aboard the ship. Archippo might be the answer. I did think while we were talking to Miss Ocean Blue that if Bryce was working with Archippo, the gun might actually have belonged to him in the first place, and the weapon was turned on him.'

Kitt nodded. 'I really don't want to think about Bryce getting mixed up with someone like that. Organized crime, for heaven's sake. Had he not learned anything after all the trouble he's been in over the years? But when you lay it out like that there are more than a few factors pointing in this direction.'

'There's just a boldness to the criminal behaviour we're seeing that I don't think you see from people acting alone,' Rebecca said.

'I can't deny it,' said Kitt. 'I suppose I'd just rather not believe that Bryce was involved with such a sinister figure. People like that, as Bryce ultimately found out in the hardest possible way, don't take any prisoners.'

'I know,' said Rebecca. 'It can't be an easy thing to consider but, like Miss Ocean Blue said, who else would have the gall to shoot someone in broad daylight? Who else would have the means to get a gun on board the ship when everyone has to pass through airport-style security just to get here?'

'Based on what we've learned, particularly about the robberies – which I can't believe are a coincidence, especially after Rebecca's attacker made the reference to Georgia being a thorn in their side for the precise amount of time the robberies have been taking place,' Kitt said, 'it's looking less and less like Bryce's killing was a crime of passion based on a personal matter. If he were saying that name in his sleep, the odds are he was in some way involved in whatever criminal actions are taking place on the ship. Though I still think it's much more likely that we're dealing with someone loyal to Archippo than with Archippo himself.' Kitt rubbed her arms. 'Oh Bryce, what the bloody hell were you up to this time?'

'Maybe the answer is in that deposit box from the poem,' said Grace. 'I don't think that you go to the trouble of writing the first poem you've ever written in your life and hiding a code in it unless it's important.'

'The poem was odd on its own,' said Kitt. 'Adding in a code that reveals a safety deposit box number only makes it stranger. Halloran is trying to track it down. He's been in touch with the North East police about it. They're starting the search in Carlisle since that's the only place mentioned in the letter. But they're having to go through every bank based there. It's not a big place, but this search is also not something they can prioritize over their other cases right now so it's probably going to take a few days.'

'Wait!' said Rebecca. 'My attacker claimed they were an

important person on the ship. From what Miss Ocean Blue said about Archippo, it would appear we're looking for a man. Perhaps he and my attacker are one and the same. Someone high-ranking who is also a notorious criminal.'

'It makes sense,' said Grace. 'Attacking a passenger like that was beyond bolshy. If someone like Archippo is operating off of this ship, they'd need to be high up in the ranks. Someone who people trusted implicitly and wouldn't question . . . maybe someone who people would turn a blind eye for if they were ordered to.'

'Lends weight to the theory that Captain Dominic Ortega might yet have some role to play in all this,' Kitt said with a nod.

'You really think the captain took the risk of attacking Rebecca on his own ship?' said Evie. She had finally swallowed the last mouthful of ice cream and was thus more able to chip in. 'I mean, that is a huge risk, and that's putting it lightly. If he got caught, he'd lose everything. His marriage. His position. His freedom. I can understand someone wanting to cover up a devious act at any cost if they committed a murder. But I just can't quite see the captain doing that himself.'

'And thinking about it,' said Grace. 'If he did risk something like that, would he actually drop a clue that it was him behind it by telling us that he's a person of great importance?'

'You're assuming that the captain thinks getting caught

and having to face the consequences of his actions is within the realm of probability. The thing about power is when people get too much of it, they think they can do anything,' said Kitt. 'Out here, on the sea, when you're in a position of authority far away from land law enforcement, there's a good chance you'll start to think it's acceptable to make your own rules.'

'Maybe I can buy that. Especially if you're already working with a notorious organized crime boss who would likely put an end to you if you stepped out of line,' said Grace. 'Or, I suppose, we can't rule out the fact that the captain could be Archippo himself. Most captains have been at sea for years. It takes great experience to drive a boat like this. And Miss Ocean Blue said Archippo had been in operation for around twenty years, right?'

'That's what she said,' Kitt agreed. 'I suppose if an organized crime gang did manage to get a crime boss promoted up to the position of captain, they could potentially ensure people on the ship turned a blind eye to a lot of bad behaviour.'

'But don't you find it kind of unthinkable?' said Evie. 'That a crime gang, no matter how strategic, could really pull that off.'

'The fact that it seems unthinkable might be the very reason he's got away with it for so long,' said Kitt. 'And if he is pulling all the strings in this situation, if he attacked Rebecca and had Bryce killed, that's probably not the only criminality he's involved with. People like that aren't in it for the small wins. They're always looking for the big hauls.'

'Robbery, money laundering and arms dealing are all big business, I'm sad to report,' said Grace. 'If there's a crime ring operating out of this ship, they could be committing all kinds of crimes right under our noses.'

'And if the captain is involved, there might be some clues when we visit his cabin,' said Rebecca.

'Yes, but it's unlikely he'll leave them in clear view. You don't get to the top of a crime ring by being sloppy. Which means we need an opportunity to conduct a search without Mrs Ortega noticing. Given that even the most spacious suites on this ship aren't exactly what you'd call free-range, that might be something of a challenge,' said Kitt.

'Fear not,' said Grace. 'I've just the plan. What would you do without me, eh? Yet again it's Grace Edwards to the rescue!'

CHAPTER TWENTY

It had taken a good few minutes, but Kitt had at last managed to calm Grace down enough so she might relay the plan she'd formulated. Despite the overexcitable manner in which her scheme was conveyed, Rebecca had to admit that on hearing it she was more than impressed by the ingenuity on display. It was clear that Grace, though young in years, had picked up some impressive strategy while working with her sister at the agency for the past eighteen months. So long as Yvonne didn't recognize Grace from last night's party, everything should go off without a hitch.

'Forgive me for pouring a drink before dinner,' said Yvonne, filling one of the largest wine glasses Rebecca had ever seen almost to the brim with a crisp Sauvignon Blanc. 'Whenever I come on these cruises I remember that the one thing worse than being apart from your spouse for months on end is being with them at all hours. Not that I see Dominic all the time because naturally he has his duties to fulfil but when you barely see your spouse, seeing them every day can be a bit of a rude awakening. I've spoken to the spouses of other cruise ship workers and many of them feel the same. They can't quite work out if they're happier with their partner around all the time or if they'd rather only see them when they're on leave. Must all sound very strange to you, I'm sure.'

Kitt, Rebecca and Yvonne were perched around a small round table on the cabin balcony and the sun was a warm and welcome presence, given how nervous Rebecca was just then. Could they really pull this off? Conduct a search of the, rather luxurious, captain's cabin under Yvonne's nose? To be safe, Rebecca didn't refuse when Yvonne poured a splash of wine into her glass. She'd need a bit of courage for this.

'Proximity in relationships is a difficult thing to master,' said Kitt. 'As you've already discovered for yourself, you're not alone in matters like that.'

'So true, so true,' Yvonne said with an almost weary shake of her head. 'Though I have to say, I never minded how close I was with your friend Bryce. The sparkle in his eyes ... I don't think I'd ever quite seen eyes like his. The deepest blue. Bluer than the ocean.'

'Yes, he could turn on the charm when he wanted to,' Kitt said, with a knowing smile.

'That fact didn't pass me by.' Yvonne took a sip of her wine and looked out to sea as though remembering those illicit, stolen moments with Bryce. 'I still can't quite believe he's gone.'

'You and me both,' said Kitt. 'If anyone in this world had the nine lives of a cat, I thought it would be him.'

'How did you meet Bryce?' Yvonne asked.

'I used to bartend at a pub in the north of England, just for a short spell in my early twenties. Bryce was one of the more colourful customers,' Kitt explained. Rebecca noticed that Kitt had omitted the treasure hunt portion of the story. Probably for the best. The lines of the linen dress Yvonne was wearing were unmistakably designer and she'd bet her life savings that her shoes were Louboutins. Money was clearly of high importance to a woman like Mrs Ortega and the last thing they needed was for this conversation to get sidetracked by a treasure hunt gone wrong.

'And you've known him all these years?' said Yvonne.

'We were more penpals than anything else in recent times. But he was still a very important figure in my life.'

'I know he ruffled some feathers, not least my husband's, but even now I find it unimaginable that somebody on board this vessel could have done something like that to him. It was so . . . brutal. I would go so far as to say callous, in fact.'

Rebecca did her best to hide her thoughts on that matter. Given Yvonne's blatant and unabashed affections for Bryce, had it really never entered her head that her husband could be responsible in some way for the death of someone who was essentially a lover? It didn't seem as though the pair had ever made it to the bedroom but, from the sounds of things, if Captain Ortega hadn't discovered them when he did, that's where things were heading.

Then it occurred to Rebecca that perhaps Mrs Ortega did suspect her husband could have been involved but, for all her protests about how bored she was, she did not wish to give up the life of luxury her husband afforded her. This cabin alone was thrice the size of the one she and Kitt were sharing. She wasn't an expert on thread counts but the bed looked undoubtedly softer and had many more throw-pillows. Even the paint looked fresher than that in their cabin. Perhaps, when you got used to the best, you held on to it at all costs. Even if it meant a lonely, loveless life.

When Rebecca's eyes returned to her companions, rather than idly surveying the cabin, she noticed Kitt's eyes were fixed on her. Reminding her that she too had a role to play in this little charade, and had better get on with it.

'Excuse me,' said Rebecca. 'I just need to use your facilities, do you mind?'

'Please, go ahead,' Mrs Ortega said, waving in the direction of the door leading to the bathroom.

Rebecca offered a polite smile and then made her way over to the bathroom. Once there she locked the door and, as per Kitt's instructions, began opening cupboards and drawers as quietly as she could, looking for any disturbing signs or anything suspicious that the captain might be hiding.

She paused for a moment, straining to hear what was

being said on the other side of the door. But she couldn't make anything out. The bathroom was too far away from the balcony. She could only hope that Yvonne was a safe person for Kitt to be around on a one-to-one basis. So far there were no red flags when it came to what Grace had found online about her but at present it was difficult to think of anyone on this ship as trustworthy. Still, Kitt had insisted she needed to be alone with her, theorizing that Yvonne might be more forthcoming if they had a chance to talk with just the two of them. Thus, as well as secretly hunting for any incriminating evidence, Rebecca was to delay returning from the bathroom as long as possible to give Kitt the best chance of drawing the truth from her.

Easing open the drawers and cupboards, Rebecca checked each one, looking for anything untoward that had been stashed away. Or any medication that might hint that the captain wasn't of sound mind. The bathroom wasn't particularly spacious and the nooks and crannies were few. Between them she found nothing more damning than a bottle of aspirin.

Everything else was just your standard bathroom accessories. Toothbrushes, nail clippers, dental floss. Everything looked normal ... until Rebecca checked the cupboard beside the sink. It wasn't the contents of the cupboard that alarmed her but a single spot of blood, only visible at crouching height, on the side of the sink.

Rebecca's breath caught in her throat as she looked at

the spot. Which was ridiculous really and proof that this case had her incredibly on edge. It could, after all, be proof of nothing more sinister than a shaving accident. Or perhaps one of the Ortegas had gum problems. That said, she couldn't leave it to chance. Not with everything that was going on. She looked closer at the spot of blood. It was fairly fresh and hadn't completely dried yet. Pulling the plastic bag from her pocket, one of the many investigative essentials Kitt had packed in her luggage, she reached for a cotton bud and used it to take a swab before placing it into the bag. She'd deliberately worn trousers with deep pockets for this particular mission. Not knowing what she might need to stash away as evidence.

Rebecca took one last cursory glance around the bathroom to check everything was as she'd found it and to confirm there were no other red flags. Once satisfied, she took a deep breath while avoiding her own eyes in the bathroom mirror before flushing the toilet, washing her hands and exiting the room. Hoping beyond hope that, when she came face-to-face with Yvonne Ortega again, her little discovery wouldn't be written all over her face.

CHAPTER TWENTY-ONE

Rebecca had barely sat back in her seat at the table when a hard knock came on the door. Even though Rebecca had been expecting it, she still jumped when she heard it. Luckily, Yvonne's eyes were fixed on the door so she didn't notice Rebecca's little slip. Though she probably could have explained it away easily enough, for this next part they needed Yvonne to feel easy in their company. Jumping out of your seat at the slightest sound probably wasn't going to achieve that.

'I don't know who that can be,' Yvonne said with a frown, before standing and heading towards the door.

When she opened it, Grace was standing there holding the biggest bouquet of tiger lilies the on-board florist had been willing to sell them.

'Flowers for Mrs Ortega?' said Grace, in the same broad West Yorkshire tones she always spoke in. Mercifully, Kitt had managed to talk her out of the idea of adopting an Italian accent for this particular undercover role.

'My goodness,' Yvonne said, glancing back at Rebecca and Kitt in astonishment. 'Who can have sent these? Is there a card?'

'Er, no, no card, madam, but the buyer did admit to being an admirer of yours. He asked me to relay the fact that, if you approve of the flowers, he will be waiting just down the corridor in the main piazza for the next ten minutes holding a pink rose, and if you meet him, he ... well, he will more directly relate his admiration for you. Yes, those were the words he used.'

'Oh.' Yvonne toyed with a jewelled necklace she was wearing. She fell silent for a moment, clearly contemplating the invitation. Grace, on noticing that Yvonne was wavering over whether to meet this mysterious admirer, whispered slyly, 'He was very young and good-looking to boot. I have to say, I'm a bit jealous. Nobody's ever sent me flowers. Maybe it's because I'm an orphan.'

Uh-oh.

Kitt had managed to talk Grace out of the accent but not out of the backstory that she was an orphan, whose parents had died in a freak storm, and that she had over-compensated for the lack of parent-child relationship by having seven children of her own which she was now struggling to support on a florist's wage. The fact that she was only twenty-five and would have had to have birthed those children at a rate of around one a year for seven years to make that story plausible hadn't deterred Grace from the idea that this would give real depth to her under-cover performance.

Rebecca looked over at Kitt to see she was wincing. If Grace gave the game away now, my goodness was she in for it when Kitt got hold of her.

'I'm . . . sorry to hear you're an orphan,' Yvonne said, the uncertainty more than evident in her voice. 'I'm not sure how that would result in you not being sent flowers.'

'Yes, well, it's . . . a long story, one of the many things people don't realize orphans suffer through, but the bottom line is, I wish someone like your admirer was sending me flowers,' said Grace.

Kitt put her head in her hands. Surely they were going to strike out after this?

'He's . . . that handsome, is he?' Yvonne said.

Rebecca and Kitt froze. Was there still hope?

'Oh, I should say so. I got rather tongue-tied while taking his order.'

'Hmm, well, these flowers are a very kind gesture,' she said, accepting them and laying them down on a small table near the door before turning to Kitt and Rebecca. 'I think I'll just quickly go and see what this is about,' said Yvonne. 'I'll only be a minute. You'll be all right with your drinks, won't you?'

'Of course,' said Kitt. 'Take your time . . . we're happy to relax here. What's not to love about this view? We can see for miles from here.'

Yvonne paused for a moment as though suddenly realizing she was leaving strangers in her cabin unattended, but then shrugged and followed Grace out into the corridor.

Was it cruel of them to prey on the loneliness of a woman in a difficult marriage? Perhaps. Would it be worth it if they uncovered that the captain was behind all the theft and death on this ship? Absolutely.

The moment the door clicked closed Rebecca and Kitt jumped to their feet. Kitt turned the radio on so they could hear what was happening with Grace and Yvonne.

'And my third child, Chi-chi, she's just adorable,' Grace said amidst the static. 'She could do a handstand at eighteen months. The doctors had never seen anything like it.'

'Oh, dear God,' said Kitt. 'Some days, I tell you, she really tries my patience. You do realize she just nearly blew that whole operation for us? All because she can't keep her silliness in check.'

'At least if she wants to bide more time to let us search, she's got four more kids to work through,' Rebecca said with a chuckle. She must admit she'd thought her sister might have been exaggerating when she had told her past stories about Grace and her audacious ways but after this trip she would never doubt another word Kitt said about her again.

'Anything in the bathroom?' asked Kitt as she began her search of the room.

'Nothing except a spot of blood.'

'Did you take a swab?'

'Please, I'm a doctor. I live for taking swabs, don't you know.'

'That's so wrong.'

'This coming from the woman whose dating life is like a sequel to *The Story of O*.'

'Making up for lost time. Maybe it's time you followed my lead?' Kitt said, pulling her sleeves over her hands while opening the drawers in the bedside table.

'You made me snoop on the last person who showed any interest in me. Not exactly the basis of a solid relationship. Especially as I'm still lying to him about the case being closed. Dating is a brutal sport.'

'It's not for the faint-hearted, that's for sure,' said Kitt. 'I got more than I bargained for with Halloran.'

'And I'm fairly sure he says the same to others about you,' Rebecca said. 'I'm not sure that the blood swab will be that useful. It probably just belongs to either the captain or his wife,' Rebecca said. She knew the subject change was obvious. She didn't care. She had enough conflicting feelings towards Errol right now without going three rounds with her sister about her dating life.

'It's always useful to have something like that. If we find any other DNA on a weapon, for example – remember the police never found the gun that killed Bryce, it's probably at the bottom of the ocean but you never know – then we might be able to make a match.'

'Oh, I hadn't thought of that,' said Rebecca.

'It's almost like I was paying attention during my training,' Kitt said with a knowing smile, getting down on her hands and knees to look under the bed.

Using the same trick Kitt had with her sleeve to avoid leaving any traces of her own DNA, Rebecca opened the cupboard to find the captain's uniforms hanging, crisp and clean, and several of Yvonne's evening gowns. She brushed them aside to check the back of the cupboard. But there was nothing there.

'What did Yvonne say to you whilst I was in the bathroom, anything useful?' said Rebecca.

'Maybe one thing of note. She didn't outright admit it, which is not surprising given I was a friend to Bryce and her actions might have cost him his life, but from the way she was talking, I got the impression she had blamed Bryce for what happened between them when her husband discovered them. As though she was the innocent party and hadn't really wanted to engage with him. She said Bryce helped her put on a bit of a show so she wouldn't get into trouble with her husband, but I don't believe that. Bryce was all about self-preservation. I can't see him taking the fall for anyone – let alone a woman he barely knows whose husband could get him fired at the drop of a hat.'

'So you think that she just made out to the captain that Bryce came on to her and she didn't know how to get rid of him?'

'That's the impression I got.'

Rebecca's stomach clenched. 'Kitt, if she managed to absolve herself with the captain and lay all the blame at Bryce's door. If she even made out that he'd forced her into the situation, that it was non-consensual, that's pure motive. Very few people would tolerate someone putting their spouse through that. And if the captain is connected to organized crime or is just drunk on his own authority, well, that could have ended very badly for Bryce.'

'That's what's been running around my head for the past ten minutes. Her blaming Bryce for what passed between them only strengthens the captain's motive for taking matters into his own hands. I have wondered if that safety deposit box from the poem held some kind of incriminating evidence against the captain but the incident with Yvonne only happened on the crossing before this one and Bryce wrote that letter to me six months ago so the timeline doesn't fit,' said Kitt as she opened up Yvonne's handbag and pulled out a hairbrush, a wallet full of credit cards and several lipsticks. 'I just wish I knew what was in that box. I've a feeling it contains some vital piece of evidence that would make all the pieces of the case fit together.'

No sooner had Kitt shook the last couple of items out of Yvonne's handbag than she heard Grace apologizing over the radio: 'I really don't know what could have happened to him, madam. He promised to be right here. I'm so sorry for wasting your time. Would you like me to walk you back to your cabin?'

'No, thank you, but I should get back to my guests,' came Yvonne's response.

Rebecca and Kitt looked at each other.

'Damn it, we didn't get anywhere near as long as we needed,' Kitt said, quickly throwing all of Yvonne's belongings back into the bag and closing the zip.

Rebecca checked the cupboard door was closed properly and smoothed some ruffles from the sheets which Kitt had disturbed to look under the bed.

Red-faced and somewhat out of breath, the pair had just managed to dash to the balcony and sit back down at the table when the door to the cabin opened. But the person who walked through it wasn't Yvonne, as they had been expecting. It was Captain Ortega himself.

CHAPTER TWENTY-TWO

Rebecca did all she could to steady her breath as the captain stared at them with cold, grey eyes. She was trying not to think about what could have happened if the captain had entered even a minute earlier. He would have caught them rifling through his stuff. Rebecca's heart almost stopped at the thought. They had been lucky, this time, but that had been far too close a call for comfort.

As the captain stood there in the doorway, the frown on the captain's face seemed to run deeper than confusion, at least from where Rebecca was sitting. Was he just angry to find a couple of strangers sitting in his cabin unattended? Or was there more to it than that? Did he suspect what they'd really been up to?

'Can I ask what you are doing in my cabin?' the captain said, his voice just the wrong side of civil.

'Your wife kindly invited us for an afternoon drink and has just popped out for a moment,' said Kitt. Rebecca couldn't help but marvel at how casual she sounded given what they'd just been up to. Here she was falling to bits under the surface while Kitt had never seemed more calm and collected. She really had this undercover work down. 'She said she wouldn't be long. May I pour you a drink in her absence?'

'No, you may not,' the captain said, the edge to his voice getting sharper.

At this point Yvonne arrived back through the door. Rebecca tried to hide her sigh of relief. She'd corroborate their story and then hopefully that would be the end of the matter . . . hopefully.

'Did you invite these people in here?' the captain said, turning on his wife. As they stood in the door frame together, he and Yvonne, Rebecca couldn't help but notice how much bigger than her he was. Almost twice as broad and a good foot taller. Rebecca wondered how brave she'd feel, standing up to a man of that physical stature if she'd done something that displeased him. Yvonne, though at times somewhat demure in her mannerisms, had seemed confident when they'd spoken to her, perhaps even a little blasé about her indiscretions with Bryce. So it hadn't occurred to Rebecca that Yvonne might actually fear her husband. Was that a defensive raise of her chin or a fearful glance upwards to a man who intimidated her? From this angle, Rebecca couldn't work it out.

'Yes,' Yvonne said, giving a dismissive wave. 'You know I get lonely when you're working your shifts. I invited them over for a drink. It's just a bit of girl chat, Dominic. What's the problem?'

'Only that, according to our security team, these are the people who are doing an investigation into Bryce Griffin's death.'

So it was someone on the security team who talked to the captain about their investigation. Errol said they had been informed and it made sense to Rebecca that Georgia and her colleagues would no doubt be the ones to report to the captain on a number of matters. But the question was, once armed with the information that a civilian investigation was taking place, had he instructed someone to attack Rebecca to ensure the truth about Bryce's death never came out?

'What?' Yvonne said. 'You never mentioned any investigation. If you've been using me to spy on my own husband, I'll—'

'There's no need for any threats,' Kitt said to Yvonne quickly before turning her attentions once again to the captain. 'We're actually not investigating Bryce's death any more. We decided not to pursue the matter any further for personal reasons. I merely came here to hear from your wife about any memories she had about my deceased friend. It had been a while since I had last seen him when he died. I just . . . wanted to know what life was like for him before the end. That's all.'

'I see,' Captain Ortega said. Kitt's explanation seemed to give him pause and she wasted no time whatsoever on pressing her advantage.

'Even if we were investigating Bryce's death,' she pushed, 'which, as I've explained we are not, surely there wouldn't be any reason to keep us out of your cabin?'

Rebecca held her breath as she saw a thunderous look form on the captain's face. If Kitt kept on like this, they'd wind up swimming back to England.

Captain Ortega cleared his throat in such a manner that it was obvious Kitt had hit a nerve. 'No, there would not. But I didn't part on the best of terms with Mr Griffin and I don't need anyone getting the wrong idea just because I saw fit to protect my relationship with my wife. Many of the staff know you launched an investigation but most of them don't know you had already closed it – I wasn't even aware of that. So if other staff members see you knocking on my door, they might start to think I had some kind of role in what happened to Mr Griffin, which I absolutely did not.'

Rebecca looked the captain up and down as he delivered his little speech. He'd taken pains to make it clear he didn't know their investigation had folded. If he was the person who attacked her, he might be hoping that claiming not to know they'd ended the investigation was the perfect way to make himself seem more innocent. And considering what Yvonne had told Kitt about the fact that she blamed Bryce for their indiscretions, Rebecca had only become more suspicious of the captain since she'd stepped over the threshold of his cabin.

'I am not in the least bit interested in sullying the

reputation of a man as respected as you are, Captain Ortega, I can assure you. I'm under no illusions about how difficult a personality Bryce was,' said Kitt. 'And I hardly think such a small altercation would be enough to make you a suspect. Surely you were on the bridge at the time Bryce was killed, guiding this vessel into port?'

'That I was, that I was.'

'So anyone with half a brain, who had no idea about your wonderful reputation as captain, would have no reason to suspect you of anything sinister. Everybody knows where you were at the time of Bryce's death. Guiding several thousand people safely into port. If the police gave you a hard time about an argument you had with Bryce, I'm sorry to hear about that, but no person with an ounce of sense would think you capable of such mindless cruelty,' said Kitt.

The captain's expression seemed to soften at this and Rebecca did her best not to roll her eyes. She wished, not for the first time in her life, that ego-stroking hadn't been the answer. Still, at least, she supposed, it was a fairly easy solution to a problem.

'In spite of all that, as you might imagine, that man is something of a sore subject for my wife and me. What passed between us was very unfortunate, not least because our private business became the talk of the ship. Quite humiliating for someone in my position, I can tell you. So the last thing I need is his friends hanging around my cabin as a reminder of all that went on. With that in mind, I think it's best you leave.'

'Of course,' said Kitt. 'The last thing we wanted was to be an imposition. I'm so very sorry if I, in any way, upset you. I assure you it wasn't my intention. It's just been difficult thinking about my lost friend. Not really knowing what happened to him.'

'I can imagine,' said Captain Ortega, his voice utterly devoid of feeling. 'But you won't get any answers here, I'm afraid.'

'Understood,' said Kitt, rising from her chair. Rebecca followed suit and walked quietly behind Kitt as they left the cabin.

The second the door was closed behind them, an argument of epic proportions broke out on the other side. From the muffled accusations and outrage, it was clear enough that the captain had a possessive streak and was making no bones about the fact that Yvonne wasn't to invite any more strangers into their private quarters.

Kitt and Rebecca lingered for a couple of moments, but dared not stay there any longer in case either the captain or his wife stormed out of the cabin in anger and caught them listening in. The captain had seemed to believe the story that they'd given up the investigation but that would be a lot harder to sell in the long-term if he discovered them lurking and eavesdropping on his private conversations.

'Sounds like they've got a complicated relationship, to say the least,' said Rebecca as they set off down the corridor to rejoin Evie and Grace, who they'd agreed to meet by the fountain at the main piazza once the sting was over.

'That much we agree on,' said Kitt, keeping her voice low. 'And did you hear the way he talked about Bryce's death? He said it was unfortunate but didn't show any remorse for Bryce's passing. He spoke only about how it affected his reputation and how humiliating it was. But there was no evidence of foul play in his cabin. No weapon. No money stashed under the mattress. No suspicious documents of any kind.'

'And, playing devil's advocate, given the way things were left between the captain and Bryce before he died, it's perfectly plausible that he would turf us out just for being friends with the deceased,' said Rebecca. 'He doesn't have to entertain friends of people he was on bad terms with, even if they are dead.'

'I agree,' said Kitt. 'But we can't dismiss the idea that the big speech he made to shoo us out of the cabin was just a cover story to lead us off track. There's still a chance the captain took matters into his own hands, strong-arming someone else to do his dirty work while relying on his reputation to save him. Or, if he is part of an organized crime ring, that he used Bryce's advances on his wife as a smokescreen for what their altercation was really about. The lack of evidence doesn't rule him out as Archippo either, assuming such a person exists. After all, a seasoned crime boss would know just how to cover his tracks.'

CHAPTER TWENTY-THREE

A hard rapping on Rebecca and Kitt's cabin door the next morning jolted the pair awake. They had been up late with Grace and Evie going over all the evidence collected so far and deciding on research priorities. Grace had been hitting one dead end after another in her search for information about Archippo and had thus moved on to looking into the mechanic angle. She had made a solemn vow not to fail in her quest after Kitt had played war with her over her use of the orphan backstory during yesterday's sting operation. Could someone in the engine room have left their post for just long enough to pull off a murder? Grace had promised them all that she would not rest until she found out. Even though engineering manuals weren't exactly her first choice for bedtime reading.

At some point during their discussions a bottle of vodka had been thrown into the mix and, consequently, Rebecca had no recollection of what time they'd actually rolled into bed.

Squinting at her watch, however, she could see that it was now only just coming up to half past six. A time of day she really hoped she wouldn't see when on a luxury cruise. Unless, of course, she was on her way home from a party.

The knock came again and the twins groaned in synchrony before Kitt reluctantly threw off the covers and lolloped over to the door in her pyjamas.

'Errol,' Rebecca heard Kitt say. Rubbing her eyes, Rebecca hastily ran her fingers through her hair, trying to smooth it out before rolling out of bed. It was only when the cold air of the cabin hit her bare legs that she remembered what she was wearing and she began pulling at the T-shirt and shorts she had thrown on, trying to make them cling slightly less to her body, while wishing she had packed a dressing gown.

There was something about the look in Errol's eyes, however, that almost at once stopped her from fussing. Such raw emotion swirled in them – anguish and disbelief. On closer examination he looked very pale to her too. In fact, he almost looked like he might keel over at any moment.

'Have you heard?' he croaked, his words hollow. As though he were in shock.

'We ... haven't heard anything,' Kitt said, glancing at Rebecca before fixing her eyes on Errol again. 'As you can probably tell by the cut of us, we've only just got out of bed. What's going on?'

He took a deep breath before speaking again. 'Sorry, I

didn't even look at the clock before I left my cabin. I don't even know what time it is. I just heard about it and I had to come and tell you. I mean, I thought you'd want to know as soon as possible . . . there's been another murder.'

'What?' said Kitt, her mouth hanging open. 'When? Who? No, wait, come in. I'm going to need to take some notes on this.'

While Errol did as instructed and took a seat in the chair next to the writing desk, Rebecca slumped on the end of her bed, not quite able to grasp what Errol had just said. Another body. That hadn't even entered her head as a possibility. They had assumed Bryce had just got on the wrong side of someone. That it was a one-off. If they had known there was a danger of that, they would have worked quicker, regardless of the risk. A cold, tingly feeling came over Rebecca. She'd slowed the investigation down. If they hadn't taken things at a slower pace, they may have already uncovered who was behind Bryce's death. But everyone had been too afraid for her welfare – and now the killer had claimed another victim.

'Now,' said Kitt. 'Let me get some details here. First, who was murdered? Do we know the victim's identity?'

'It was another staff member,' said Errol. 'A hospitality steward. In fact, you met him briefly. He showed you to Wendy's dressing room that night you went to talk to her. Timothy Perkins. Remember him?'

'He's dead?' Rebecca said. 'He searched me as I boarded

the ship, he was so nice about it. Made so many cracks I suggested he might be wasted as a ship's steward and that maybe he should try his hand at stand-up.'

'That's Tim. Or . . . I suppose I should say that was Tim,' Errol said, swallowing hard. 'My God, I'm sorry, I'm still trying to make sense of this. I was only speaking to him yesterday. That's how it was with Bryce too, everything seemed fine. Nothing out of the ordinary at all and then the next thing I know, they're dead. Why does this keep happening?'

'I don't know,' Kitt lied, at once making it clear she still wasn't going to trust Errol with the information that they were still working the case and now suspected that an organized crime ring might be behind it all. 'But considering another staff member has been targeted, I think it's safe to say there's some bigger picture relating to the crew members on this ship that we perhaps don't understand yet.' Kitt shook her head and wrote down the name in a notepad. 'And here was me assuming that Bryce's murder was an isolated incident because, well, it's just the kind of trouble Bryce would have got himself into. I truly never thought we'd find ourselves in this position. Did they know each other? Bryce and Timothy? Ever any trouble between the two?'

'They definitely crossed paths,' said Errol. 'We often need hospitality to support us before one of our shows because people get lost around the ship and can't find their way to our little performance area. That kind of thing. But I never got the impression they were good friends. If anything, I always thought there was a bit of tension between them.'

'What kind of tension?' said Kitt.

'I don't know exactly,' said Errol. 'I think Tim had quite fancied his chances with Carla – er, Miss Ocean Blue – and didn't take too kindly to it when she chose to go out with Bryce. I never really understood it because anyone could see they didn't have a chance with her as long as Bryce was around but that's what people say. I mean, that's the gossip.'

Rebecca pursed her lips. Miss Ocean Blue had had an alibi for Bryce's murder – Errol had said she was hanging out with Wendy. But it did seem an interesting turn of events that her name was coming up in this investigation a second time. They had two bodies now, and Miss Ocean Blue was connected to both of them. And Errol had made it clear that Miss Ocean Blue's behaviour at the end of her relationship with Bryce was not particularly reasonable and perhaps might even have been described as obsessive. Rebecca couldn't quite figure out how any of this could have led to Timothy's death but if she did kill Bryce and thought she'd got away with it, perhaps she tried it again for reasons yet to be revealed.

'Did you ever see them fight about it?' said Kitt.

'No, not openly. I think most of us just knew about it because of the rumour mill. They were civil enough to do their jobs and help each other out professionally when they needed to but I couldn't say they were friendly.'

'What about the crime scene? What do you know about it?'

'What kind of information do you want?' Errol said, shooting Kitt a dubious look.

'Basic details will do for now. I know that talking about things like this, especially when they've just happened, can be very painful but even if you knew where the body was found, for example, and when? That would be a good start,' said Kitt.

'He was found . . . floating in the top deck pool by cleaning staff at around four this morning. They realized that the water was . . . dark. Darker than it should have been.'

'Because there was blood,' Rebecca said.

Errol nodded. 'That's when they looked a bit closer and saw the body. They ran down to the reception desk for help and they managed to fish him out. Once they'd done that, that's when they realized it was Tim. He hadn't been on shift at the time so nobody had noticed he was missing.'

'Do you know exactly which staff member discovered the body?' asked Kitt.

'I don't, sorry. Just that it was one of the custodial team, just like it was last time.'

'If there was blood,' Rebecca said, finally managing to think straight after the shock of learning of yet another killing, 'I'm assuming the victim didn't just drown in the pool.'

'They say it looked as though he'd been stabbed.'

At once an image flashed into Rebecca's mind. She was standing again in that shadowy hallway, a blade pointed straight into her heart. Her attacker had threatened to stab her. The attack on Timothy, that was the same MO, as Kitt would say. Rebecca glanced over to her sister to see if she'd made the connection. In response, Kitt offered her an almost imperceptible nod to confirm that, yes, a disturbing pattern was emerging. People were being attacked with sharp objects. Unlike Tim, Rebecca had been fortunate enough to survive her brush with this individual. It was almost certain that this person was either the person who killed Bryce or was in league with whoever had.

'Stabbing still might not be the official cause of death,' said Kitt. 'Until a pathologist looks at the body, it will be speculation. He may have been stabbed and fallen into the pool and drowned – unable to save himself because of the wound. I'm sorry,' Kitt said, noticing the fact that Errol was wincing. 'I don't mean to be so matter of fact when you've lost a colleague. I just know that getting the facts straight now really does help in finding the person responsible.'

'I understand,' Errol said. 'I'm glad you're here, honestly I am. Somehow, I know that with you looking into this there's much more chance of Timothy's killer being brought to justice.'

'I'm not sure we're going to go so far as to launch an investigation,' said Kitt. 'You heard what happened to Rebecca. You understand why we stopped looking into Bryce's death.

Bryce's killer and Timothy's killer are almost definitely one and the same. As such, we might not be able to risk following this up. My sister's safety has to come first.'

'Of course,' said Errol, glancing over at Rebecca. 'I wouldn't want it any other way. I already feel guilty enough. If I had just left well enough alone, you'd be safely back in your homes right now. Not here, asking for the details of the crime scene.'

'In fairness to you,' said Kitt, 'given my line of work, I could just as easily be at home asking someone else for the details of a crime scene. So don't beat yourself up about that.'

In spite of himself, Errol cracked a smile.

Satisfied that she'd raised Errol's spirits a little, Kitt continued with her questions. 'Now, did you hear anything about a weapon? Any idea if they found one with the body?'

'Not as far as anyone can see,' Errol said, rubbing a hand across his face as though hoping that would wake him up from the nightmare. 'I'm not sure how thoroughly anyone's searched for a weapon at this point, though, so one might yet turn up.'

'What about video footage?' said Kitt.

'I don't know. Georgia came to see me this morning, that's how I found out. She didn't want to disturb you any earlier than necessary but said she was going to review the footage. She asked if I'd give you a knock and request that you come to the safety command centre at eleven. By that point she thinks she'll have had time to pull out any relevant footage from the cameras and the on-board doctor is looking at the body in case there are any obvious clues about what might have played out.' Errol paused, pushing his hands through his long, sandy hair. 'I know I shouldn't have knocked so early. I'm sorry about that. I was just in shock about the news. I don't mean to speak ill of Bryce. I got on with him just fine but he did have a habit of getting into trouble. The same just wasn't true of Tim. He got along. Kept his head down. Never bothered anyone so far as I know.'

Rebecca looked down at the laminate flooring. She couldn't meet Errol's eye at the moment. She wanted to confide in him, about what they'd found out about Archippo, about the search they'd made of the captain's cabin and how keen he'd been to get rid of them. He had no idea that his workmates were likely caught up in a much darker network of lies, death and deceit than he knew about. Tim may have seemed like a person who just got on and kept his head down. Maybe that's because he was doing his best not to draw attention to something else he was up to. His death, and all they had uncovered about Bryce's, certainly hinted that Tim might not have been what he seemed. Though Rebecca longed to share this with Errol she knew Kitt wouldn't think it wise. Especially right after the discovery of another body. They were going to have to be really careful about who they trusted with any information relating to the case.

'It's totally understandable that you didn't want to wait to come and tell us about this, and there's no need to apologize,' said Kitt, interrupting the little war Rebecca was having with herself. 'We were up till late drinking so I'm not sure how much use we'll be but if we can help with any of the basics, then of course we will.'

'Well, Georgia doesn't have a trained private investigator on board very often. So many crimes on cruise ships just never get solved. But between you and the efforts of the security team, Georgia's determined that this time, whoever the culprit is, they won't get away with it.'

CHAPTER TWENTY-FOUR

On hearing the news that another body had been found and that they were likely to soon be embroiled in an even more complicated investigation than the one they had set out to solve, there was only one place Kitt had wanted to go and that was the on-board library.

After Errol had left, they had got themselves dressed and ready, explained the new situation to Evie and Grace – who were at this moment back in their cabin researching Timothy Perkins and seeing what they could find out about him from his online profile – and then, at Kitt's request, set off for the library. They still had a good half hour before they were due to meet Georgia and Kitt had made it clear she needed somewhere comforting to think.

Though the on-board library was not large and certainly not quiet, the staff who sat behind a desk in the centre of the circular room had without doubt made the most of the space. The walls that surrounded them were lined floor-to-ceiling with books and had been fitted with a couple of rolling ladders so that the volumes on the topmost shelves could be reached with ease. Thanks to the large skylight, the whole room was bathed in golden sunlight. The warmth taking the edge off the cold, hard reality of what had happened to Timothy Perkins.

'Thanks for coming here,' said Kitt, cradling a nature book on the North Sea that she'd stumbled across in the brief walk from the library entrance to the table at which they now sat. 'I know it's a funny habit to find solace in places like these.'

'Yes, a librarian who likes to spend time in libraries, who'd have thought it?' Rebecca teased.

'Most people don't find their place of work comforting, smart Alec,' said Kitt. 'But for me, being surrounded by books is like being surrounded by fortress walls. I feel safe inside.'

Rebecca raised her eyebrows. 'If this trip has taught me anything, it's that there are very few truly safe places in this world. If you find one, it is worth holding on to it with both hands . . . Is it worth it?'

'Is what worth it?'

'Finding justice, I suppose,' said Rebecca. 'Obviously I've heard all your stories. And I even managed to help you a little bit on that case with Ruby. But this is the first time I've really seen what an investigation looks like up close. And I have to say, it's a lot more gruelling than I realized. No wonder you're on the sleeping pills.'

'A little louder, I don't think the girl four tables down quite heard you.'

'Sorry, tired,' Rebecca said, stifling a yawn. 'Not always totally aware of the volume I'm operating at when I'm functioning on this little sleep.'

'But in answer to your question, yes. It is worth it. Just as all the late hours, missed social events and general stress is worth it to you in your line of work. If we don't stand with the people going through terrible times like these, who would they turn to? Everyone's so busy. They don't have time for other people's woes. Investigation is a business but it's also a calling. Righting wrongs isn't easy. But it is worthwhile.'

'And I suppose you do get to play with walkie-talkies. That's a perk that shouldn't be underestimated.'

Kitt was just nodding her agreement when her phone buzzed and she jumped to attention. 'It's a video call from Mal. I suppose he must've got my latest email then.'

Swiping the screen, Kitt turned the phone so both she and Rebecca could speak to Halloran.

'Are you two all right?' he asked, when his face at last surfaced on the screen. 'I have to say that Kitt's email wasn't the most calming I've ever read.'

'We're fine,' said Kitt. Rebecca had lost track of the number of times in her life Kitt had spoken for her and did her level best not to roll her eyes at her doing it yet again. Technically speaking, she was right. They were fine. In one piece at least, which is more than anyone could say for Timothy Perkins.

'From the sound of things this trip is only getting more dangerous by the day,' said Halloran. 'And that's not even taking into account the fact that Grace and Evie are sharing a room, getting up to God knows what.'

'I think it's better that we're all kept in the dark about that,' said Kitt. 'And as for this trip becoming increasingly dangerous . . . well, be that as it may, we can't exactly ask to get off the boat in the middle of the ocean. We're just going to have to batten down the hatches and do what we can to play it safe. We're just contemplating the next move,' said Kitt.

'Are you in the library?' Halloran said, a knowing tone to his voice.

'Yes,' said Kitt, a slightly defensive note creeping into hers. 'The library is a perfectly legitimate place to contemplate your next move. It's worked for me on a number of occasions, thank you very much.'

'All right, pet, all right,' Halloran said with a light chuckle. 'No judgement. I'm just pleased to see you're both OK. Any word on the connections between this victim and the last one? Obviously the likelihood of two killers on board is slim so if you are able to make a connection between them, it will probably lead you to the killer.'

Kitt shook her head. 'We've nothing more to go on than what was in my email. Errol thinks there might be some rivalry over a girl but we've no concrete evidence of that. Grace and Evie are looking into it back at the cabin. We're due to meet Georgia in . . .' – Kitt paused to glance at her watch – 'just over twenty minutes. Though it will be useful to get another look at the other people working in the security command centre, we're going to have to be careful. There's still a chance that one of the people working there attacked Rebecca and if they think we've restarted the investigation in light of this new body, they might come after us.'

'I should never have let you board that ship without me . . . I mean . . .' Halloran stuttered as he noticed Kitt's expression change at the idea that he was in a position to 'let' her do anything. 'What I meant was, I should have come along.'

'Oh, and I'm sure Chief Superintendent Ricci wouldn't mind you taking seven days off work at short notice to hunt for a killer on a luxury cruise ship on a case that's well and truly out of your jurisdiction.'

'Yes, thank you. We're all aware of the logistical limitations of my job. How I have to book leave months in advance and how much more freeing it is to be a freelance private investigator like you.'

Rebecca couldn't help but cover her mouth to smother a chuckle at Halloran's tone. He said it in such a way that it was clear Kitt had boasted about her freedoms in the private sector on more than one occasion.

'Let's not get into a debate about that right now,' said Kitt.

'We haven't time and you always lose. Let's just cut to the part where you tell me that you've found Bryce's deposit box, uncovered a vital clue and are happy for us to take all the credit when apprehending the true killer.'

Halloran smirked at Kitt's teasing. 'I have passed the information on to North East police and they are looking for the box but it's not at the top of their case load and I am really swamped at the moment to be offering extra support. But we are looking as fast as we can. The banks in Carlisle are being approached systematically. So far none of them have a safety deposit box that corresponds with the number hidden in the poem.'

'Even if you find it, won't you need a key?' said Rebecca. 'I don't know, I've never had anything worth putting in a deposit box.'

'If Bryce had a key, I assume it would be in the envelope,' said Kitt.

'Unless someone else took it before the letter reached you,' said Rebecca. 'The letter had been opened, remember. Halloran thought it was the police looking for clues in Bryce's murder but what if it wasn't them at all?'

'Regardless,' said Halloran. 'North East police will be able to get a court order to open the box. If anyone else figured out the code in the poem and finds the box before we do, all banks have CCTV so we'll have the person accessing it on video.'

Kitt nodded. 'Here's hoping that the key is with the bank

and wasn't in the envelope. What about Archippo? Do the police have any record of this person? The more I've thought about it, the more convinced I am that Bryce's death was an organized hit and not a crime of passion so if you've any evidence to the contrary, now would be a good time to hear it.'

'I did look into it and I was quite surprised to find there were a few records on the system pertaining to him. But when I dug a bit deeper, I can see why the North East police came down on the side of assuming this person was complete fiction. The only time that name gets mentioned is during interview transcripts with a few small-time criminals. In a couple of cases, the criminals were trying to lay blame for whatever crimes they'd committed at Archippo's door. In one case the criminal in question was trying to cut a deal. Promising to give the police information on what is most likely to be a fictional organized crime boss rather than betray who they're really working for. In all of the transcripts there was only one concrete detail given – that Archippo was believed to have operated out of Australia for many years.'

'Did any of the interrogating officers ever look into the claims that Archippo was behind the crimes they were investigating?' said Kitt.

'From what I can tell, they never found any proof that such a person existed,' said Halloran.

'Which means Miss Ocean Blue is either misinformed or she was up to something she shouldn't have been around the time that Bryce died and is trying to throw us off the scent,' said Kitt.

'The latter seems more likely at this stage. If there was some kind of rivalry between Bryce and the latest victim over this . . . Miss Ocean Blue' – Halloran almost cringed as he said what he clearly thought a ridiculous name – 'then she might be involved with what happened to them both.'

'The thing is, she has an alibi for Bryce's death,' said Rebecca.

'The problem is, every suspect in this case has an alibi, at least for the first murder,' said Kitt. 'And although we went to the trouble of double-checking Georgia was where she said she was, all of these alibis have been checked by the police once.'

'Well, you saw some footage of Bryce talking to someone before he went out on that balcony,' said Halloran. 'That would suggest that Bryce's death was not self-inflicted. Somebody did it and in cases like these where everyone has an alibi, there are two most likely scenarios.'

'The first is that I have already spoken to the killer, or should I say killers,' said Kitt. 'That more than one of the people we've got close to and interviewed is involved in this death and they are all covering for each other.'

'Well, the person who attacked me is a man, I'm almost completely sure of it,' said Rebecca. 'So if Miss Ocean Blue is behind it, then she's working with at least one other person, a very dangerous man who has yet to be identified.'

'The second scenario,' said Halloran, 'is that there's a patsy. Someone carrying out the dirty work that we haven't managed to identify. Someone nobody asks any questions of. A person nobody would ever suspect. People like that don't need an alibi because nobody ever thinks to interrogate them.'

CHAPTER TWENTY-FIVE

'Ma'am, Ms Hartley's here,' the broad man who greeted them at the doorway of the safety command centre called over to Georgia. Rebecca could see Georgia sitting at a computer several feet away.

'Well, don't just leave them standing in the corridor, Marino,' Georgia called back. 'Show them in.'

Fixing an almost robotic smile to his face, he waved them in. Rebecca heard him close the heavy steel door and then watched as he marched back to his workplace. As he did so, she realized she had seen the man the first time they had paid Georgia a visit. It was the man with an anchor tattooed on the back of his neck.

He was broad. He was male. He was a member of the security team, and was thus in a position to ensure Bryce's death hadn't been caught on camera. She hadn't smelled any cigarette smoke on him when he opened the door to them but he hadn't really been standing close enough for her to gauge if he was a smoker. Rebecca's heart started beating faster at the idea that she could be at this minute in the same room as her attacker.

The criteria she was using to identify potential suspects were, of course, far too broad to be taken seriously. Male. Strong. A smoker. Hundreds of people on board this ship must fit into that category. That said, only a select few of them had come into contact with Rebecca and her friends since they had set sail and only the people who worked in this room could have manipulated the security cameras the day Bryce was killed. She found herself paying very close attention to his voice. Her attacker had done nothing more than hiss at her, so her chances of recognizing them from their voice alone was slim but she was willing to give anything a try if it meant apprehending whoever it was who had attacked her and knowing they could never hurt her again.

Of course, even when she listened closely to the tenor of the man with the anchor tattoo she was left none the wiser about whether he had any role in what had happened to her.

Doing what she could to steady her breathing, Rebecca followed Kitt as she walked over to where Georgia was now standing. As Rebecca drew closer to Georgia, she found herself quite taken aback by her physical appearance. Her eyes were red around the edges as though she'd had little sleep or had been crying long enough to leave them raw.

Though, of course, the impact of losing a work colleague in such a brutal manner should not be underestimated, Rebecca was a little surprised to see Georgia so shaken. The first time they had visited the safety command centre, she had seemed generally self-assured and in control. But then, it's not as if anyone had been expecting a second body to be discovered. And considering Georgia had made it more than clear that she felt responsible for Bryce's death, she no doubt felt the same about poor Tim. Taking all of this into account, some visible distress was more than understandable.

'We got ourselves up and organized as quickly as we could. Is there anything we might offer a useful opinion on? At this stage you'll be much better informed than we are so perhaps you could just apprise us of what you've done so far?'

'I think we're going to have to launch a full-scale investigation into Timothy's death,' Georgia said, 'and I really need your help to do it. It was bad enough what happened to Bryce Griffin. But Timothy Jenkins, he was a real gent. I admit, I didn't have many dealings with him but whenever I did have cause to speak to him, he couldn't do enough to help me. I know I'm not alone in thinking that. Nobody on the crew has a bad word to say about this man so I don't even know where to start when it comes to motive. We've been talking it through as a team for the last couple of hours and nobody can offer any solid arguments about why anyone would target him.'

'I don't know about getting involved in a full-scale investigation,' said Kitt, maintaining the cover story that their investigation was over. 'But we might at least be able to offer a bit of behind-the-scenes help. Has anyone managed to locate Timothy's mobile phone? That's often where the police will start looking – phone records. If Timothy had developed some kind of difficult relationship with somebody on the ship, the evidence is most likely to be in his phone somewhere.'

Georgia lowered her eyes and shook her head. 'Unfortunately, Timothy had the phone on him when the attack took place and he was found in the pool so . . .'

'You haven't been able to get the phone to work,' said Kitt.

'Not as yet. We're hoping when it dries out it might be more cooperative. Or when we get to Oslo we can find someone who can read the data off the card even if the phone itself won't turn on. Until then, the phone records are a bit of a dead end.'

'What about video footage?' asked Rebecca. 'Errol said you were working through it. Did you find anything?'

'Not really. I've reviewed the footage and seen enough to at least glean a time of death – five past three in the morning. But the culprit isn't visible on the footage. Most of the cameras on the top deck pool are in the bar area; only one is pointed in the general direction of the pool. Just like with Bryce's death, the angle doesn't give us anything to go on, which also makes me suspect that this was an inside job. I mean, that someone on the crew is responsible. Again, there's just no way of telling who.'

'May we see the footage?' said Kitt.

Nodding, Georgia walked over to a computer and tapped some keys on the keyboard. A few moments later, footage from the top deck pool began to play out on the screen. There was no sound but, thanks to some floodlighting, the pool was visible. Five seconds or so elapsed before a dark shape tumbled downwards across the screen, which was instantly blurred by a rush of water splashing upwards. Someone had fallen – or been thrown – into the pool. They watched the video for a minute more but nothing else happened.

Georgia paused the video. 'That's all there is of note. I scrolled through for two hours after this, and examined the feed for a good thirty minutes before this happened, but there was nothing more.'

'What time does the top deck pool close?' said Kitt.

'At eleven,' said Georgia, 'and the bar itself closes at one so the staff would have cleaned and locked the area down a good hour before this took place. My first thought in terms of narrowing down suspects was that this area can only be accessed using a particular key.'

'That would definitely help in drawing up a list of people to talk to,' said Kitt.

'But that's not the only thing to consider,' said Georgia.

'I realized this area was also accessible via the emergency ladders on the side of the ship. Now, we've never had any guests using those inappropriately. To be honest, there's not much incentive to think that's a good idea even after a few glasses of champagne. At the top of the ship, where this killing took place, it's very windy and it can be quite difficult to navigate up and down if you don't know what you're doing or don't have direction from those who do. But if you're a crew member, someone who's taken drills on how to move up and down the steps safely during your training period, then you could potentially navigate them even late at night when visibility isn't the best without anybody knowing about it, and, of course, there are no cameras out there.'

Kitt took a moment then to look at the computer screen where the security footage was sitting on pause. Narrowing her eyes, she asked, 'I'm sure you've looked at it very carefully, but would you mind playing the footage again?'

Pressing a couple of buttons on the keyboard, Georgia obliged.

'There,' said Kitt, pointing at the screen after the dark shape of Timothy Perkins' dying body flashed across it once more.

'What is that?' said Rebecca. 'A reflection in the glass panels at the back of the pool area? Something's definitely moving . . . or should I say someone.'

'Is there any way of enhancing that image or zooming in?' said Kitt.

Georgia paused the video and pressed a key that blew the screen up to a larger resolution.

'Oh my God,' said Rebecca as she looked more closely at the reflection. She had been right to say there was some kind of movement happening. No face was visible on whoever it was. But it was possible, at least, to glean that someone was walking away from the scene of the crime. She could see the reflection of their shoes in the glass.

High heels.

Covered in blue sequins.

'Miss Ocean Blue,' said Rebecca, her eyes widening. 'She's the one behind all this.'

CHAPTER TWENTY-SIX

'This isn't right!' Miss Ocean Blue shouted as one of Georgia's security guards escorted her into the ship's brig. 'I haven't hurt anyone.'

'I wish I could believe that,' said Georgia, looking over at Kitt, Rebecca and Wendy Lostbuoy, who had been sitting in one of the ship's cafés with Miss Ocean Blue when she was apprehended. Rebecca thought it understandable that Wendy would be concerned enough to follow after her friend and ensure her fair treatment, especially after what she had said to them a few days back about how she had never really been heard. But there was no mistaking the fact that it was Miss Ocean Blue's shoes reflected in that video footage. Rebecca was having difficulty piecing together how this all fit with Bryce's murder but when it came to Tim's murder, the evidence was pretty damning.

Georgia had managed to get Miss Ocean Blue to come quietly by assuring her she only wanted to talk in the first instance.

As soon as they had escorted her out of view of any passengers, however, Rebecca had watched with teary eyes as Marino, the man with the anchor tattoo, and one of the other guards Georgia referred to as Harrison, strong-armed Miss Ocean Blue down to the ship's brig.

Georgia had already given the order to cancel all her shows until they'd had time to search her cabin. And after seeing the security footage of Tim's final minutes, Rebecca was more than a little uneasy about what they might find in her quarters. Georgia had confirmed that Timothy Perkins had been stabbed. The odds were that Miss Ocean Blue was smart enough to throw her weapon into the North Sea where it would never be discovered. But in Rebecca's morbid imaginings the bloodied blade was sitting in a drawer or under the bed in her cabin, waiting to be discovered.

'There's no point arguing with us, Carla,' said Georgia. 'We have evidence—'

'What evidence?' Miss Ocean Blue cut in.

'I can't go into it now. We need to search your quarters first and get the full picture before we conduct any kind of interview,' Georgia countered.

'My cabin? You won't find anything in there. This is madness. You know me, people on this ship know me. I would never do this. I just wouldn't,' Miss Ocean Blue said, and Rebecca could tell by the break in her voice that, even though she was trying to sound angry, outraged even, she was deeply distraught at the allegation that she had killed

Timothy Perkins. Either that, or she was just distraught about the fact she had been caught.

'We'll see,' said Georgia. 'For now, I can't take the risk of leaving you to roam about the ship. Two people have already died. I am not losing anyone else. You'll have to stay here, in custody, until we're ready to have a conversation with you. I take no pleasure in this.'

With that Georgia gave a nod and the door closed on Miss Ocean Blue. A faint sobbing could be heard just before the key was turned in the lock.

Georgia turned to Rebecca, Kitt and Wendy with a pained expression. 'I'm sorry you had to see that but I didn't know what else I could do. If I gave her the benefit of the doubt and somebody else died, I really couldn't forgive myself.'

'It's the right choice for now,' said Kitt. 'The only one really. Until you gather more evidence. In cases like these it's really better to be safe than sorry.'

'I can vouch for her whereabouts on the night of Bryce's death,' said Wendy. 'Just like I could when the police came around asking. If she didn't commit the first murder, is it really likely she committed this one?'

'I take your point, I do,' said Georgia. 'But I can't ignore the evidence I've found already. I have to dig deeper on this one. Your testimony about where she was when Bryce was killed will obviously be taken into account when the time comes. But for now, I'm going to get my team to search her room. I don't think she would have stashed a weapon there.

But if she is involved – and it's still an "if" – there might be other things to uncover.' Georgia paused, focusing her attentions on Kitt and Rebecca. 'In the meantime, perhaps you could interview members of the entertainment crew and find out if they've noticed any strange behaviour from her recently. I mean, anything that couldn't be passed off as grief for Bryce's passing. I believe they were involved at some point, so she could have been acting oddly and still be innocent. Grief can do funny things. If you're free to do it this afternoon, I'll let the stage manager know you're conducting interviews, and also make it known that anyone who doesn't cooperate will be sent straight to me to explain why. Wendy, if you can do your best to spread the word that it's really important people cooperate, that'd be appreciated.'

'I'm sure everyone will help in any way they can,' Wendy said.

'We would like to do that – to help, I mean,' said Kitt. 'Really we would, but for reasons we can't disclose it might be too dangerous.'

Georgia frowned. 'Dangerous in what respect?'

'Like I say, we can't speak about it in detail, but essentially' – Kitt lowered her voice at this juncture, muttering so Marino and Harrison couldn't overhear what she was about to say – 'we've been warned off this case and I won't risk the safety of my friends.'

'Warned off?' said Georgia. She kept her voice low, clearly

understanding that Kitt was concerned about anyone else besides her hearing. Even at that low level, however, there was no mistaking the anger in her voice. 'You mean threatened, don't you? Who's threatened you?'

'We ... don't know, it was an anonymous threat,' said Rebecca. 'We haven't said anything until now because we're trying to make sure nobody else gets hurt or finds themselves being intimidated in the same way we were. We don't know exactly who but we've hit a nerve with someone and it is too dangerous to continue.'

'Oh, dear Lord,' said Wendy. 'This just gets worse and worse.'

Georgia took in a deep breath and slowly puffed it out. 'All right. I understand. I can't ask you to put yourself in harm's way when this is my responsibility. I appreciate you coming to look at the footage anyway. Without you, I never would have spotted that reflection. I was so tired, stressed out. I will try and get to the bottom of what ...' – Georgia paused to look over her shoulders at Marino and Harrison but they were engrossed in their own private conversation – 'of what you just told me, though. That is disturbing behaviour, to say the least.'

'We'd appreciate it, we'd certainly sleep easier,' said Kitt. 'And we're pleased to have helped but I'm afraid this is as far as we can go.'

'Sounds like I'd better get to work then,' said Georgia, before turning to Marino and Harrison and waving at them to follow after her. As they passed by, Rebecca made sure to take a deep breath.

No nicotine.

At least not strong enough to smell without invading their space.

The moment Georgia was out of earshot, Wendy turned to Rebecca and Kitt.

'I get that you're scared, after being threatened and all, but I wish you wouldn't give up the case. I know for a fact these tragic events had nothing to do with Miss Ocean Blue. They say you can't truly know a person. That they can have all kinds of secrets behind closed doors. But I know her. She wouldn't do this, and she definitely wouldn't have killed Bryce. She was over the moon in love with him.'

Rebecca ached to tell Wendy the truth: that they hadn't given up the case. She seemed so concerned for her friend it pained Rebecca to think that she would be agonizing over the fate of Miss Ocean Blue when she, Kitt, Evie and Grace would be working behind the scenes to make sure that justice really was served. But Kitt had been clear that nobody could know what they were doing. That it could cost them their lives if they confided in the wrong person, or if information was unwittingly passed on by a well-meaning party. Consequently, against her better judgement, Rebecca kept her lips sealed.

'I wish there was more we could do,' said Kitt. 'Really,

but I saw her walking away from that crime scene with my own eyes.'

'No you didn't,' said Wendy. 'From what I've heard, all you saw were her shoes walking away from that crime scene. Her face wasn't in the frame. Unless I've misunderstood what you've all been talking about?'

'So, what are you suggesting?' said Kitt. 'That somebody stole Wendy's shoes and wore them at the murder scene to frame her?'

'It wouldn't be difficult and it makes a damn sight more sense than the idea that Carla killed anybody,' said Wendy. 'She doesn't wear those heels for every performance. They could have been borrowed from backstage after her late-night show and returned without her noticing before she'd even got out of bed the next morning. All I can tell you is, Carla is no killer.'

With that, Wendy slowly turned away and walked along the corridor, taking the stairs up to the main deck. Rebecca went to follow her but Kitt held her arm, prompting her to hang back a minute.

'Don't you think it's weird that when Bryce was killed and when Timothy Perkins was killed, security footage in both instances was patchy?' said Kitt.

Rebecca shrugged. 'Not considering a crew member is likely to blame in both cases. And we've already suspected for a while that someone from the security team might be in on it. Even the average member of the crew with nothing to do with security might know where camera coverage is better and worse across the ship. So no, it doesn't surprise me that much.'

'I'm not sure if a staff member who has never been in the safety command centre would be able to gauge that. It would be quite difficult to know exactly what each individual camera might pick up unless you reviewed footage from said cameras every day.'

'Well, if you're looking at a member of the security team, my money is on Marino.'

Before Kitt could either agree or disagree with Rebecca's accusation, a scratching sounded out and Grace's voice said, 'Jane, are you reading?'

'Yes, Lyra?' Kitt said, pulling the radio from her.

'Something's come up. I need to see you back at the cabin, now.'

CHAPTER TWENTY-SEVEN

'Grace Edwards, don't you even think of keeping me in suspense a moment longer with any of your silly antics,' Kitt said, as she burst through the door of Grace and Evie's cabin. Grace had been unable to tell them exactly what had 'come up' over the radio when they weren't sure if the line was secure, and consequently Rebecca and Kitt had dashed back to the cabin in a state of nigh on frenzied desperation to find out what exactly Grace had uncovereed. Kitt's walking pace was brisk on any ordinary day but between the brig and here even Rebecca had struggled to keep up with her. She couldn't tell if this highlighted her sister's curiosity or impatience.

'Tempting though it is, if I'm right, I don't think we've got time for any games,' said Grace, her sobriety astounding everyone in the room. She continued to speak, despite the stunned silence. 'It's about Skittles and his repetition of the word "mechanic". A mechanic isn't just someone you might call in case of technical breakdown. It's also casino slang for a dice or card cheat.'

'So, whoever killed Bryce had links with the casino?' said Kitt.

'And there's only one name from the casino that's ever been mentioned in relation to this case,' said Evie.

'Noah Davies,' said Rebecca. 'Georgia's alibi.'

'Georgia said that Noah was chief dealer,' said Kitt. 'If there was any kind of scam running in the casino, he'd be in a prime position to execute it, or turn a blind eye.'

'Do you think Bryce found out what he was doing and threatened to expose him? And maybe that's why he died?' said Rebecca. This wasn't actually her first assumption. Given Bryce's chequered past, the most likely scenario would surely be that he was part of the scam and something went wrong, but Rebecca wanted Kitt to feel her lost friend was being given the benefit of the doubt.

'Or he was mixed up in it himself,' said Kitt, shooting Rebecca a knowing look. Rebecca resisted the urge to roll her eyes. There really was no protecting this woman. She saw through all attempts to cosset her.

'But what about Tim, why would the killer target him?' said Evie. 'Bryce had a bit of a reputation, I understand that, but nobody had a bad word to say about Tim.'

'Perhaps he wasn't as pristine as everyone thought,' Kitt said. 'Or perhaps he knew about whatever scam was being run out of the casino and threatened to expose it.'

'Either way,' Grace said, 'I can't think it's a coincidence that Bryce was saying Archippo in his sleep and now we're finding out that a scam is likely being run out of the casino.'

'It is rather the kind of MO you would expect from an organized crime boss,' Kitt said with a nod. 'It's probably linked with the thefts somehow too. I sincerely doubt there's a casino scam and a ring of thieves operating independently. Of course, given that the person who told us about Archippo in the first place is currently in the ship's brig accused of murder, it's difficult to know if we can base any theory whatsoever on that information.'

'I know you wanted to keep the investigation secret to protect me,' said Rebecca. 'But I don't think that any of this is something we can handle on our own. If we go after Noah Davies and he's either a dangerous crime boss or connected to one, who knows if we'll ever see Oslo?'

'Difficult to know how we can trust anyone to help us,' said Kitt. 'If organized crime is de rigueur on this ship, then any number of people might be involved in it. I don't even know if we can bring Georgia in on what we know. Noah Davies is her alibi. Georgia said she always checks in with him around docking time, so there's a chance that Davies organized for Bryce to be killed by a patsy safe in the knowledge that he'd have a firm alibi when it took place.'

'And not just with anyone,' said Grace. 'With the head of security, one of the most trusted people on the ship.'

'But there's also a chance, especially given how little

security footage is available of the murders, that Georgia and Davies are in on it together. That Davies is perhaps masterminding the scam but coerces or pays off Georgia to ensure there is no evidence. She said they'd never managed to get usable footage of the thief or thieves operating on board. Just like they've never caught the face of the killer. We can't jump to any conclusions until we find some way of confirming Georgia's allegiances but we have to at least entertain the possibility that she is involved.'

'With all this in mind, are we assuming that Miss Ocean Blue has been framed as a scapegoat?' said Evie.

'Again, difficult to answer until we gather more evidence,' said Kitt. 'She certainly seemed horrified at the allegations. But people who work in organized crime are known for their sharp intellect. It's how they manage to operate so long without being caught. There is a small chance that Miss Ocean Blue agreed to take the fall for a payoff. I don't want to think it of her and certainly Wendy's insistence that she's innocent has me leaning more towards the idea that she is being framed.'

'So what's our next move?' said Rebecca. 'I realize we're in over our heads here but we can't just sit and do nothing.'

Kitt paused for a moment, musing. 'If we're going to bring down a notorious crime boss, we're going to need some outside help, you're right. And the most logical person to help us do that is the ship's head of security.'

'But we don't know if we can trust her,' said Evie.

'No, but we can find out,' said Kitt. 'If Georgia is in any way connected to the killings, the thefts and the casino scam, it's likely she'll do something at some point that gives herself away. There was a killing just last night. If Georgia was involved in that killing, she will have had a very busy morning covering things up and will likely make contact with Davies, or whoever else she might be working with.'

'So we get to do surveillance?' Grace said, doing an excitable little dance on the spot that Kitt chose to ignore.

Kitt took her phone out of her pocket and glanced at the screen before sighing. 'I had a vague hope that we might hear from Halloran about the contents of that safety deposit box. For all we know it holds all the answers. But he hasn't come back to me and we can't afford to wait any longer. He said it could be a while before they locate the box anyway. Right now, surveillance it's our best bet,' Kitt said. 'If we watch Georgia closely for a couple of hours, I'm sure it won't be long before we find out where her true allegiance lies.'

CHAPTER TWENTY-EIGHT

'Dorothy has left the farm,' Grace's voice said over the scratchy walkie-talkie.

A couple of moments after Grace had noted that 'Dorothy' was on the move, Georgia came into view. Rebecca made sure she was shielded behind the newspaper she was reading. A trick she had seen in many a spy movie. If it was good enough for Hollywood, it was good enough for her.

Discreetly, Rebecca eyed Georgia over the top of her newspaper. She had stopped at a coffee stand to buy herself a drink. There was still a good chance that Georgia wasn't playing a part in the organized crime taking place on board the *Northern Spirit*. That some other member of the security team had been paid off to ensure nothing untoward was picked up by the security cameras. If Georgia was involved, however, she would be kicking herself and she had no doubt that Kitt would be too.

The thought that the key to the whole case could have

been in front of them from the very beginning was, to say the least, infuriating. Georgia had told Rebecca and Kitt about the robberies that were happening on board the very first day they set sail and although at the time they had had some sense that these robberies might be related to Bryce's death, they hadn't imagined an elaborate scheme by an organized crime boss. If only they had brainstormed a few left-field notions then, Timothy Perkins might still be alive. Quite how Bryce and Timothy had been mixed up in all this was still a mystery and the only way of solving it was to find out precisely who they could trust. Rebecca's mind flitted back to what Halloran had said about cases in which everyone appeared to have an alibi. Had Georgia and Noah been lying to cover for each other whilst carrying out the orders of a corrupt higher power? One way or another, they were soon to find out.

Georgia was chatting away with the server behind the coffee stand in the most casual of manners. She was laughing at a joke the server had made. Was it really possible? That Georgia could have had a hand in ending a man's life last night and laugh with such cheer today? Maybe their suspicions about her were unfounded.

Rebecca held her breath for a moment as she took full stock of just how close the coffee stand was to where she was sitting. She could only hope Georgia was engaged enough by the conversation that she wouldn't turn around and notice Rebecca sitting on the nearby bench. This was the first time she'd tailed anyone and it would be a true disappointment if it was over before they'd even really got started.

After what seemed like forever, Georgia finally walked off, supping her coffee as she went.

As Kitt had instructed, Rebecca counted slowly to three and then stood to follow Georgia. She was wearing a crisp white uniform. Even though other crew members were wearing similar garments, it wasn't difficult to keep track of Georgia. Rebecca just kept her eyes fixed on that tight blonde bun and tried not to seethe too much about how Georgia may have hidden behind that uniform and betrayed people's trust. If she was even in part to blame for all that had happened, it would be a staggering abuse of power. The main thing Rebecca had to watch was how close she was getting to Georgia. If she made an abrupt change of direction at any point, Rebecca did not want to get made. Kitt, Grace and Evie were all posted in nearby positions to cover all the possible directions Georgia might take as she walked the main corridor along from the piazza so there was no need to panic and get too close. Patience was going to win out here.

The longer Rebecca followed Georgia, however, the less convinced she was this was going to lead anywhere. Georgia didn't seem to have any set purpose. She just dawdled here and there chatting to other staff members, which was odd in itself given that she was supposed to be in the midst of an urgent murder investigation. As the body had been found by staff members, it seemed the crew had managed to compartmentalize information about Perkins' death, but according to Kitt, that wouldn't last forever.

Sooner or later a passenger would overhear a conversation between crew members, and when that happened, the rumours would spread pretty quickly. With this in mind, you'd think that Georgia would be frantically assessing whatever evidence they'd uncovered in Miss Ocean Blue's cabin or, at the very least, interviewing their chief suspect. But Georgia was idling around as though it was any other day.

'Dorothy is caught in the tornado,' Evie said over the radio. Code for the fact that Georgia had stopped walking now and was hovering near a corridor that was marked 'Crew Members Only'. Georgia gave one last look over her shoulder before starting off down the corridor.

'Dorothy has gone to Oz,' said Evie.

Rebecca sauntered towards the corridor, and then waited, looking at her watch as though she were meeting a friend. A couple of minutes later Kitt joined her.

'Stay in Kansas for now,' Kitt said into the radio so Evie and Grace would know to hold their positions.

'What if she spots us?' said Rebecca, glancing into the relatively dark corridor. It was quite similar to the corridor she'd been attacked in and she really didn't fancy a repeat of that episode.

'We can just pretend we were looking for her,' said Kitt. 'We'll tell her we changed our minds about the investigation and want to take part. That we felt bad leaving it all to her, et cetera.'

That seemed like a fairly safe plan. Nodding, Rebecca followed Kitt down the corridor, ensuring they walked in complete silence.

They were just in time to see Georgia turn left around a corner. They sped up a little so that they wouldn't lose her trail but came to an abrupt stop just before the turn when they heard voices.

'Good job on Carla's cabin,' said Georgia. 'Between that collage of Bryce and the bloodied skewer, she'll definitely go down for both murders.'

Timothy was stabbed with a skewer? A skewered steward?

'It was nothing,' said a man's voice that sounded familiar. 'You gave me plenty of time to set everything up once you'd hauled her off to the brig. I was out of there a good ten minutes before I saw your goons arrive.'

Rebecca mouthed the name *Noah Davies* to Kitt and Kitt nodded. Yes, at a guess, that's who Georgia was speaking to. So they had conspired to set Miss Ocean Blue up, just like Wendy had said. She'd probably seemed an easy target. She had opportunity and motive when it came to killing Bryce. And they'd probably think of some way of framing her for Timothy Perkins too, given the rumours floating around the ship about Timothy having affections for her.

'Good, that lowers the probability that you made any mistakes,' Georgia said, a harshness rising in her voice.

'What about the little resident Scoobie gang, do they suspect anything?'

Rebecca could only assume that they were talking about her, Kitt, Evie and Grace.

'They won't be a problem any longer. They think they've cracked the case. I even let them believe they saw the reflection of Carla's shoe on the video footage.'

'Nice touch.'

Kit shook her head and Rebecca could hardly believe what she was hearing either: even the discovery of Carla's reflection had been organized in such a way that it seemed a natural part of the investigation. Georgia hadn't called them into the safety command centre because she wanted their help. She just wanted to manipulate what they saw and how they processed the information. Georgia had been one step ahead of them this whole time.

'One tries,' said Georgia. 'All we have to do now is sit tight, document the evidence and she'll go down for it. Everything. I will keep an ear out on the various on-board radio channels. Just in case this second body sparks their virtuous instincts and they try to covertly restart the investigation. I haven't heard anything untoward so far but I haven't been able to monitor all channels at all times. It's just a precaution though. As far as I can see I've thought of everything . . . Including making sure you keep your mouth shut. If you breathe a word, well, you saw what happened to Timothy when he tried to step out of line . . .'

Rebecca's eyes widened at this, and when she glanced at Kitt she noticed an equally surprised expression on her sister's face.

Timothy Perkins, who everyone had such high praise for, he too was beholden to this crime ring. But it didn't sound as though he had been willing to go along with it forever. And so, he was killed. Maybe he was even going to come forward with whatever he knew about Bryce's murder. Now that Rebecca really thought about it, killing Timothy Perkins must have been an act of desperation for Georgia and Noah. Though they thought that Hartley and Edwards Investigations had stopped looking into Bryce's death, they would still no doubt have preferred to lie low until the ship docked in Oslo and they could be doubly sure Kitt was no longer monitoring their activities. Throwing another dead body into Kitt's path was probably the last thing they intended to do but Perkins forced their hand and he paid the ultimate price.

'Haven't I shown you that I'm loyal to Archippo?' said Noah Davies.

Kitt and Rebecca exchanged a look. There it was. Evidence of who these two were working for.

'You've made a good start,' said Georgia. 'But I can't hang around, I'm supposed to be investigating a murder.'

A shuffling sound made it clear that the pair were heading back in Rebecca and Kitt's direction. If they tried to make a run for it, they'd likely be seen, so they dashed into a janitorial closet that stood a few paces away and pulled the door to, leaving only a small crack of light.

Rebecca held her breath as she heard footsteps approach. The sound of her own heart was like thunder and she was convinced it was loud enough to give them away. To her horror, Georgia and Noah paused just beyond where they were hiding. Had they heard them? Or did they sense they were being watched?

'You'd better put that thing out,' she heard Georgia say at last, 'we'll be in range of the smoke alarms in a minute. I've spent all morning making sure we can fly under the radar from here forward. I don't need you drawing attention to us.'

Rebecca watched Noah Davies through the crack in the door as he stubbed a cigarette out on the wall. As she watched him a numb feeling that started in her chest but soon spread to the end of every limb came over her.

So, Noah was a smoker? Of course, why didn't she put the pieces together sooner? Noah was the man who had attacked her.

CHAPTER TWENTY-NINE

Errol was just saying goodbye to the last audience members who had watched his afternoon show when Rebecca approached. The small performance area in which Errol worked smelled strongly of stale popcorn and beer. Long, blue curtains hung around the edge of the room and a recording of ocean waves crashing against the shore played in the background. She noticed Skittles perched on a stand in front of a seating area shaped like a small skiff. She gave his chest a little stroke before looking for somewhere to sit. Barely able to breathe for fear of what might happen next, she sat down in one of the front rows and waited for Errol to sit down next to her.

'Is everything OK?' Errol asked.

Rebecca couldn't bring herself to look at him. Not because he was wearing a ridiculous pirate costume and this situation was absurd enough as it was but because she was at the end of her tether with this case and could feel tears pricking the back of her eyes.

'No, it's not.' As she said these words, her voice didn't even sound like her own. 'I have to tell you something.'

'Sounds serious.' Errol was trying to keep his tone light but there was a note to it that betrayed the fact he knew trouble was coming.

'It is, I'm afraid.'

'Mechanic,' Skittles said, somewhere in the background.

'Oh God,' Rebecca said, putting her head in her hands and trying to wipe away a couple of tears she couldn't stop.

'Hey, hey, come on now,' Errol said, putting an arm around her and pulling her against him. Rebecca breathed in the scent of cedarwood and allowed herself to feel a little relief at being so close to Errol. His body was warm, inviting. She'd better make the most of it. After what she had to say, he probably wasn't going to be in the mood to comfort her.

'You're scaring me,' he said, snapping her out of her thoughts. 'There hasn't been another murder, has there?'

'No, that's not it,' Rebecca said, biting her lip. Once the words were out of her mouth there was no taking them back. Kitt had been dead against bringing Errol into this at all. She had argued that they needed to keep the number of people who knew to a minimum.

But Bryce's murder had had so many unexpected threads. It was bigger than them. Much bigger. They couldn't handle this alone and they had to trust someone, sometime, if they had any hope of bringing this matter to a close.

At last she steeled herself and looked at him. 'The thing is, we never really stopped the investigation into Bryce's death.'

Errol frowned. 'But you said it was too dangerous. That you couldn't take the risk.'

'I know. I . . . I lied. And after what you told me about what happened with your wife I know that was an unforgiveable thing for me to do. And I don't expect you to believe me, but I'm not in the habit of deceiving anyone. But we had to pretend as though we had stopped so that the real killer wouldn't find out what we were really up to.'

Rebecca, having not paused once throughout her confession, was panting now. Trying to catch her breath as shame and mild panic hit her in equal force.

'I still don't understand why you couldn't have just told me that you were continuing the investigation. I wouldn't have told anyone. And it's not like I'm the killer.'

Rebecca looked at him.

'Oh my God,' Errol said, pulling away from her. 'You suspected me, didn't you? You thought I might have had a hand in what happened to Bryce? And with your attack.'

'No, well, no, not for long. It was just a brief theory in the beginning but I knew that you wouldn't do something like that.'

The pain in Errol's eyes startled Rebecca and it was only

in that moment that she realized what a terrible mistake she had made in not confiding in him. In her defence she had only known him a matter of days but she had to admit that during that brief period he had done nothing but try to protect and help her. He just happened to meet her at a time when she couldn't be sure who she could trust. Still, she was surprised by how cut up he looked about it. Anger she had been expecting, but sadness? She hadn't thought that would be a significant factor given how little they knew each other.

'You really entertained the thought that I could do something like that?'

'Not in any serious way. You have to understand, after I was attacked I felt very vulnerable. I don't know you that well. I didn't know what to think.'

'But I tried to look after you. I was the one trying to keep you safe,' said Errol. 'And if my involvement in Bryce's death was just a brief theory, why didn't you tell me after you'd decided I was innocent?'

'We had to keep the information compartmentalized. If anything had slipped out or—'

'That's great, so as far as you're concerned, I'm either a suspect or someone who doesn't have the intelligence to know when to keep my mouth shut.'

'That's not . . . We just couldn't risk telling you. We'd only just met you. Can't you understand?'

'I should have known,' said Errol. 'Whenever I take a shine to someone they always disappoint me.'

'I didn't mean to hurt you.'

'Don't worry, you didn't,' he snapped, but even Rebecca could tell he was lying. 'Whatever, you did what you thought you had to do. But I'm not going to hang around. Call me old-fashioned but I'm not a big fan of people making a fool out of me.'

With that Errol got up to leave and began to walk towards Skittles who he was probably planning to take back to his cabin.

'Errol, please don't walk away,' she called after him. 'We could really use your help right now.'

'You want my help after this?' he said, glancing back at her for just a moment as he offered his shoulder to Skittles. 'All I have done is help you and you couldn't even trust me. No offence but I don't think you deserve any more of my help.'

With Skittles now perched on his shoulder, he turned to walk away.

'We know who Bryce's killer is,' she called after him in panic. She shouted this a little louder than she knew was sensible given that there were people walking by.

Errol stopped in his tracks.

'And we know who it was who attacked me.'

Slowly, Errol turned to her, the lines on his usually soft face hardening.

CHAPTER THIRTY

The next time Rebecca saw Noah Davies, he was smoking a cigarette out on the balcony in the lower deck rec room. Standing on the very spot where they assumed he had killed Bryce Griffin. As she watched silently from a safe distance, Rebecca felt sickened by the sheer audacity on display. It didn't help, of course, that she knew he was the man who had threatened her. That he had been under their noses all along. It was clear from the conversation she had overheard with Georgia that he had no scruples and was happy to deceive or cheat anyone if it saved his own skin. But now they knew the truth about him. They had a plan and they had him surrounded. As such, saving his own skin wouldn't be so easy.

When Kitt gave her the nod she, along with Errol, Evie and Grace, advanced towards the unsuspecting subject. His back was turned to them as he looked over the ocean.

There were a couple of other crew members in the rec

room but when they saw that Rebecca and her friends were with Errol, they paid them little heed.

The group waited until they had Noah completely cornered on the balcony before drawing his attention to their presence. Standing this close to someone who had threatened her so violently suddenly put her on edge. Rebecca could only hope there was safety in numbers.

'Noah Davies?' Kitt said.

Noah swung round and his face at once paled when he saw quite how many opponents he was facing.

'I am making a citizen's arrest for the murder of Bryce Griffin and Timothy Perkins. If you resist, we are permitted by UK law, to which this ship is bound as it flies the British flag, to use reasonable force to detain you, but I would advise you to come quietly and not make a scene.'

'What are you talking about?' said Davies, looking at Kitt as if she were cracked. Rebecca had to admit that he was making a very good show of innocence indeed. If she hadn't overheard his conversation with Georgia for herself, even she might have second guessed their plan here.

'It's too late for denial,' Kitt said, initiating phase two of the plan they'd cooked up to ensure Noah Davies gave his partner up. 'Georgia has already told us everything.'

'She *what*?' Davies said, taking a threatening step towards Kitt.

'I wouldn't move any closer if I were you,' Errol said. Despite the more than painful scene that had passed between them at his performance area he had ultimately decided that his anger towards Davies outweighed his anger towards Rebecca and Kitt and had agreed to help them in apprehending the suspect, hopefully putting an end to whatever crime ring Archippo had established on the *Northern Spirit* for good. Knowing first-hand just how strong Davies was, Rebecca was glad of Errol's support. He would probably never speak to her again after this but at least he'd been able to put aside his differences long enough to make sure justice was served.

'If you try anything, there'll be serious consequences,' said Evie. Though her face was fixed in a determined frown it was quite funny to think of her doing any real damage to anyone. She was five foot nothing and couldn't weigh more than eight stone dripping wet.

'We know Georgia's been covering for you. That you killed Bryce because he owed you money and that you threatened Georgia's life if she didn't cover it up. Well, after this second body's been found, she can't do it any more. She's with the captain right now, apprising him of everything you've done. She instructed us to come and arrest you and escort you straight to the ship's brig.'

Rebecca thought her sister did a good job of selling the lie they'd concocted. From the look on Noah's face, he certainly didn't think Georgia was above sending him down the river.

'No, no, no,' said Noah, running a hand through his hair. 'This can't be right.'

Rebecca wasn't a vindictive person by nature but she didn't mind admitting privately to herself that watching panic set into a man like Noah Davies was a joy to behold.

'I'm sorry but there's no way out now. Georgia's already made some calls about incarceration back in England. You'll be kept in the ship's brig until the return voyage is over. Come quietly now.'

'But I'm not the killer!' Davies sputtered, panic starting to set in.

'That's not what we've 'eard,' said Grace. 'Georgia says you shot Bryce and killed that poor steward.'

'I only shot Bryce because she told me to. And she killed Timothy Jenkins, not me.'

Kitt shrugged. 'That's your version. And I don't really see why I should believe it.'

'You don't have any evidence,' Noah said, pointing hard at Kitt.

'I'm afraid we do. Georgia's testimony for one and Skittles for another.'

'That stupid parrot Bryce was always carrying around?'

'Skittles is not stupid,' Evie said. 'He's got more brains than you, and more heart too by the look of things.'

Kitt glared at her friend for interrupting at a crucial moment but then continued with her verbal assault. 'Mechanic. That was the only word Skittles could say, over and over again. A mechanic, as you well know, is a casino cheat. You. You've been fixing games. Running a scam. Bryce was in on it, things went south and you killed him.'

'You got that all wrong,' Davies half shouted. 'Georgia – she's the one running the scam. She's the one . . . no . . . I can't say anything else. It will mean the end for me, and my family.'

Without another word Davies swung around and began to clamber towards the ledge on the balcony. He had one leg dangling over the North Sea when Errol grabbed hold of his collar and pulled him back.'

'Oh no you don't,' said Errol. 'You're not getting out of this that easily.'

Davies was panting now and pulling at his collar, hysteria was well and truly setting in. 'Easily? You think anything about my life has been easy?'

'If you've got some evidence that in some way counters Georgia's statement, then we will find a way of keeping you safe,' Kitt said, switching gears now. Trying a softer, reassuring voice on for size.

'No chance, nobody can keep me safe. Not from her.'

'A little bit dramatic, don't you think?' said Grace. 'Why are you so afraid of her? Has she got something else on you? Something we don't know about?'

Noah's eyes widened and he shook his head.

'Then why would you be so . . .' Kitt stopped in her tracks and frowned. A look of sheer disbelief fell over her face.

'Wait a minute. She doesn't just work for Archippo, does she? She is Archippo.'

Rebecca looked over at her sister, digesting this revelation. She didn't know much about organized crime in general, just that it relied on corrupting a trusted system. In this case, Georgia had controlled her operations by establishing herself in a position of authority – the ship's head of security. It will have taken her years of work to reach a place where she could really call the shots but the payoff was all the motivation she would have needed. And by the time she was in such a position of respect and authority nobody would have thought to question what she did or how she did it. Then there was her accent ... Rebecca had thought that Georgia must have spent time in South Africa. But Halloran had said Archippo was rumoured to have worked out of Australia for a while. It was quite common for people to confuse the more diluted versions of those accents. Could it really be true? Had they been in the presence of Archippo all along?

'She tasked you to kill Bryce, and attack Rebecca. She told you to say that you were a person of importance on the ship and that Georgia was a thorn in your side in case we found out about Archippo, so our suspicions would be diverted elsewhere. But ... she's really the one behind it all ... Am I right?' Kitt pushed.

Noah gave an almost indiscernible nod. 'I used to work on the front desk in hospitality. I've never been good with money but over the last five years, I developed a real gambling problem. I kept thinking I could win it back but each time I lost even bigger amounts. I took a loan from Georgia – I didn't know who she was, I just knew she was someone who could arrange a loan from rumours I'd heard – but then I couldn't pay it back. And I found out that the last person in the world you want to owe money to is Georgia Rhames.'

'How much are we talking?' asked Errol.

'Twenty grand,' Noah replied. 'She said she'd arrange a job move for me from the front desk to the casino. That all I had to do was follow her instructions and I could pay off my debt. It was either that or pay the penalty for owing money to Archippo.'

'Death?' Kitt said.

Noah nodded. 'People like that, they make an example of you when you can't pay up. Make sure everyone else keeps up with their payments.'

'Bryce owed her money too, didn't he?' said Kitt. 'He and Georgia never argued about a missing watch. They argued about him paying off his debt to her.'

'He lost big in a card game during a trip to the Gulf of Aden,' said Davies. 'He bet more than he had. Wound up borrowing the difference from Georgia and paying in more ways than he imagined. He helped her with the scam of fixing games and robbing guests who won big for a while, but ultimately, he said he wasn't going to do it any more. That he'd been legit for years and didn't want to go down that path again.'

'Oh Bryce,' Kitt said, shaking her head. 'So, the thefts stopped after Bryce's death because Georgia had to lie low after ordering you to kill him. Not because he was the main culprit of those crimes . . .'

'I'm sorry about your friend,' Noah said.

Tears rose in Kitt's eyes. Rebecca reached out to her, took her hand and squeezed it. Smiling somewhat bitterly, Kitt squeezed her hand in return.

'If you're really sorry about what happened to Bryce,' Kitt said to Davies, 'if you want her to pay for all the pain she's caused and to minimize how long you'll spend behind bars, you'll tell me everything I need to know about Georgia Rhames. And spare not one detail.'

Davies shrugged. 'I might as well tell you. If you've found her out, I'm as good as dead anyway. We all are.'

A frown passed between the group.

'What do you mean by that?' said Kitt. Davies looked from left to right, anywhere but at Kitt. His attempts at avoiding eye contact, however, did not deter Kitt from issuing one of the hardest stares Rebecca had ever seen from her. 'You'd better take a seat, Noah,' she said. 'You're going to tell me everything. Right now.'

CHAPTER THIRTY-ONE

Given all that Noah Davies had told them about Archippo's operation and the fact that she'd had two people killed in the last six weeks (and those were just the ones they knew about), the last thing they could afford to do was underestimate Georgia Rhames.

Even if they did outnumber her.

They believed Davies had cooperated with them fully. Since, however, they couldn't use the ship's brig without alerting Georgia they were on to her and they couldn't risk Davies trying to get some kind of message to her to save himself the repercussions of revealing her true identity, they had handcuffed him to the radiator in Errol's cabin and left Wendy to watch over him.

Kitt had only crowed about her foresight to bring handcuffs with her for about ten minutes, which for her was quite modest.

As a further precaution, they had used the radios as

sparingly as possible – only ever talking in code – in case she had found their channel and arranged to meet Georgia in the most public place they could think of: the Top Deck Bar. When they at last showed their hand, with so many witnesses around, she'd be very unlikely to try anything they hadn't already anticipated.

Thus, Errol, Rebecca and Kitt sat at a table on high stools whilst Evie and Grace remained posted further afield, awaiting a signal to move in once they had Georgia cornered.

'Dorothy is in the Emerald City,' Evie said over the radio.

Trying not to react too abruptly to the news that a wanted crime boss was in the vicinity, Rebecca looked casually around the bar. Skimming the crowds, she glanced this way and that but couldn't immediately see Georgia.

'Whereabouts?' Rebecca asked.

'I see her,' said Grace. 'Advancing from your three o'clock. Dressed in a yellow sweatshirt.'

At this, Rebecca and Kitt looked in the direction Grace had indicated as naturally as they could. They at once locked eyes with Georgia. She stopped in her tracks and glanced downwards at her chest. No, not quite at her chest. At a lump beneath her jumper. When she looked back up at them, her eyes were narrowed and her jaw set.

'She's got a radio under there. She's listening in on our frequency and that reference to her clothing has tipped her off,' Kitt said to Errol and Rebecca. 'She knows. Come on, we've got to move in.'

But they hadn't got three paces in Georgia's direction when she flashed a smug smile and turned to run.

'Why can they never come quietly?' Kitt said in a weary tone before hitting a button on her radio. 'Grace, move in now. Evie, now's the time to alert security that Georgia has gone rogue. Suspect heading towards the fire exit steps on the starboard of the ship, likely heading for the tender boats or a lifeboat. Tell the security team to radio it into the coast guard, just in case . . . in case we fail.'

'Received,' came Evie's scratchy response.

Kitt jogged lightly towards the steps. Rebecca and Errol followed and Rebecca soon overtook her sister. When she reached the emergency steps, however, she hesitated as she stared down into what looked like a labyrinth of spiralling metal.

'What if she's armed?' Rebecca said, once Errol and her sister had caught up with her.

'Doubtful she'd have a gun on her in such a public place,' said Errol.

'What about a knife?' Rebecca said, remembering the blade she'd been threatened with when she was attacked.

'Just don't get too close to her,' said Kitt. 'Come on, we can't let her get away. She'll be gone in minutes if she gets to a boat. We can't wait.'

Nodding, Rebecca scampered down the steps as quickly as her feet would carry her, listening to the clanging of iron as her friends did the same. Grace couldn't be far behind but she didn't have time to look back and check. All that mattered was trying to catch Georgia, who was a good two decks down from them now. Rebecca could make out the boats that Errol had indicated. It would probably take a few minutes to lower one into the sea and that would be their window to try and apprehend her. Assuming their plan to do so played out as they hoped. If not, well . . . if not, then nothing much would matter to them any more.

It was windy out on the steps and Rebecca found herself clinging on to the banisters to deal with that and the perpetual zigzagging from one deck to the next; the abrupt turn and drop was starting to leave her feeling quite dizzy but she had to stay steady on her feet. She thought about how Georgia had put Davies up to attacking her. Feeding her lies to throw her off the scent. Like that, he was a person of importance on the ship. Georgia was a thorn in his side. On reflection, considering that Davies had been coerced, perhaps that last part was true. In any case, he had made her feel like she was helpless. A victim. That's not something Rebecca would easily forgive.

'She's just reached the tender boat,' Kitt called out.

This news spurred Rebecca to scurry faster and faster, the last couple of decks passing in something of a blur, until she reached the bottom where Georgia was fiddling with the controls on her getaway boat.

'I wouldn't advise coming closer,' Georgia said. She was

panting, out of breath. But then Rebecca was also managing the effects of the exertion and Errol, Kitt and Grace weren't faring any better than her.

'What's to stop us?' said Kitt. 'We're not in your pocket. We don't owe you anything. You're unarmed.'

'Not quite.' Georgia reached into her pocket and pulled out something so small Rebecca could barely see it.

Georgia pressed a button on the device and a small beeping sounded out. 'This is a detonator and now it's armed.'

Rebecca and Kitt exchanged a look. Rebecca stiffened, barely daring to breathe.

'A detonator to what?' said Kitt.

'Some very strategically placed C4. A contingency, you would call it. A get-out-of-jail-free card. In case anyone ever found out about me.'

'You can't be serious,' said Errol.

'Deadly serious,' said Georgia. 'If I press this button, there'll be one almighty explosion right near the central hub of gas pipes. Whatever's left of the ship after the bomb goes off will go down. And everyone on it. I've made sure of that.'

'You're bluffing,' said Kitt. 'You couldn't plant a bomb like that on a ship like this without somebody noticing. Not even if you're head of security. There would be maintenance checks. Someone would have spotted an explosive device, I'm sure of it.'

'But I'm the one who walks every inch of this ship every

day to make sure nothing untoward is happening. And I'm kept informed of any maintenance checks. So if my contingency needs to be temporarily removed, I can do that without anyone knowing. And if all else had really failed, well, who would have guessed that the head of security would have planted something like that? So I can assure you I'm not bluffing and you really don't want to test that theory.'

'I'm not going to let you get away with this,' said Kitt, taking a step closer to Georgia.

'Oooh, think very carefully about your next move,' Georgia said, hovering her finger over the button. 'A fortunate few might get to the lifeboats. How many do you think out of four thousand? Maybe five hundred. Maybe. But a lot of people will die. So do the sensible thing and let me sail off into the sunset. You're risking a lot of people's lives if you don't let me get away.'

'So you can blow us up once you're making tracks to paradise?' said Grace. 'There's no way you'll leave anyone who knows your identity alive.'

'I might. It's not like you'll ever find me once I get into that boat. But that's a risk you'll have to take.'

'If you press that button, you'll go down with this ship, just as we will,' said Kitt.

'Are you blind?' Georgia said. 'I've got my escape route ready. And funnily enough, I didn't plant the bomb on the same side of the ship as my intended getaway boat.

You might even make it yourselves if you jump overboard straight away. But most of these people won't.'

Kitt took a step towards Georgia.

'Don't push me,' Georgia said through gritted teeth. 'That's what Bryce did and look how he ended up.'

'And I suppose Timothy Perkins pushed you too, did 'e?' said Grace.

'That idiot was threatening to go to the authorities about me. It's the last threat he ever made.'

'How long, Georgia? How many people have you killed?' said Kitt.

'You're going to be waiting a long time if a full confession is what you're after,' said Georgia.

'With an attitude like that, I can only assume that who-ever introduced you to crime found you at a very young age,' said Kitt.

Georgia curled her lip but didn't verbally respond.

'Someone like you, who's willing to heartlessly kill this many people, with no remorse. They don't just learn that on their thirtieth birthday. More often than not, they wit-ness cruelty and abuse and exploitation before they even hit double figures. They don't stand a chance really of ever being anything other than the lowest of the low.'

'You don't know a thing about me,' Georgia said, her voice quiet, menacing.

'Of course I do,' said Kitt. 'You think you're so clever. That nobody can touch you. Well, I'm here to prove you wrong on that score and, what's more, I'm well-read enough to tell you you're just a textbook case. Just another statistic for a criminologist to write up in a report. You are clever, I'll give you that. You've been patient. You've been strategic. But it's all a waste. Because you could have used your intellect to create a better world. And instead you just decided to get rich. You could have given to this world instead of walking around behaving as though you had the right to take whatever you wanted. I don't fear you. I don't respect you,' Kitt paused before at last spitting out, 'I pity you.'

'Is there an easy way of shutting this woman up?' Georgia said, scowling at Rebecca.

'Not that we're aware of,' she replied.

Rebecca watched as Kitt took another step towards Georgia.

'You've clearly got a death wish,' Georgia snarled. 'One more step and I'll—'

But she didn't get a chance to finish her sentence before Kitt lunged at her, making a grab for the detonator. Georgia was too quick, however. She moved her hand out of reach and, after shoving Kitt backwards with impressive force, she pressed down hard on the button.

CHAPTER THIRTY-TWO

The second Georgia's finger met the detonator, Rebecca grabbed hold of the nearest railing, just as they had planned. Rebecca was vaguely aware of the others doing the same, and of Errol grabbing her arm to keep her steady. None of them knew exactly what was going to happen next but holding on to something just seemed like good common sense.

What did happen was that a large boom sounded out. Rebecca was no expert on gauging distance but, at a guess, she would have said the explosion was coming from about two hundred yards out to sea beyond the stern. She narrowed her eyes in that direction and watched a plume of water ripple out from where the blast had taken place. But the *Northern Spirit* remained steady and on course. Rocking only gently from the waves the detonation had caused.

'What?' Georgia screeched, eyes also turned to the spot where the bang had sounded out. 'No, no, no, it can't be.'

She pressed the detonation button over and over again but nothing more happened. She watched on helplessly as black smoke curled up from the empty lifeboat which they had pushed out to sea just five minutes before they were due to meet with Georgia.

'Noah Davies is already in custody,' Kitt said to Georgia who was, by this point, tugging on her hair in frustration. 'He told us all about you, Archippo.'

At the mention of this name, Georgia's eyes looked even colder than they had when she was pushing the button on the detonator.

'We know about all of your crimes. The money laundering. The arms dealing. The robberies and the way you murdered anyone who tried to speak out or escape you. Just like Timothy Perkins did. Just like Bryce Griffin did. Noah told us all about the explosives you planned to use. Your get-out-of-jail-free card, as you put it.'

'What did you do with the bomb?' Georgia snarled.

'After some research to check how to safely move explosives, Wendy called in a favour with a couple of stewards she trusted. They placed the bomb into a hardened container to minimize any potential damage should an explosion occur and then stowed it aboard a lifeboat. We just had to make sure we pushed it out to sea close to our meeting so it stayed out there for as little time as possible to prevent another vessel from running into it. The stewards in question were watching over the boat for us, to make sure someone else didn't pay the price for your cruelty. So you see, there is no get-out-of-jail-free card, not for you. You won't sink this ship. Not while I'm on board.'

Georgia half wailed, half screamed and then made a last scramble for the tender boat. Errol grabbed hold of her, but she kicked and scratched at him. Rebecca and Grace closed in, then held Georgia's arms and legs steady. She struggled for a good few minutes. So long, in fact, that Rebecca wondered if she was ever going to give it up. Eventually, though, her body did go limp.

'Georgia Rhames,' said Kitt, 'I am making a citizen's arrest for your part in conspiracy to murder Bryce Griffin, for the murder of Timothy Perkins and for several other felonies, including conspiracy to mass murder, to be confirmed by the UK police force when you are taken into custody in England. You will remain in the ship's brig until this vessel docks in Newcastle. There, the police will make a formal arrest.'

'Whatever,' Georgia spat. 'Nobody's going to testify against me, I'll promise you that.'

'I will,' said Rebecca.

'And that goes for all of us,' said Kitt. 'You're not going to hurt anyone else. We're going to make sure of it.'

CHAPTER THIRTY-THREE

'This song goes out to some very special friends of mine,'
Wendy purred into the microphone as she began a special
set at the Top Deck Bar the following evening. As it was
the venue for the 1960s dance night Evie had been looking
forward to since they had first boarded, the bar had been
given something of a special makeover.

Large banners hung all around featuring the faces
of 1960s icons, everyone from John Lennon to Elvis to
Marilyn Monroe. A large dance space had been cleared and
a circular wooden board laid down that had been painted
to look like a vinyl record. Tiny lanterns had been posi-
tioned all around in psychedelic Sixties colours and lots of
people, Evie included, were wearing Sixties-style clothing.
As Rebecca, Kitt and Grace were hardly vintage clothes
horses like Evie they had to settle for having their hair and
make-up done in the Sixties style. Since Rebecca's hair was
quite short, Evie had styled it in the way Twiggy once wore

her hair. It wasn't a look Rebecca would usually go for but it was quite a welcome change and frankly, after almost a week of dealing with suspicion and death, it was a relief that she had nothing more pressing to think about than how she was going to wear her hair.

'Thanks to Rebecca, Kitt, Evie and Grace for being such great friends to the *Northern Spirit*,' Wendy said, before launching into the opening lines of 'With a Little Help from My Friends' by The Beatles. Rebecca smiled and shook her head. A strangely fitting theme to the cruise they had just experienced. She had no idea how she would have survived hunting down a mysterious crime boss and averting near death via an explosive device had it not been for the companionship of Kitt, Evie and Grace.

Still, Rebecca could now say she had been on at least one adventure. Whether it had been quite all she imagined it would be was another matter.

Of course, Wendy couldn't publicly announce why she was doing this song in their honour. It was, in fact, by order of Captain Ortega himself, who had been the very embodiment of gratitude once he learned of Georgia's grand betrayal. If the truth about what had happened on board since they left Tynemouth harbour had got out before they docked in Oslo, it would undoubtedly have caused panic on board. Grace had done a fair bit of grumbling about the fact that, by the time any of the wealthy passengers on the ship learned what a service they'd performed, it would be too late for any thanks, preferably in the form of a generous cheque for saving their lives. But Rebecca, for her part, was uninterested in compensation.

Perhaps one of the best things to come out of them getting to the truth was that it had turned out that Bryce Griffin wasn't the villain of the piece after all. He had, true to the word he'd given Kitt, done all he could to stay legitimate and tried to stand up to one of the most intimidating figures in organized crime. Gratifying news for Kitt. Although rather than reflecting on her friend's moral fibre, she had instead spent quite a bit of time talking about how Halloran had been wrong about Bryce and how thoroughly she was going to underline this to him when they returned to York.

Still, Rebecca had seen a little of the rosiness return to her sister's cheeks over the last twenty-four hours and, from a few passing comments she'd made here and there about how proud she was of Bryce for doing what he'd done, Rebecca knew there was hope for her sister's faith in humanity yet. It also warmed her heart to know that Miss Ocean Blue, who it was now clear Bryce had truly broken up with because he wanted to protect her, would avert an unlawful prosecution. This thought, and knowing that Bryce and Timothy's killer had been apprehended, kept her mind off the fact that Georgia Rhames and Noah Davies were at this minute incarcerated in the lower decks. Just thinking about them made Rebecca shiver. In that respect, docking in Oslo couldn't come soon enough.

The sight of Kitt, Grace and Evie swaying in the crowd to Wendy's charismatic crooning snapped Rebecca out of her thoughts.

'Oooh, Skittles!' Evie cried a moment later.

Rebecca turned to see Errol in full pirate garb. He'd have not long finished his early evening show and, due to his work commitments, they hadn't had much chance to talk since they'd apprehended Georgia . . . although maybe that was in part because she had done her best to avoid any circumstances where they might cross paths.

He had said very little to her after Georgia had been taken down to the brig and he certainly hadn't asked to see her or talk to her about all that passed between them earlier yesterday afternoon. She took that as a sign that he still needed space to process everything that had transpired. She imagined that he might calm down about the fact they hadn't been able to trust him after seeing the lengths Georgia had gone to in order to conceal her identity and keep her crime ring in operation. But she strongly suspected that was as far as his forgiveness would go. The hints of romance they had shared when they first crossed paths were probably dashed now. Which was likely to lead to moments of extreme awkwardness in his presence. As such, avoiding him had seemed like the easier option.

'Pretty girl, pretty girl,' Skittles said to Evie, who blushed a little bit as he hopped on to her shoulder and pressed his beak against her cheek. Just touching the edges of the facial scars that reminded Rebecca of just some of the dire consequences this group of women had endured to ensure justice was served. The first case Kitt had ever worked had had some irreversible effects on her best friend, and from the odd comment her sister had made, she'd never really forgiven herself for that.

'Ey up.' Evie chuckled and stroked the bird's chest. 'I usually make someone take me to dinner before they get this up close and personal. My girlfriend might not be too happy when I tell her about you.'

'He's a terrible flirt,' said Errol.

'Not unlike his master,' Rebecca said with a smile. It was a risky thing to say given their argument. But trying to move back to a place of easiness around him after their disagreement was surely the mature thing to do.

'A bit rich coming from a woman who showed quite a bit of interest in my jawline a few days ago.'

Rebecca could feel the heat in her cheeks at the reminder of how outrageously she had flirted with Errol that first day on the cruise. It wasn't something she would normally have felt comfortable doing – even in a plight to tease her sister – which, she realized now, must have been an early sign that she felt comfortable around him. She couldn't help laughing along with Grace, Evie and Kitt, all of whom were lapping up Errol's banter.

Rebecca cleared her throat and decided to quickly

change the subject. 'He's saying something different besides "mechanic", then?'

'Yes, "pretty girl" is about the limit to his vocabulary right now but I'm hoping it's a positive sign that he's branched out a little bit.'

'Oh, I didn't know you were saying it to all the girls,' Evie said to the bird. 'And I thought I was special.'

Errol chuckled. 'Maybe you can get to know each other better whilst I have this dance with Rebecca. I will want him back at some point, though.'

Rebecca felt her mouth drop at Errol's offer of a dance. She tried to close it as quickly as she could, hoping he hadn't noticed.

So, it looked as though they would bury the hatchet even quicker than she'd anticipated. That was no bad thing. There were only three nights left until they reached Oslo and she didn't want to disembark the ship on bad terms with Errol. Not when he had tried so hard to help them and had been instrumental in cornering the hardened criminals who had attempted to escape custody.

Evie gave Errol an excitable nod at the prospect of being trusted with Skittles' welfare. It looked as if the pair were destined to become fast friends.

Errol offered his hand and Rebecca put hers in his. He drew her into his arms and for the first time since they'd met, she didn't resist. She simply breathed in that now familiar scent of cedarwood and tried to think about what she should say.

'I know I apologized yesterday, but I wanted to say again just how sorry I was for, well, everything really,' she said, looking up into those sea-green eyes that seemed more mesmerizing now than ever.

'Yes, well, I've had some time to think, and it's not often I'm wrong, mind, but perhaps I could have been a little more understanding yesterday afternoon,' Errol said. 'After what happened to you, just being on the ship must have been scary. Made you feel like you couldn't trust anyone.'

'That is the way I felt. But I was wrong not to trust you. Unfortunately, that's only something I could see with hindsight. Hard to believe now how lost I felt only yesterday.'

'Well, of course, I'm not sure I shall ever recover from such a heinous heartbreak. It may very well destroy my faith in humanity and cause me to become a jittery old recluse who can't even remember his own name and forgets what bread tastes like,' he said with a grin.

'You're enjoying this,' Rebecca said, giving him a playful shove.

'Would I?' Errol said. 'I'm merely amused that you didn't see what was really going on here.'

'And what was that, exactly?' Rebecca said, fighting a smile.

'Well, you meet this devilishly handsome man. He's dashing and charming and you think to yourself, if I let myself fall for this one, I will fall hard. So you put an obstacle in the way, and that made you feel safe. Safe from my charms. Safe from love. Safe from heartbreak.'

'A little bit early to be throwing the L word around, don't you think?' Rebecca said.

Errol shrugged. 'Maybe a little, but I regret nothing.'

'So if I've understood you correctly,' Rebecca said, really having to work hard not to laugh now, 'my suspecting you was just an emotional defence mechanism.'

'I have seen quite a lot of American chat shows that would support this theory. And also my reaction yesterday may not have been completely levelled at you. You know what happened in my marriage.'

'Yes, that's part of why I felt so terrible keeping the truth from you.'

'I may have overreacted yesterday as my own defence mechanism. I just don't ever want to go through something like that again. Where somebody so completely deceives me. I don't believe you would do that but in the moment I was telling myself you would because it was easier than admitting I found you . . . reasonably attractive.'

'Reasonably attractive? Oh, be still my heart. How can I resist you when you shower me with such passionate compliments?'

Errol smiled. 'I may be underplaying it slightly. I hear playing it cool in the beginning is how it's done.'

'The beginning?'

'Yeah,' Errol said, his smile widening. 'The beginning of your dating life with a ruggedly handsome fellow, the very thought of him almost making you faint. The—'

Rebecca shook her head. 'Just shut up and kiss me, will you?' She grabbed hold of Errol's lapel and pulled his mouth hard against hers. Though the little jump he gave indicated some surprise, he soon relaxed into the kiss, running his hands through her hair and pulling her body closer against his. His lips were just as firm as she had imagined they'd be and he tasted sweet, like pineapple juice. A wonderful byproduct of the fact that fresh fruit juices were served in abundance at every bar on the ship. As his tongue found hers, their kiss became more urgent. His hands gripped the back of the shift dress she was wearing and he clawed at the fabric in such a way that Rebecca began to think of all the fun ways they might find to pass the time over the last few days of the cruise.

When their lips at last parted, Rebecca stared dreamily into Errol's eyes for a moment before realizing that Kitt was standing next to them, watching and waiting.

'Argh!' Rebecca said, jumping in shock.

'Sorry to interrupt,' said Kitt, 'but I've just picked up the most cryptic email from Mal.'

'Aren't you supposed to be dancing? You know, relaxing, having a good time,' Rebecca said, less than pleased that Kitt was infringing on the most romantic scene of her life to date, with yet more mystery.

'I get good Wi-Fi signal here so I just thought I'd check in,' said Kitt.

'Well, cryptic *how*?' Rebecca said when Kit showed no signs of leaving her and Errol in peace.

'He says he's found the deposit box from Bryce's poem.'

'What's inside it?' said Errol.

'He won't tell me. Not until I get back from Oslo. He says he wants to make sure I actually do fly back from Oslo and don't get involved in some other investigation. Can you believe that?'

Rebecca giggled. 'Yes, I can actually. He's really got you pegged, hasn't he? Knows exactly how to keep you around. Just stimulate your curiosity.'

'Cruelty is what it is. Making me wait three whole days for answers. It's going to feel like a lifetime.'

'If it was urgent and integral to the case, Halloran would have told you what was going on,' said Rebecca. 'So it looks like for once you're going to have to keep your curiosity in check.'

Kitt sighed and looked wistfully off into the distance. 'In that case, I think I'm going to need a few more drinks.'

CHAPTER THIRTY-FOUR

'Mal! Mal?' Kitt called as she bustled through the door of thirteen Ouse View Avenue, straight into the living room without even attempting to help Rebecca, Evie and Grace with the bags.

'Don't worry, Kitt,' Rebecca said. 'We'll sort your luggage.'

'Yes, yes, yes, thank you,' was all she got in return.

After they had all ambled over the threshold behind Kitt, they slumped into the nearest available chairs exhausted, while she marched over to Halloran. He was sitting in one of the armchairs by the hearth, reading a newspaper. It was evident just how much he'd been enjoying winding Kitt up about his discovery in the deposit box when he made a show of being surprised to see her.

'Oh, hello, my dearest darling, how was your trip?'

'Mal,' Kitt said, putting her hands on her hips. 'Don't play games. You know very well what I want to hear about.'

'Isn't it polite to at least acknowledge that you're home

first, and to tell me about Oslo? I hear the Viking Ship Museum is a true treasure and the Royal Palace is supposed to put Buckingham Palace to shame.'

'Yes, it was a very enlightening end to the trip,' Kitt said. 'A true cultural paradise. Now, if you'll just—'

'And what about the flight back? How was it?'

Halloran was really pushing his luck and everyone in the room knew it but the smile on his face made it abundantly clear he didn't care one bit.

'Cardboard food and interminable curiosity.' The sterner Kitt's voice became, the harder Grace and Evie giggled.

They had all heard little else other than how Kitt couldn't believe Halloran was keeping such a big secret from her for three whole days. Rebecca wasn't convinced she'd ever seen her sister so worked up about anything, and that was a strong claim given that Rebecca had been present when Kitt first learned that ebooks were going to be launched as a reading format. Though not everyone was keen to embrace such brave new technology at the time, Kitt was always looking for fresh ways to get people reading.

'I thought before we look at the contents of Bryce's box you might want to give me a kiss first. Have we really got to that point in our relationship where I can no longer get a kiss from my girlfriend when she comes home from an extended trip?'

Kitt chuckled. 'You are a terrible tease, Malcolm Galfrid Halloran.'

Grace clamped a hand over her mouth. It seemed Halloran's middle name was a source of endless amusement to her.

Kitt leaned in to kiss Halloran while the rest of them averted their eyes. At the same time, Rebecca tried not to think about how difficult it had been parting ways with Errol when she left the ship. He still had six weeks left on this rotation. After which he'd promised to come and stay in Northumberland for a while and take her out to dinner. Given how much fun they'd already had together in the privacy of his cabin, the end of his rotation couldn't come fast enough as far as she was concerned.

'Oh, come on now, my love, just one more kiss,' Halloran said, looking a bit too pleased with himself.

'Oooh, give over, will you? You've had your fun, don't push it,' said Kitt.

Raising his hands in a signal of defeat, Halloran stood from his chair and walked over to the sideboard. He pulled a small velvet pouch out of the drawer, along with a piece of paper that had no envelope but was folded in half.

Though Kitt arguably harboured more curiosity in her heart than all the rest of them put together, Rebecca, Grace and Evie were intrigued enough to pull themselves up and gather round to read what the letter said.

A BODY BY THE LIGHTHOUSE

Dear Red,

If you are reading this, that must mean I'm no longer here. Which is rather tough luck but I suppose it happens to us all. Sooner or later. And my time must have come.

As you know, I've lived a bit of an unsettled life and you are really the only person who has remained a staple all these years. Because of that, I felt bad (yes, I know you will be shocked to learn I actually have a conscience) for double-crossing you all those years ago in Seaton Carew. I can't say that I regret much in this life but I do regret that. It's why I asked you to stay in touch with me. I suppose I hoped at some point if we stayed friends, I would at least have an opportunity to earn your forgiveness. Perhaps even your respect. I hope by the time you read this I've managed to go up in your estimation.

I've never been good at holding on to money but I've made a point of holding on to this for you. Even when I was in dire straits and needed the brass. It's going to sound strange but I wanted to leave something to somebody when I was gone. To be remembered. I suppose in some strange way, that became more important to me than money. An unexpected notion for an ex-smuggler if ever there was one.

I have no doubt that you won't use this to get stinking rich as most people would but I suppose that's one of the reasons I'm giving it to you and not gambling it away somewhere or using it to pay off one of my many debts.

I should have given this to you a long time ago. I never

would have found it without you. Take care of yourself,
Red. And if there is something on the other side of all this,
come and find me at the bar. I'll be there, drinking with
Bartholomew Roberts, exchanging tips on the quickest route to
wealth in case we get sent back here for a second chance.

In closing, I think it's important you know that although
I've had many adventures in my life, the adventure I treasure
most is the one we shared all those years ago. You're a very
special person, Kitt. There is nobody quite like you. And I for
one am a better person for having known you.

With love – yes, really, love – to you Red.

Raise a glass to me.

Bryce

When Rebecca looked up from the letter, she noticed her
sister was crying and Rebecca had to admit she felt rather
teary herself. She had never met Bryce but Kitt had clearly
been a light for him in an otherwise dark life.

Though they were identical twins physically, apart from
some simple cosmetic differences, Rebecca had always considered herself quite a different personality to her sister.
One thing they did have in common is that they had both
chosen paths that gave them an opportunity to help other
people. And reading Bryce's letter, Rebecca realized the
value of this could not be overstated.

She heard the compliments from patients at the hospital when they were offered. but she didn't really listen to

them. She was too busy trying to meet the next deadline or filling in forms to make sure everyone got everything they needed as quickly as possible. Next time someone had something good to say about her practice, however, she would really listen. She'd seen how quickly her sister had spiralled towards cynicism. For now, she believed she'd done enough to pull Kitt back from that particular cliff edge, but really heeding others when they made it clear you'd made a difference in their lives was surely the ticket to keeping optimism alive in the long-term.

Kitt started then, as a realization struck her. 'My God, Mal,' she said, staring at the pouch. 'Is this what I think it is?'

Halloran nodded with a knowing smile on his face.

Pulling open the pouch, Kitt let the contents fall into her palm. It contained a single coin, the likes of which Rebecca had never seen before.

'A silver dollar,' said Kitt.

'Is this the treasure?' said Grace.

'Part of it, yes,' said Kitt.

'The treasure you found when you deciphered the map Bryce had and he double-crossed you?'

'Yes,' Kitt said, an edge of irritation growing in her voice.

'The treasure that is worth more money than any of us can ever imagine?' said Grace.

'For heaven's sake, Grace, yes. Would you give over?'

'We're rich,' said Grace, punching her fists up to the

ceiling. 'Which is opportune because we need a new printer at the agency.'

'We're not rich,' said Kitt. 'This belongs in a museum. With a plaque next to it that has a fitting dedication to Bryce. He's really to thank for finding this treasure. I didn't even believe the map he had was going to lead anywhere at the time. He was the one who embraced adventure. And people will remember him for it, even if it's in a small corner of the world.'

'That's a lovely gesture, pet,' Halloran said, kissing Kitt on the forehead while Grace did her best not to look disappointed.

Rebecca picked up the letter from Bryce again and reread his words. An unsettled life. That's how he had described his time here. That she could believe, being at the mercy of a character as twisted as Georgia Rhames, someone who sucked you in with a friendly face and scratched you out when they were finished with you. Thankfully Bryce was only acquainted with Georgia for a very short period of time. And maybe having an unsettled life wasn't a bad thing? Perhaps too many people were over-settled and didn't always make the most of opportunities for adventure when they came knocking.

Though Rebecca's little adventure had been a lot more than she'd bargained for, she could see how the feeling of solving a case might have become something of an addiction for her sister and Grace. It was much akin to how she felt when treatments at the hospital were a success. There really was no better feeling than giving whatever you could of yourself for the greater good.

There was no doubt that, after this experience, Rebecca would be returning to the wards with renewed energy. Raring to face whatever new challenges awaited her there.

Still, hospitals were places of routine and it would be a shame to think there wouldn't be any more opportunities for far-flung escapades. With a bit of luck, if things worked out with her new pirate boyfriend and she didn't stray too far away from her sister, there would be yet more adventures to come.

ACKNOWLEDGEMENTS

I remain incredibly grateful to my publisher Quercus Books, specifically Stef Bierwerth and Kat Burdon for their ongoing enthusiasm for, and belief in, The Kitt Hartley Yorkshire Mysteries. And to my agent Joanna Swainson for all her support in ensuring Kitt continues her adventures book after book. Returning to these characters time and again is pure joy and without these people it simply would not be possible.

The enduring support of my writing partners Dean Cummings and Ann Leander, not to mention their top-notch critiquing skills, is also a blessing this writer simply could not live without. Moreover, much appreciation is due to Hazel Nicholson for her sage guidance on police procedure.

I am also thankful to all readers and reviewers who take the time to pick up my work and spend a few hours in the company of these characters for themselves. I know there are a lot of stories out there to choose from and it means the world to me that you persistently choose mine.

And lastly to my darling Jo, thank you for the love, the patience and the kindness. All of it.